The Nominee

By

Robert M. Crowder

Preface

This is the sequel to "We Can Fix America," a book that I wrote about the political and economic situations in our country. Over the last four years, I watched the Progressive Movement in this country pass the heinous ObamaCare legislation through tricks; watched as billions and perhaps trillions of dollars have been stolen from future generations and wasted on poorly laid-out stimulus plans that appear to have been paybacks for Obama's victory in 2008; and watched as the American people have been pitted against one another—Tea Partiers vs. Occupy Wall Street, white vs. black, rich vs. poor, and old vs. young. The methods used by the Progressive Movement have been shocking and should scare all of us.

In "We Can Fix America," John Robert Randolph retires from a Wall Street investment firm and becomes a college professor teaching about capitalism. As the semester unfolds, John comes to realization that America is broken and needs immediate help. He formulates a plan for fixing America and, with the promised help from his twin brother, announces his candidacy for President of the Unites States.

This book continues the story of an unknown candidate and his journey through the quagmire of American politics. The Nine-Point Plan to Fix America is introduced and laid out as a means to correct the ills that have befallen this great country. The journey will take him across America in an effort to convince the electorate he is the right choice as The Nominee.

The calendar of primaries and caucuses in this book do not correspond with the timing of actual events in 2012. After that portion of the book was written, several states changed their election dates. I did not feel it was necessary to make those changes. In addition, direct donations to candidates are limited under current federal law. The majority of money used to fund elections is found in PACs, Super PACs, and other "non-direct" organizations. For the purposes of this book, I included all of those funds as contributions to the individual candidates.

As with my first book, the purpose here is to document my opinions about what it will take to stop the Progressive onslaught on this country and most importantly to fix the many ailments facing the country. This book also points out that, without a serious resetting of our core values, the country is in for a very rude awakening. This book is fiction; however, I did use actual current events and public figures in the story. I hope you enjoy this sequel to "We Can Fix America."

Chapter 1

On Thursday, April 28, 2011, John disembarked from the airplane in Des Moines, Iowa. He had left Williamsburg that morning to start his campaign for president of the United States. Hank Johnson, his campaign manager, met him at the airport. Once they were in the car, Hank started debriefing him on activities since yesterday morning, when John Robert Randolph had announced his candidacy for president on the steps of the J. Christopher Wren Building at the College of William and Mary. After the announcement, Hank hopped on an airplane and headed for Iowa to set up an office and to "get the ball rolling" in the first caucus state. Hank told John that he had rented a vacant, former Western Auto building in downtown Des Moines. He had also called a couple of people that he had worked with on other campaigns in the past. Hank had made a career out of getting Republicans elected in about thirty states in America. He knew a lot of people in the party, and it was one of the reasons John had selected him as campaign manager.

As the car slowed in front of an old, vacant building with a homemade sign that read "We Can Fix America—John Randolph for President in 2012," John felt a sick feeling in his stomach. While he knew this was a starting point, he had no idea the beginning would be so modest. Hank was continuing to talk about several planned events and saying the campaign had certainly hit the ground running. They walked into the building.

Hank introduced John to Jen Harrison, who was the Campaign's Director of Scheduling and Advance, and to Henry Washington, the campaign's Iowa coordinator. John smiled and thanked both for joining the campaign, and assured them that the ultimate goal was winning this election and fixing America. John and Hank walked to the back of the store and sat down at a card table. There were papers everywhere; Hank quickly organized the loose papers into a single pile.

Hank said the first goal was to get some order in the process. He emphasized that the bulk of John's time was needed in introducing himself and his plan to America. Hank, who knew John was an early riser, suggested the daily staff meeting would take place at 7:00 a.m. each morning. This meeting would focus on the schedule for the current day and three days out. The goal was to be finished by 7:15 a.m., at which time there would be a meeting between William Randolph, Hank, and John to discuss the message of the day. William was John's Chief of Staff and also his twin brother. William would typically be located at campaign headquarters in Williamsburg. By 7:30 a.m., John needed to be either in a car or in front of people discussing his plan for fixing America. John liked the schedule. While he was Chief Executive Officer of Smith Goldman, his daily calendar had been broken down into fifteen-minute increments.

Hank screamed across the relatively empty space and asked Jen to join them. Jen hurried over and put the following schedule in front of John and Hank:

Thursday, April 28, 2011

3:00pm	Meeting with Iowa Republican Chairman - Matt Strawn
6:00pm	Dinner with VFW in Des Moines
8:30pm	Drive to Cedar Rapids

Friday, April 29, 2011

7:00am	Scheduling Meeting
7:15am	Message Meeting
8:00am	Moose Breakfast Meeting in Cedar Rapids
10:30am	Meeting with Cedar Rapids Mayor - Ron Corbett
12:15pm	Lunch Meeting with Local Republican Party
3:00pm	Drive to Davenport
6:00pm	Dinner with local Republican Party
8:30pm	Drive to Iowa City

Saturday, April 30, 2011

7:00am	Scheduling Meeting
7:15am	Message Meeting
8:30am	Meeting with Local Republican Party
11:00am	Drive to Des Moines
2:00pm	Interview with Des Moines Register
4:00pm	Drive to Airport
5:15pm	Flight to Richmond

John looked over the schedule and wondered when he would be able to give speeches directly to the American people, and not just civic and political groups. Hank anticipated the thought and explained this trip was a quick introduction to the state of Iowa. The key was to meet the Republican leaders. Hank stated that John was unknown to Iowans. He needed to meet people, get to know them, and to introduce his plan for fixing America. This trip would focus on Des Moines and the eastern part of the state. The

3

next trip would focus on the remainder of the state. On Saturday, John would return to Williamsburg. After only two days on the campaign trail, being recalled to campaign headquarters was not what John had expected. Jen stated the Greenville, SC Republican Party had invited John to take part in the first debate on May 5th. It would be covered by Fox News and would be held in the Peace Center in downtown Greenville. Tim Pawlenty, the current frontrunner, was expected to be there. William wanted John back in Williamsburg for debate preparation on Sunday. John sat there in the chair while the team was planning his agenda. He was starting to feel like he wasn't running the campaign, but the campaign was running him. Hank asked John if the schedule was acceptable, and John agreed. Of course, John did not know what other response to give.

Hank grabbed a telephone and called William, who was in Williamsburg. William asked John how things were going, to which he responded "fast." William said John needed to focus on the Nine-Point Plan: specifically talk about the slow-moving economy, ObamaCare, and how he plans on fixing America. William stressed the word "fix" should be used as much as possible. He stated Americans like the idea of someone fixing broken things. John asked William why it was necessary for him to come back to Williamsburg so quickly. William replied they needed every moment to get ready for the debate in Greenville, SC. It was absolutely critical that John "slam dunk" the debate so he could start making a name for himself. John asked whether it would take four days to prepare. William said four days was all that was available; he had wanted about seven-to-ten days for debate preparation. John was surprised by the abrupt answer.

Hank jumped up and said they needed to go in order to meet with Iowa Republican Chairman, Matt Strawn. Hank and John hopped into the car and set off for the offices of the Iowa Republican Party. On the way, Hank was coaching John on how to conduct the meeting. It was to be informal, but formal at the same time and needed to be general, but specific, short, but thorough. John wondered how he could manage each of these competing directives. When the car stopped in the parking lot adjacent to the building, Hank gave one more instruction—"Just be yourself." John laughed nervously and walked into the building with Hank tagging along. John met with Matt Strawn for over an hour. He introduced himself and gave a brief background of his college life and his professional career. He talked about teaching at the College of William and Mary last year. Finally, John described his Nine-Point Plan for Fixing America. Matt listened to John as he went through the discussion and stated he thought it would be extremely difficult to get term limits for congressmen. John agreed. As the meeting concluded, John stood up and said he would be honored if Matt would give the Randolph campaign some consideration. He stated again that the ultimate goal of his campaign was to fix America. John and Hank left the office; as they walked out, John asked Hank what he thought. Hank said the meeting had gone well. John wasn't so sure.

At 6:00 p.m., John and Hank went to a VFW hall in the western part of Des Moines. John felt like he'd shaken the hands of at least fifty people. He sat beside two gentlemen who had served in Vietnam during the 1960s and enjoyed talking to them about their experiences. After dinner, John was invited to give a "short" speech about his candidacy. He spoke of his childhood, his college experiences, and his professional career. He also talked about his love for America and how poorly America had been led over the last several years. He spoke briefly of his Nine-Point Plan for Fixing America. John estimated the word "fix" was used twelve times in the speech. William would be so proud. In conclusion, he asked everyone in attendance to give his campaign a try. He was convinced if they understood his plan for fixing America, they would agree. He thanked them for their hospitality.

John and Hank left Des Moines around 8:45 p.m. and drove to Cedar Rapids. It took about two and one-half hours. They checked in to a Comfort Inn around11:30 p.m. John said he would meet Hank for breakfast at6:00 a.m.

Friday was a complete blur. John's hand was starting to become sore with all of the handshaking. He figured he had shaken more hands in two days than he had in the past year. John kept giving the same speech over and over again. By the time they arrived at a Comfort

Inn in Iowa City late that night, he was almost asleep. John and Hank repeated Friday's schedule again on Saturday as they met with the local Republican Party. John kept hammering the phrase "fixing America." On Saturday afternoon, he had his first newspaper interview. The interview went remarkably well. The questions focused mostly on background information. John did give some details into his Nine-Point Plan. At 4:00 p.m., Hank and John left the *Des Moines Register* and drove to the airport. The flight was on time and they arrived in Richmond at 11:00 p.m. John was exhausted and ready to get home. The "We Can Fix America" campaign had begun.

Chapter 2

John woke up on Sunday morning. He was still tired from the whirlwind of starting the campaign. John and his wife, Jenny met the children and grandchildren for church and went to lunch afterwards. At 2:00 p.m., John and Jenny drove back to The Willows, and William and Hank arrived shortly thereafter. John was curious how he had come to be invited to the South Carolina debate when usually only candidates that met certain polling criteria were asked to attend. William told John that Hank had called in a few favors for the invitation. John was exceedingly fortunate he had picked Hank as campaign manager.

William started by saying the debate would be ninety minutes long and would be moderated by Bret Baier of Fox News. The panel consisted of Juan Williams, Shannon Bream, and Chris Wallace. The other candidates scheduled to attend were Herman Cain, former governor Gary Johnson, Congressman Ron Paul, former governor Tim Pawlenty, and former senator Rick Santorum. William stated the purpose of today's meeting was to put together a debate strategy. John thought the campaign needed to present the Nine-Point Plan and talk about fixing America. William and Hank both chuckled. William explained debates were not speeches, but instead very quick sound bites that could either make or break a candidate. John nodded his head as though he understood the discussion. William stated the key items needing to be stressed were:

1. John was an outsider to politics, and 2. He wanted to "Fix America." John asked about Herman Cain, who was also a former businessman. Both William and Hank stated Cain did not have a detailed plan, and they would deal with that situation later. Hank noted the key was to peck away at Pawlenty, Santorum, Paul, and Johnson who were career politicians. John would discuss how successful Smith Goldman was during his tenure and how unsuccessful career politicians had been for America. Secondarily, he would briefly introduce his concepts for fixing America.

John watched and listened as William and Hank discussed the goals and objectives of the debate. He understood a victory would not be winning the debate, but instead would mean articulating a significant difference between the other people on stage and himself. He was to describe himself as a non-politician with a plan for fixing America. William and Hank were convinced he could accomplish both of these goals and establish himself as a legitimate candidate. Hank was going to go to South Carolina on Monday to set up an office in Greenville. He was also going to get people to attend the debate who would support the Randolph campaign.

William said debate preparation would start on Monday. John asked what that entailed. William replied he would have to be ready to answer any questions the panel threw at him, including about his wealth. John stated he was already prepared for the debate and would do just fine. He had a vision and a plan for how to fix America. William asked if he believed America should eliminate the Department of Education. John started on a five-minute discussion of the many failures of the department. He spoke of massive increases in funding and continued poor performance on test scores. He continued by stressing how unions have destroyed the educational system in this country. After he finished, William said the buzzer would have stopped him about three and one-half minutes ago. John's answer would have been incomplete, and the American people would not have known what the Randolph campaign's position was. John looked a bit defeated. They would transform five-minute answers to one-and-a-half-minute sound bites.

John continued to sit and feel rather useless, listening to William and Hank make debate preparation plans. At about 5:00 p.m., Hank said he needed to go and pack for his trip to South Carolina. William and John agreed to meet at the new campaign headquarters located in an office building off Richmond Road at 8:00 a.m. the next morning. After both William and Hank had left The Willows, John walked into the kitchen and looked at Jenny. He had second thoughts about running for president.

John did not sleep well that night. He was thinking about his complete flubbing of the question that William had posed to him that day. He had never considered himself a long-winded person, but perhaps he was. John was worried he would not be able to get his points across in one and one-half minute segments. If he was not able to get his points across, how could he possibly explain his vision for America?

John got out of bed at around 5:00 a.m. and worked out. By 7:00 a.m., he had eaten breakfast and was ready to go to campaign headquarters. He decided to call Hank to check in. Hank did not pick up his cell phone, so John concluded he was in an airplane en route to South Carolina. At 7:30 a.m., John could not wait any longer and drove to campaign headquarters. When he arrived at the building, he looked for William's automobile, but it was not there. At 8:00 a.m., John saw William drive up in his car. John met him at the front door, and they walked in together. John expected the office would be empty, except for maybe a couple of tables and chairs. He walked in, and the room was abuzz with activity going on everywhere. John knew his mouth was wide open. William walked ahead of him and publicly introduced him to everyone in the office area. One by one, John was introduced to about fifteen individuals. William announced each of their roles, but it was impossible for John to remember everyone. As they walked into William's office, William could see the look of surprise on John's face. He said he had hired all of these people last week. He jokingly remarked he had been working last week too. John was amazed. William pulled out the following organization chart:

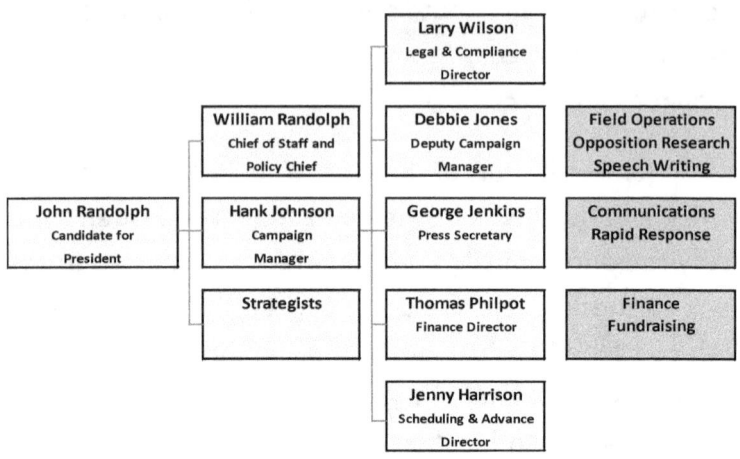

William said John should spend some time with the department heads over the next couple of days. Afterwards, he led John to a conference room about fifty feet from his office. George Jenkins, the Press Secretary, and Debbie Jones, Deputy Campaign Manager, joined them in the conference room. They shared some small talk. A few minutes later, Sophie Lee, a Republican debate strategist came into the room. At approximately 8:30 a.m., they started working on John so he could be successful in the debate on Thursday night. It was quickly determined that he could answer the questions, but he was having a hard time meeting the ninety-second time requirement. All of them provided guidance on how to limit the responses. William seemed to be the "bad guy" in the room, as his questions hit some of John's potential weaknesses. By noon, John was weary of the process. At one point, he stated the answers were not policy positions, but simply campaign slogans. Since all of the people around the room were experienced in debate preparation, they let the statement go unanswered. By 5:00 p.m., John was utterly frustrated with the process, and with the people in the room. He was scheduled to meet with WAVY TV10 for an interview at 6:15 p.m. Since Hank was in South Carolina, Debbie drove John to Newport News. On the way, Hank called and asked how it was going. John was not happy with the day's events and let Hank know about his displeasure.

The interview was a cream-puff piece; it consisted of fifteen minutes talking about John's background and why he wanted to be president. As they were leaving, several people in the television studio came up and engaged him in a conversation about the economy. John spent the next forty-five minutes talking to them about which Obama policies had failed and what his plan was to get the economy growing again. He touched on certain areas of the Nine-Point Plan. As he was leaving, he thanked them for their questions, and said he hoped they would consider voting for him. A couple of people said they would. John felt energized again.

As they got in the car, John talked about his exchange with the backstage people. Debbie heard the fire in John's tone about how worried they were about the economy and the future of America. John "preached" all the way back to Williamsburg about how the economy could be fixed. Having already read the Nine-Point Plan, Debbie smiled politely and nodded. When they got back to campaign headquarters, William met them and asked why they were so late. John explained and retold the entire story. At around 9:00 p.m., William said they should start again tomorrow by 8:00 a.m. As John drove home, he was still thinking about the people he had talked to and how he knew he could help them. He could help them as long as he could get through the next two days with the debate hounds.

The next morning, John moaned as he walked into campaign headquarters. The entire team was already in the conference room. Sophie Lee, the debate strategist said John had done a lot of things well yesterday, but there were some things to work on. Over the remainder of that day and the next day, John was asked every question that could be asked. He honestly felt the actual debate could not be as horrific as this process was. He noticed by the end of Wednesday, the hit squad started to react more favorably to his responses, even though they were the same as previous days. They kept asking questions, and John kept providing commentary. At the end of Wednesday's session, William asked everyone to leave the room so he could talk to John privately. William told John to stay on message "no matter what." If a question was asked for which an answer was not forthcoming, he should simply refer to a previously asked question. Do not fidget, do not get angry, do not show emotion, and, most of all, stay calm. Do not address any of the competitors unless a question is asked directly. While they are answering a question, just look at them as if you care what their responses are and never nod or shake your head. John sat there for a minute, trying to take in all of these final instructions. William looked at him and said he would be great. John left campaign headquarters and drove to the Richmond airport for his flight to Greenville, South Carolina which was leaving at 4:00 p.m. He called Hank on his drive and asked how things were going. Hank said an office had been set up in Greenville, and he had arranged for a couple of meetings with some South Carolina Republican leaders for Friday. Hank reminded John that he would pick him up at the airport in Greenville at 6:30 p.m.

John boarded the plane, connected through Charlotte, North Carolina and arrived in Greenville on time. As he made his way through the airport, he saw Hank at a distance. They looked at each other, smiled, walked out to Hank's rental car, and departed for the hotel. John told Hank he was terribly tired from the debate preparation and wanted to chill out that night. John and Hank decided they would watch a baseball game on television.

The next day, John woke up around 7:00 a.m. and went down to the lobby for the hotel's continental breakfast. Hank joined him at 7:30 a.m. They sat around the hotel that day and discussed the campaign, but they did not touch on any issues, policies, or anything else that might be discussed later that night. Hank knew that was the last thing one wanted their candidate doing directly before a debate. Around 7:00 p.m., John and Hank drove to the Peace Center in downtown Greenville where the debate would be held. They were ushered to a holding room where they sat and joked around. At 8:45 p.m., someone knocked on the door and asked John to follow him to the stage for some last-minute instructions. Hank said "good luck," and John smiled.

John walked up to the other candidates—Herman Cain, Ron Paul, Tim Pawlenty, Gary Johnson, and Rick Santorum—and shook their hands. John had met Herman Cain once a couple of years ago, but the others were first-time introductions. A few minutes before 9:00 p.m., the candidates walked onto the stage. Bret Baier started the debate at 9:00 p.m. The first question John was asked was related to his Nine-Point Plan, specifically his suggestion that congressional members should have term limits. John gave the following answer:

Thanks Bret. I first want to thank the Greenville Republican Party for inviting me to this debate. As the newcomer to this process, I was thrilled and honored by the invitation and I look forward to sharing my vision for fixing America. As for congressional term limits, I think they are crucial in our work to fix America. A lot of our problems are not being addressed, because Congress forgets who puts them there. It is time for Congress members to work for the people who put them there and not special interest groups and lobbyists.

The response drew a massive applause from the crowd in attendance. Juan Williams, another of the panelists and a known liberal, stated that Ron Paul had been in Congress for a much longer period of time than was being proposed in John's Nine-Point Plan. John responded:

I met Congressman Paul for the first time tonight on stage and did not know much about him other than what I have read. I do not know if Mr. Paul takes money from lobbyists and special interest groups, but if he does not, he would surely be in the minority of congressional members. It is time to stop this behavior, and the only surefire way to stop it is to limit the amount of time that people can stay in Congress. After you fix that, you can go after comprehensive lobbyist reform.

There was more massive applause.

Later in the debate, a question was asked about the huge annual deficits and debts being amassed by the country. John was the only person on stage who believed a combination of tax increases and spending cuts would solve the problem. He stated:

I know I am the only person on stage proposing additional taxes to fix our debt problems. People, we have a $14 trillion problem. Cutting all the spending in the world is not going to fix this problem. My tax increase proposal is very straightforward—a VAT tax would be implemented and the additional revenues could only be used to pay down debt. There would be "poison-pill" provisions in the bill that *would repeal the tax if future Congresses used it for current-year appropriations. Further, I propose we sell some of the land holdings of the United States government. Our government owns 782 million acres of land in this country. Why not sell 200 million acres and make a down payment on debt reduction? This is common sense to me. You use all resources available to you to fix your problems. Fourteen trillion dollars is too vast to hope spending cuts can solve the problem.*

Surprisingly, the Republican crowd enthusiastically applauded his response. John was the first Republican candidate to propose additional taxes to fix the debt problem.

Finally, no one on the stage actively agreed with John about eliminating the Department of Education, except Congressman Paul. John stated the Department of Education was just a start; he thought several federal agencies and departments needed to be either combined or eliminated. Congressman Paul added he would eliminate the Federal Reserve, to which John also agreed.

Otherwise, there was little in the way of noteworthy exchanges between the candidates. John thought the debate passed very quickly. After the session, John stayed and talked with the other candidates and the panelists. He also talked with several members of the Republican Party. Hank finally pulled John out of the Peace Center at 11:30 p.m. As they were driving back to the hotel, they received a call from Debbie who stated Fox News had set up an independent group of people who thought Herman Cain had won the debate, Ron Paul had come in second, and surprisingly, John Randolph had come in a close third. The respondents were impressed with John's articulation of his plan. They specifically liked the idea of congressional term limits and were even positive about a VAT tax as long as it was used to pay down debt. The entire team was energized by the news. As soon as they had finished the telephone call with Debbie, William called and congratulated John on the debate. Personally, William thought John had the best reaction from the audience. When John got back to his hotel room, he called his wife, Jenny. They talked about the debate, and John asked her opinion. Jenny, who had always been an extraordinarily straight shooter with John, said he had done great. John told Jenny he would see her tomorrow night. He was so excited by the events of the evening that he had a difficult time falling asleep.

The next morning John and Hank met for breakfast downstairs at the hotel. At breakfast, three different people came up to the table and told John that they had enjoyed the debate the previous night. John engaged the people on what they did for a living, where they were from, and their family situations. He stood there and talked to each of them for quite some time. Hank finally interrupted and said John needed to meet with some Republican Party leaders. John thanked each of the people for talking with him and said he would appreciate their support in the upcoming South Carolina primary. Hank joked with John on the elevator about his outgoing personality and "never knowing a stranger."

John met with several Republican Party leaders who were highly complimentary of his debate performance. John talked to the leaders about his Nine-Point Plan and asked them what they thought. Most of the comments were positive, but they were concerned about campaign finance-reform and wanted to know more details. John stated he was a proponent of limiting the amount of money that could be spent in elections. He could tell that some of them were not comfortable with that stance. All in all, the discussions were very good. Several of the people told Hank to stay in touch about future campaign visits to the upstate of South Carolina.

John and Hank went to the Greenville-Spartanburg airport in the early afternoon for the trip back to Richmond. Hank talked constantly about New Hampshire, which was next week's trip. At around 7:00 p.m., John drove his car down the driveway of The Willows. He noticed several cars near the house. As he parked the car, Jenny, the children, grandchildren, and several friends ran out of the house. William, his wife, their children, and grandchildren were also there. Jenny had prepared a grandiose celebration party. During the party, John had a telephone call from Hank. Hank was almost yelling, saying the May 6th CNN poll had John at 5 percent of the national vote and he only trailed Mitt Romney, Sarah Palin, Newt

Gingrich—none of whom had announced their candidacies—Ron Paul, and Herman Cain. John could not believe it. He told William who nearly fell out of his chair. A complete nobody had taken 5 percent of the vote in a little over a week. Hank came over and joined in the celebration. The party broke up around 11:00 p.m. John walked upstairs and fell asleep quickly. It had been a long, great first week.

Chapter 3

On Saturday, John called William and asked how someone could get an amendment added to the United States Constitution. William said the process would be a long and hard struggle. The United States Constitution basically provides two ways in which an amendment can be added. The first method involves the passage of a proposed amendment by two-thirds of both Houses of Congress. Afterwards, the bill is given to the state legislatures, and the Constitution requires three-fourths of the state legislatures to pass the amendment. Historically, this method has been used exclusively. John stated Congress would never pass a bill that would limit its ability to stay in office. William, however, said there was another way spelled out in the Constitution. Two-thirds of the state legislatures could call for a special constitutional convention. If this constitutional convention passes the amendment, it is sent to the state legislatures and will need a three-fourths vote for ratification. William pointed out this method has never been used. Some historical scholars believe calling a special constitutional convention may bring about more, unintended consequences. The group may convene and vote to disband the Supreme Court or something more drastic. John asked whether the state legislatures could allow discussion only on congressional term limits. William said yes, but once the convention started, the session would take on a life of its own. He pointed out it would still take three-fourths of the state legislatures to ratify any measure out of the convention. John asked William to start thinking how they could get this done.

For the rest of the weekend, John thought how reckless the founding fathers had been in not foreseeing how corrupt Congress could become. With the fledging country just leaving a monarchy, John thought term limits would have been one the first things considered. He had read several books on how presidents had grabbed non-enumerated powers such as Wilson's creation of the Federal Reserve, and the many harmful policies and new federal departments of Franklin Roosevelt. No one, however, had ever written a book on the silent power grabs and personal enrichment schemes that Congress had set up for its members. It was time for the US to stop being a country for those who could buy access, and go back to its historical roots—a country for and by the people. John knew all congressmen were not corrupt—as far as he knew there were only several dozen. However, the environment existed for such corruption to be cultivated. It was time to fix that problem. Based on what William told him, it was not going to be easy.

After church on Sunday, Hank called John to make final arrangements for the campaign's inaugural trip to New Hampshire. Hank told John that New Hampshire considers being the first primary state almost a birthright. John said a lot of time next week would be "meeting and greeting" the Republican Party leaders in the state. Hank e-mailed the schedule for next

week:

Sunday, May 8, 2011
5:55pm   Leaving Richmond Airport
10:37pm   Arriving Manchester Airport

Monday, May 9, 2011
7:00am   Scheduling Meeting
7:15am   Message Meeting
8:00am   Meeting with Jeffrey Frost, Chairman of Manchester GOP
11:00am   Lunch with Manchester Rotary Club
1:30pm   Meeting with Ted Gatsas, Mayor of Manchester
4:30pm   Meet with local field office personnel
6:00pm   Dinner with Manchester Chamber of Commerce
8:00pm   Leave for Concord

Tuesday, May 10, 2011
7:00am   Scheduling Meeting
7:15am   Message Meeting
8:00am   Meet with Jack Kimball, Chairman of Republican State Committee
11:00am   Interview with WKXL 1450 AM (News Talk Information)
1:00pm   Meet with local field office personnel
3:00pm   Radio interview - Sean Hannity
4:30pm   Interview with WWHK 102.3 FM (Talk Radio)
6:00pm   Dinner with Concord Chamber of Commerce
8:00pm   Conference Call with US Senator Kelly Ayotte
8:30pm   Conference Call with US Congressman Frank Guinta
9:30pm   Conference Call with US Congressman Charles Bass

Wednesday, May 11, 2011
6:30am   Leave for Portsmith, NH
7:00am   Scheduling Meeting (by cell phone in car)
7:15am   Message Meeting (by cell phone in car)
9:00am   Meet with local Republican Party Leaders
12:00pm   Meet lunch patrons at local eatery
1:00pm   Leave for Nashua, NH
3:00pm   Meeting with Nashua Mayor Donnalee Lozeau
6:00pm   Dinner with Nashua Chamber of Commerce
8:00pm   Leave for Derry, NH

Thursday, May 12, 2011
7:00am   Scheduling Meeting
7:15am   Message Meeting
8:30am   Meeting with Derry Mayor Brad Benson
10:30am   Meeting the Derry Chamber of Commerce
12:00pm   Lunch Meeting with Local Republican Party
2:00pm   Drive Back to Manchester
6:00pm   Dinner with Manchester GOP
8:00pm   Conference Call with Reince Priebus, Chair of GOP

Friday, May 13, 2011
7:00am   Scheduling Meeting
7:15am   Message Meeting
9:50am   Air Flight from Manchester, NH
2:17pm   Arrive in Richmond, VA

John looked over the schedule and said it was

24

going to be an eventful week. Hank said he would meet him at the Richmond airport at 5:00 p.m. John went upstairs and finished packing. He drove to the airport, parked his car in the long-term parking lot, and walked into the airport. When he went through security, he noticed several of the TSA agents recognized him. One of them mentioned he had seen the South Carolina debate and thought John had won. John thanked him and asked him to vote for him in the Virginia primary. As he boarded the airplane, he noticed Hank was already seated. John and Hank talked about the schedule during the flight to Manchester, New Hampshire. They arrived at the airport around 10:45 p.m. and at the Hampton Inn around 11:30 p.m. John told Hank that he would be downstairs at 5:00 a.m. the next morning for a workout and at breakfast at 6:30 a.m. Hank stated his room would serve as the place for the 7:00 a.m. and 7:15 a.m. meetings.

At 7:00 a.m., John walked down to Hank's room, and they jointly took part in the scheduling meeting. Jen went through the schedule for the day, and John could only think of how many new people he would meet. William jumped in and said the goal for the week was meeting as many people as possible. John smiled at that statement. The ultimate goal was to get major Republican leaders to realize the Randolph campaign was for real. New Hampshire was all about "retail politics." The people of New Hampshire needed to know the candidate before voting for him. William said focusing on term limits for congressmen would be the best thing to talk about; the elimination of the Department of Education would be a bad discussion topic in New Hampshire. Hank interrupted and said they needed to stop this meeting, and John and Hank left the hotel to get the day and the week started. John was a little worried Hank would drag him all over the state in five days.

The week was a complete blur—John shook the hands of a least two thousand people during the week. He ate so much "rubber chicken" that he thought his taste buds would never recover. Hank kept encouraging John, telling him that he was hitting "home runs" all week. John was not so sure. He did not hear any of the power brokers say they were going to support him. Mitt Romney had not announced yet. Romney would be favored to win New Hampshire since he was from Massachusetts.

John never understood the press. They picked winners based on what they thought, whether the person had announced his or her candidacy or not. There should be a law. If people had not announced their intentions, it should be illegal for the media to include them in their polls. This was, in effect, an enormous financial benefit for the undeclared candidates. Declared candidates had to pay for special polling. Even after the South Carolina debates, Romney and Palin were running unusually high in opinion polls, even though neither had declared as official candidates.

By Friday, as John was boarding an airplane to return to Virginia, he was thoroughly exhausted. There was a staff meeting on Saturday at 9:00 a.m. to discuss the scheduling details for the next week; the campaign would return to South Carolina. The week after that would be a return trip to Iowa. John decided, after the 9:00 a.m. conference call, he was going to relax for the rest of the weekend. There would be absolutely no campaign business.

Chapter 4

John drove his Ford F-150 pickup truck to campaign headquarters on Saturday morning. It was about 8:30 a.m. when he arrived, and he noticed both William's and Hank's cars in the parking lot. As a matter of fact, there were many cars in the parking lot. John went into the building, and Debbie Jones, Deputy Campaign Manager, almost knocked him down. She screamed he had been invited to be a guest on NBC's "Meet the Press" on Sunday morning. William noticed John had just walked in the office, and he quickly ran over. William stated they had a lot to do to get ready for the television show. John sighed. He had been looking forward to a quiet weekend with Jenny and possibly the grandchildren. John followed William into a large conference room where Hank and Debbie were already sitting. They started discussing the agenda for Sunday's program. Jen Harrison, Director of Advance and Scheduling, ran into the conference room, saying John's airline ticket was booked, and he was leaving the Richmond airport at 4:00 p.m. which was only several hours away.

"Meet the Press" is a liberal political show on NBC. The host, David Gregory, is known for attacking Republicans when they are guests on the show. William, Debbie, and Hank started quizzing John on all of the issues. They agreed John needed to keep the discussion centered on the economy. They felt David Gregory would try to steer the conversation toward John's previous occupation as CEO of a Wall Street firm during the financial meltdown. After three hours of intense preparation, John said he was ready. John walked with Hank to his office. Hank said fundraising had substantially increased since the South Carolina debate. Campaign funds totaled $8 million. Hank also said the campaign had leased a Boeing 737 airplane. John looked up. He asked Hank how costly the airplane was. Hank stated it would cost $25,000 per month plus operating costs. John asked if this was necessary and Hank chuckled. Hank said over the next six months John was going to live on the airplane. John reluctantly agreed to the expenditure, but it still perplexed him why a private airplane was necessary, particularly an airplane of this size.

John called Jenny on his drive back to The Willows and told her about the invitation to be on "Meet the Press." He asked Jenny if she would start packing for the overnight trip to Washington and for next week's trip to South Carolina. He also told her about the Boeing 737 airplane the campaign was going to lease. She said she was glad. This surprised John, because Jenny was exceedingly frugal. After hanging up the cell phone, John called William and asked his opinion of the aforementioned expenditure. William said Hank knew what he was doing, to stop worrying about it, and to trust him. William was always immensely direct. John left The Willows at 2:15 p.m. for the short drive to Richmond. When he got there, he noticed Hank waiting for him at the gate. Hank told John this would be the last trip out of Richmond flying commercial. John liked the idea, but was not sure if renting an airplane was spendthrift.

When they arrived in Washington, John said he wanted to spend some time looking at the possible questions that Debbie had put together. As they left for their individual hotel rooms, Hank mentioned that he had a lot of calls to make to South Carolina for next week's visit, but to call him if he wanted to discuss anything. John ordered room service and nibbled on his dinner. He was nervous about "Meet the Press," because the host was known for trying to stump the guest, in particular any Republican. He decided to go to sleep at 9:30 p.m., but it was a not a restful night. John woke up at around 5:00 a.m., worked out in the hotel's exercise room, came back to his room for a shower, and called room service for breakfast. At 7:00 a.m. his telephone rang, and it was Jenny who wished him luck. At 7:15 a.m., William called and offered some further advice. At 7:30 a.m., Debbie called. John was getting more nervous as each person wished him luck. He concluded they must be worried if they felt like they needed to call and wish him luck. Finally, Hank knocked on the door at 8:00 a.m., and they departed the hotel for NBC's Washington's news studio. When they arrived at the studio, they were ushered into the green room, which is a holding room for guests. Fifteen minutes before the show, David Gregory walked into the room to introduce himself. There were a few jokes and some laughter. John thought Gregory was trying to loosen him up before the kill. At ten minutes before the show, the show's producer walked in and gave John some final instructions. The producer led John out to the studio, "wired him up," and showed him where the cameras would be. At one minute before the show, the host walked in, already wired, and smiled at John. It was game time.

The show's theme music came on, and he heard his name mentioned as today's guest. The subject—should congressmen have term limits. David Gregory greeted the television audience and welcomed John, and the discussion began.

HOST: *Mr. Randolph, you announced you are running for president. You have announced a nine-point plan that you believe will fix America. You took part in the South Carolina debate and did remarkably well. And your polling numbers continue to rise.*

John: *We have had some good weeks.*

HOST: *Why do you think it is so essential for Congress to have term limits? Even the founding fathers served multiple terms in office, and many were lifelong congressmen. Men like Daniel Webster and Henry Clay. Why now?*

John: *You must admit the times are vastly different as compared to the 1790s through the 1830s. America was a fledging republic being held together by Band-Aids and rope. However, there were considerable disagreements. Some of the disagreements still persist today—too much government and not enough government. Slavery was of course one of the most contentious issues. Congressmen of that day did not have lobbyists and other special interest groups constantly in their collective ears.*

HOST: *Are you saying that we need term limits because congressmen today are on the take?*

John: *Of course not. I am saying the environment is ripe for such behavior. I may be naïve, but I do not think people aspire to be in Congress in order to enrich themselves with lobbyists' and special interest groups' money. I believe over time, congressmen forget why they are there and whose best interests they serve.*

HOST: *Getting a constitutional amendment requires approval of Congress. How could that possibly happen? They would basically be kicking themselves out of a job.*

John: *I agree. To ask Congress to do something about this would be a non-starter. There is another way in which a constitutional amendment can be originated. It would require a special constitutional convention originated by two-thirds of the state legislatures.*

HOST: *Do you think that is even possible?*

John: *I do not know. But America needs sweeping changes in the way we are doing things. I personally think it is outrageous for people to be in Congress for twenty, thirty, or forty years. Maybe, just maybe, the threat of a special constitutional convention would persuade Congress to vote for what is right vs. its own self-preservation.*

HOST: *Term limits for Congress is the first part of your nine-point plan. The second point is lobbyist reform. The Supreme Court ruled lobbyists and special interest groups have the right to petition and contribute as they see fit. What do you propose that would be different from what has already been overturned?*

John: *This may require another constitutional amendment. I agree the Supreme Court said lobbyists could spend whatever they wanted, but I would levy a tax of 50 percent on all contributions to PACs, re-election funds, anything in which lobbyists are buying influence. The federal government, under Barack Obama and Harry Reid, is exceptionally proficient at taxing. Under the Constitution, taxing is allowable as long as it is done equitably.*

HOST: *Since congressmen will again be hurt, I think this is an uphill climb as well.*

John: *David, our problems are enormous, and the solutions will need to be enormous to fix them. If it were easy to fix our problems, I would not need to run for president. Lobbyist reform could be issue number two at a special constitutional convention. I personally think Congress would be much more worried about a special constitutional convention than having either of these items as constitutional amendments.*

HOST: *Why do you say that?*

John: *Let's say that all of the procedural steps are taken to have a special constitutional convention. Everyone is told that its purpose is to propose constitutional amendments for both congressional term limits and curtailing the activities of lobbyists. While the convention is in session, new amendments could be proposed and passed in open sessions, assuming enough support is present. Think about some of the amendments that could see the light of day in a special constitutional convention—a balanced-budget amendment, an amendment making it illegal to have firearms, an amendment to disband the military, etc. The sky is the limit on what could be proposed.*

HOST: *So you think that Congress will bow down and agree to have amendments for term limits and the curtailment of lobbyists so they there will not be a special constitutional convention.*

John: *No. But in my opinion, the existing power brokers in this country would do anything to keep a special constitutional convention from happening.*

HOST: *The third point in your nine-point plan is campaign finance reform.*

John: *It is. We are sitting here talking about an election that is eighteen months in the future. I understand the president has already started receiving record-breaking contributions. My opponents have also started bringing in* contributions. In 2008, the president raised over $800 million. Eight hundred million was spent for a job paying $450 thousand. We have utterly lost our minds.

HOST: *What specific changes do you want to make?*

John: *1. Contributions cannot be collected until 365 days before the election. 2. Candidates cannot announce their intentions until one year before the election. 3. After the individual parties* select *their candidates, the presidential candidates must take federal funds, and they cannot supplement those funds. 4. All funds not spent must be handed to the federal government and must be used to pay down the debt.*

HOST: *Some say that this favors the "rich" candidates. You even have disclosed that you will personally contribute up to $100 million to your own campaign, if necessary.*

John: *I would not have to if I had been a career politician. The president and all of my opponents have run for office before. All of them had funds left over from previous campaigns. I have to contribute money to balance the playing field.*

HOST: *Most Americans would never be able to do what you are doing.*

John: *That is why we need massive campaign finance reform.*

HOST: *You have also proposed massive changes to entitlement programs. Some believe this could bring your campaign down when you spell out more details.*

John: *David, what you call massive, I call necessary. Entitlement spending encompasses one-third of all federal spending, and the percentage will rise to one-half in the next ten years. Some of my Republican opponents and all of the Democrats like to politicize entitlements. We need to fix them. I personally believe FDR was wrong to start them, but the federal government made promises that I, as president, will keep. The problem with entitlements is that they were created over the last one and one-half generations. It will take that much time to get them fixed.*

HOST: *A lot of people need Social Security, Medicare, Medicaid, etc. You are saying that you are going to get rid of them.*

John: *You must be working for the Democratic Party, because, that is the same kind of rhetoric they employ. My plan is anyone receiving or about to receive Social Security or Medicare will see absolutely no changes. For those that have not gotten to retirement age, we will allow them to save more in 401(k)s or some type of deferred tax instrument. The scale works itself down so that sooner or later entitlement programs will be only for those who truly need them. We will also change entitlement programs for Congress and federal workers to match the general public's programs.*

HOST: *We are running out of time. There are people who are criticizing you about the money you made while working at Smith Goldman. Your financial disclosures have stated you are worth around $900 million. You were also at the reins of the company during the economic meltdown in 2008, and your firm took $10 billion from TARP. It has also been said your firm engaged in transactions involving mortgage-backed securities. What is your response?*

John: *Several things you just said are unequivocally true. I was the CEO of Smith Goldman in 2008 during the financial meltdown, and the firm did trade in mortgage-backed securities. However, our firm never exceeded a leverage ratio of 16 percent. By the time the meltdown happened, our leverage ratio was well under 10 percent. This was lower than the "big commercial banks." The entities that failed or should have been allowed to fail had leverage ratios of 30–to–50 percent. As for the bailouts, our firm did not need the money that Hank Paulson and Tim Geithner forced upon us. We did not want or need the money. We were the second firm to repay the money with interest.*

HOST: *Why are you not a fat-cat Wall Streeter that is running to make sure Wall Street gets back to its proper place? You earned $900 million through salaries, bonuses, and stock options.*

John: *You know I retired in October 2010, and I have no financial interests left in the firm. I did make a lot of money during my time at the firm, but it was over many, many years. I worked my entire career there. I am also keenly aware of the things Wall Street did that were not good. I can fix them, because I already know what caused the financial meltdown. And I should point out the majority of my assets were generated when I sold my stock as I left the firm. It was not mostly created by massive bonuses as you alluded to. It was due to stock appreciation.*

HOST: *What is next for the Randolph campaign?*

John: *We will be in South Carolina next week and then a trip to Iowa. Afterwards, we will have a week in Virginia to get ready for the New Hampshire debate. Our polling data continues to show improvement, and we are continually working on getting our message out. After the New Hampshire debate, we are planning on introducing more details on entitlement reforms and more details on our roadmap to get America's financial health fixed.*

The host thanked John for being on the show. John shook Gregory's hand and walked out of the studio to the green room. Hank was there with a huge smile on his face. Hank just about talked John's ear off as they left NBC, got in the car, and drove to the airport. On the way, Jenny called John and said he'd done great. William and Debbie, who were now together at campaign headquarters, both called and said how well he had done. John asked William how the details were coming with the entitlement programs. William said there was still a lot of work to do. John said details were needed in two weeks. He and Hank arrived at the airport, returned the rental car, boarded a US Airways commuter airplane, and departed for South Carolina. The last "first" state, South Carolina, was going to hear from the Randolph campaign.

Chapter 5

John awoke in Charleston, South Carolina. This was going to be another extremely hectic, but eventful week. On Monday and Tuesday, John and Hank were going to be in Charleston, Florence, and Myrtle Beach. On Wednesday and Thursday, they would be in Columbia. On Friday, they would call upon the fine people of Greenville they had met several weeks ago.

The key goal of the week was to introduce John to the local Republican officials and office holders. John was also going to spend time visiting the "Randolph for President" field offices that were already in full operation in the state. John was impressed Hank and his team had accomplished so much in just a short amount of time. The campaign was also going to visit several civic organizations to introduce the Nine-Point Plan for Fixing America. Jenny had packed Tums so John was ready for the proverbial rubber-chicken dinners all week.

The morning scheduling meeting began promptly at 7:00 a.m. and at 7:15 a.m., William started the "message of the week" meeting. The message of the week was John's Nine-Point Plan. John knew the speech verbatim and did not need notes any longer. Debbie mentioned town hall meetings would be held in Charleston, Myrtle Beach, and Columbia. William also suggested John take part in daily pressers. This is when the candidate stands in front of the press pool and answer any questions they may have. Debbie and Hank were both against that strategy. They thought that was too much time for the press to fire questions. John said he would like to try it for a week to see what happened. Finally, Debbie said John would be interviewed at local Fox stations in both Charleston and Columbia, on Tuesday and Thursday respectively. John and Hank left the hotel shortly after the conclusion of the message meeting.

The first part of the week went exceptionally well even though John continued to have difficulties remembering all of the people he was meeting. Hank had assured John that campaigning would get easier. Hank kept John on schedule, and he stayed on message. He lost count of how many hands he shook during the week. As the week wore on, John started to get into a groove. Even during the daily pressers, he was able to deflect any unwanted questions by returning to the message of the week.

On Wednesday night, John and Hank had a conference call with Thomas Philpot, the campaign's Finance Director. Since being a guest on "Meet the Press," the campaign had brought in another $3.5 million. Total contributions and loans were $11.5 million, of which $9.2 million was available in cash. Hank said this news was positive. John asked Thomas specifically the source of the funds. Many contributions were of the maximum sort, but the campaign's website was also bringing in considerable numbers of ten, twenty, and fifty-dollar contributions. The direct mailings were also doing well. Thomas was complimented on his exemplary work and was instructed to continue his efforts. Thomas also mentioned the first month's rent had been paid on the Boeing 737, and the airplane would be delivered to the Newport News airport next week. Hank looked relieved, but John still had reservations.

On Thursday morning, John visited the South Carolina statehouse and attended a meeting sponsored by several of the state Republican legislators. That afternoon, John met with several Republican leaders. He also made a call on Nikki Haley, South Carolina's governor, at the governor's mansion in Columbia. He was greeted warmly everywhere he went, and several people inquired whether the campaign needed any assistance. John also met privately with several donors after dinner.

On Friday, John and Hank drove to Greenville to meet with people they had met earlier, during and after the debate. John continued to talk about the Nine-Point Plan on fixing America. While in Greenville, the campaign visited Senator Lindsey Graham's office. The senator congratulated John on the successes of the campaign, but made it known he disagreed with term limits for congressmen. The senator and John debated the issue for over an hour. At the end of the discussion, both men agreed to disagree. After the meeting, John and Hank went to the Greenville-Spartanburg airport and departed for Richmond, Virginia. John was so tired he dozed off on the return trip.

After arriving at the Richmond airport and driving back to Williamsburg, John drove his Ford F-150 down the driveway of The Willows. Jenny met him at the door. John was exhausted from the last ten days. He said he would go into the office the next day for the morning meetings, and he would finally get to have that relaxing weekend he had desperately wanted last weekend. Jenny demanded he follow that schedule. John fell asleep immediately after lying down in his bed. It had been another fantastic week. Next week, the campaign would visit Iowa again.

Chapter 6

When John arrived home from Iowa for the Memorial Day weekend, he was exhausted. The week had gone remarkably well, and John was beginning to feel more and more at home in Iowa. However, he was eagerly anticipating the Memorial Day weekend with Jenny, their children, and grandchildren. It would be an enjoyable weekend of playing in the pool, riding horses, and pleasurable eating. On Saturday afternoon, William and Sarah dropped by for a visit. It didn't take long for John and William to begin discussing campaign business. Jenny noticed the guys huddled together on one side of the pool patio. She immediately broke it up. John made baby back ribs for dinner. The grandchildren were allowed to sleep over at The Willows on Saturday night. On Sunday morning, John and Jenny went to church. As John and Jenny were helping the grandchildren get ready, Jenny mentioned the experience brought back distant memories of when they had gotten their own children ready for church. On Sunday afternoon, John played golf with William. On Monday, he gave a couple of Memorial Day speeches—one at the Norfolk Shipyard and one at a Memorial Day celebration at Fort Eustis, a US Army base near Newport News, Virginia. Later on Monday, John and Jenny discussed what the campaign activities were for the upcoming week—a week of preparation for the New Hampshire debate.

John got to campaign headquarters around 7:00 a.m. on Tuesday. He noticed several cars already in the parking lot. When he walked in, Debbie met him at the door and directed him toward the large conference room. The room had been set up like a debate hall and had handmade posters around the room. Debbie told him that everyone would join them in a few minutes. She said this would be called the "war room" for the next week. John thought war room was an appropriate name as he knew tempers would flare.

Hank and William walked in and were arguing about something. John tried to listen, but he knew it was a never-ending saga. William said former Pennsylvania senator Rick Santorum, Texas congressman Ron Paul, former Minnesota governor Tim Pawlenty, and former CEO Herman Cain, all of whom were at the South Carolina debate, would be at the New Hampshire debate. William also said former Speaker of the House Newt Gingrich and former Massachusetts governor Mitt Romney would be at the debate. Congresswoman Michele Bachmann, who had not declared, would also be there. William was betting she was going to use the debate to announce her candidacy, and she would get an immediate bump in the polls.

The following chart highlighted the polls since the last debate:

Poll	CNN	PPP (D)	Gallup	PPP (D)
Date	5/26/2011	5/25/2011	5/24/2011	5/8/2011
Romney	15%	16%	17%	24%
Palin	13%	16%	15%	17%
Cain	10%	12%	8%	0%
Gingrich	8%	9%	9%	20%
Paul	12%	9%	10%	12%
Bachmann	7%	9%	5%	8%
Pawlenty	5%	6%	6%	8%
Santorum	2%	2%	2%	0%
Randolph	8%	8%	7%	5%

William stated he was pleased with the progress the campaign had made; he knew they needed to slam-dunk the New Hampshire debate. The strategy was to promote the Nine-Point Plan and to attempt to get the overall discussion focused on that. The ultimate goal was to be in the top three, based on the exit polls, to continue focusing on the weak economy and the plan to fix it, and to continue making distinctions between John and the other candidates. If the polls were in the low-to-mid double digits after the debate, the campaign would be in outstanding shape for the rest of the summer.

William stated John King of CNN would be the moderator, and he would ask questions on several subjects: the economy, the deficit/debt, ObamaCare, foreign policy, and social matters (abortion, gay marriage).

All subjects were available for question. William suggested spending the next four days focused on:

Tuesday – Economy and the Deficit/Debt

Wednesday – ObamaCare

Thursday – Foreign Policy

Friday – Social Agenda and Other

William and Hank would take turns asking John questions. They coached John on how to answer the questions quickly and direct the discussion back to the Nine-Point Plan. William and Hank would cut John off whenever they felt he was getting too wordy. At lunch, John walked out of the building. He was becoming irritated at the process. He felt a little bruised and battered by William and Hank. At 1:30 p.m., they started the process again of shaping the answers for the debate. At the end of the day, William and Hank tried to stump John with some out-of-the-box questions. Overall, William and Hank thought the day went well. John, on the other hand, was visibly frustrated.

At 6:00 p.m., John had a radio interview with Mark Levin, a conservative talk-show host on Patriot Radio. After finishing the radio interview, he walked into William's office and asked whether "beating him up" was necessary for debate preparation. He pointed out this tactic had not taken place during the first debate preparations. William explained that John Randolph was a complete unknown at the first debate. This time, John King or one of his competitors may come after him. He needed to be thoroughly prepared on how to get the discussion back to what he wanted. John accepted that explanation and left for the day.

The rest of the week was a complete bloodbath in John's view. He was asked every question that could be asked. William and Hank critiqued every step of the way. The harshest area was foreign policy. John had no specific experience with foreign policy, and Hank felt it might be an area that his competitors would attack. William and Hank brought in a consultant at the end of the week. Victor Miller had been a former member of the state department under the Bush administration. As William, Hank, and now Victor started asking questions, John could see his shortfalls in this area. He also noticed how well versed Victor was in foreign policy. Victor kept walking John through the main trouble spots around the world. John knew his positions on certain foreign policy areas were different from Victor's. The most noteworthy example was America's involvement in Libya; Victor had confessed he thought America's involvement in Libya was the only way in which the region could be stabilized. John, on the other hand, was staunchly against engaging Libya. Libya was of little danger to America or its vital interests. During lunch, John spent the hour asking Victor questions about different "hot spots" around the world. He also asked Victor who he thought American's true friends were. The afternoon was similar to the morning—a lot of questions and constant criticism from the panelists. John resented the entire process.

By Friday, John and the panel had grown tremendously weary of each other. John had started getting testy with William and Hank, and they—in particular William—were returning the favor. By Friday afternoon, William and Hank decided it was time to start building John up. The William-and-Hank debate-preparation process consisted of "humbling" then "building up" the candidate. The humbling portion took three days, and the building-up portion lasted a couple of hours. The questions after lunch were "softballs," and of course, John nailed each of them. By the end of Friday afternoon, John and the panel were back to being friends. John invited William and Hank over to The Willows for dinner. Jenny was babysitting some of the grandchildren. John thought it would be an opportune peace offering to have the guys over for a steak and drinks. They accepted the invitation.

Friday night included a lot of laughing and recollection of the tense moments of the week. By airing the negatives, everyone felt better. At 10:00 p.m., William and Hank left The Willows just as Jenny was getting home. They warned her about the grouchiness of her husband as they laughed and got into their cars. John told Jenny about the events of the day. John also said the guys had started to build him up in the afternoon by lobbing softball questions at him. Jenny asked if he was ready for the debate. He said he thought so.

The weekend flew by and after church on Sunday morning, John and Jenny took the children and grandchildren out to lunch. John spent the rest of the afternoon and early evening reviewing the information from the previous week. He walked upstairs and noticed Jenny was packing for *them*. John was surprised Jenny was coming with him to the debate, but he wasn't going to complain. It would be great for her to be in the audience. The maiden voyage on the campaign's new Boeing 737 would be at 9:30 a.m., Monday morning. John and Jenny went to bed early so they would be refreshed for the trip.

The next morning, John and Jenny drove to the Newport News airport which was about twenty minutes from The Willows. As they drove to the private airplane hangars and first saw the campaign's new airplane, they were in awe. It was a Boeing 737 and painted on the side of the fuselage was "We Can Fix America – Randolph in 2012" in bright-blue letters, with "Randolph in 2012" in slightly larger letters. As John and Jenny approached the airplane, Hank walked down the stairs and met them at the bottom. Hank gushed about how wonderful the airplane was and hurried John and Jenny on board. As they walked up the stairs, they noticed a few people watching them. John turned around and waved. As they walked onto the airplane, they noticed how nice it was on the inside. To the left of the stairs was the cockpit. John introduced himself to the pilot and co-pilot and thanked them for working with the campaign. John started walking to the back of the aircraft. The first five or six rows were set up with first-class seats. Hank said the press would sit in this section on future flights. Over the wings, there was a curtain separating the next section. Hank opened it, and John noticed several additional rows with first-class seats. A food galley was positioned right behind those seats. Finally, the walkway led to a door. Behind the door was an office, or something like an office. Everywhere on the airplane, there were campaign placards. All in all, it was extremely nice.

Promptly at 9:30 a.m., the campaign's new airplane departed the Newport News airport for the two-hour trip to New Hampshire. Hank continued talking about the airplane, but John started thinking about the debate on Tuesday night. For Monday's activities, Jen Harrison had scheduled meetings with several Republican leaders John had met during the last visit. The rest of the day was busy giving mini-speeches on the Nine-Point Plan. So far, the plan was getting a great deal of positive interest from the American people. In particular, people were starting to embrace the idea of congressional term limits, and campaign finance and lobbyist reforms. The American people were beginning to see the problems with the current system, and they were beginning to see why the country was in such gridlock. This encouraged John, and he kept bringing up the issues at just about every scheduled event. People were even starting to at least talk about entitlement reform. Discussion of entitlement reform has always been considered political suicide, and it might still be. John, however, wanted to keep the discussion going. By the end of the night, he was exceedingly energized by the positive feedback he was getting on the Nine-Point Plan.

John spent the next morning and early afternoon reviewing all of the materials from the debate-preparation sessions from the previous week. He tried not to talk and to save his voice for the debate that evening. At around 5:30 p.m., John and Jenny ordered room service and had a quiet dinner. John started to feel some nervousness as time grew short. At 7:30 p.m., Hank came to the hotel room to drive John and Jenny to the convention center, the location of the debate. On arrival, they met with the members of the debate commission who gave John and Hank some final instructions. They said their holding room was located down the corridor on the right. John, Jenny, and Hank walked down the corridor and found the room marked with John's name. At around 8:55 p.m., someone from the debate commission walked in and asked John to follow. Jenny and Hank walked out of the holding room and into the main auditorium of the convention center. John was led to a room offstage. He smiled and shook hands with Tim Pawlenty, Rick Santorum, Herman Cain, and Ron Paul, all of whom he had met at the South Carolina debate in May. John introduced himself to former governor Mitt Romney, former Speaker of the House Newt Gingrich, and Congresswoman Michele Bachmann. No one was particularly talkative; everyone was nervous about the upcoming debate. No matter how extensive a front the candidates put up, everyone was anxious. At 9:00 p.m., John King of CNN went on the air. He introduced the candidates as they walked on the stage. Finally, it was time for the second Republican debate.

John King started the debate with a simple request of each of the candidates—state why you want to be president. Each of the candidates essentially gave a one and one-half minute summary of their current stump speech. John's answer was:

I want to be president so we can fix America. Over the last four years, America has been through extremely troubling economic times. Our debt has risen by over $5 trillion during this period, and unemployment has consistently been over 9 percent. Obama has purchased automobile companies that have been given to unions, wasted almost $1 trillion and called it stimulus, and managed to log more miles on Air Force One in an effort to be the most beloved US president in world history. The economic problems of America cannot be fixed by Band-Aids; they have to be fixed by adults willing to do what is right for America and its future instead of what is convenient for them today. It will take sacrifices by all Americans, not just the rich, or the poor, the middle class, or retirees—everyone will need to help us fix our problems.

I have developed a Nine-Point Plan that I believe will fix America and the problems that faces her. Primary among these changes are: (1) a constitutional amendment to impose term limits on members of Congress, (2) substantial campaign finance reform, and (3) limiting lobbyists from hijacking America. If we are able to get these initiatives in place, America can start the process of fixing itself. I am sure some of my opponents will criticize my proposals tonight. That would be the politically correct thing to do. If any candidate questions my proposal, please share your own proposal for fixing America. I am willing to discuss anything that is brought to the light of day. But your proposal needs to fix America, not simply push the problems downhill like Barack Obama's economic policies have done for the last two and one-half years.

Almost one year ago, I retired from private industry. I was looking forward to moving to Virginia and spending the rest of my life traveling with my wife and spending time with my children and grandchildren. Instead, I was given an opportunity to teach at my alma mater, The College of William and Mary. The subject matter was capitalism. After researching and preparing for the course, I realized America had gone from being the world's greatest example of capitalism to fundamentally an entitlement state bordering on a socialist state. If President Obama gets his way, a socialist society we will be. Prior to Obama, the changes were gradual and took almost two generations for the radical changes to be made. Woodrow Wilson's creation of the Federal Reserve, FDR's expansion of the federal government, LBJ's Great Society—all of these programs took capitalism and liberty and threw them in the trash. It was so gradual it was hard to see. Once you look back today and see what the ramifications of these programs were, you begin to see why the founders of this country were so specific in what powers the federal government could have. Every time the federal government tries to fix something, it spends more money and doesn't fix any of the problems. I knew I needed to run for president so we could fix America and provide hope for the American people, including my children and grandchildren.

Thank you.

The audience loudly applauded John's response, and John King motioned for them to quiet down.

The second question was how each of the candidates would have handled the Libya uprising if they were president. All of the candidates disagreed on how President Obama had handled the crisis. None of them would have involved US troops or military firepower.

The third question was whether President Obama had overstepped his constitutional authority in Libya by using US Armed Forces without congressional approval. With the exception of Newt Gingrich, the candidates believed there were no direct American interests threatened, and therefore, the president had overstepped his authority. Congressman Ron Paul added that the campaigns in Iraq and Afghanistan were not constitutional either, even though congressional approval had been gained before each military action. Paul wasn't given an opportunity to expand his thoughts.

John King announced the next series of questions were related to the economy. He stated the economy was in extremely precarious shape, and the unemployment rate was still above 9 percent. The American people were struggling to pay their bills and to stay in their homes. King asked what each candidate would do to fix the economy. Each of them had answers to this question which were full of promise, but lacking in specifics other than cutting taxes and reducing federal spending. John responded:

The easy answer is to do the exact opposite of what the president has done. It seems everything he did had a negative impact on the economy. The very first thing that needs to be done is reduce the corporate tax rate from 35 percent, which is the highest of the G-20 countries, to 20 percent. What Obama has forgotten is that the government doesn't create jobs; the free-market system and companies create jobs. We also need to make the Bush tax cuts permanent. A massive, progressive income tax increase will certainly kill any growth the economy has. The next thing we need to do is get federal spending under control. We need to push spending levels back to 2008 levels at a minimum and 2006 if possible. We need to look at every line of the budget and cut, including programs that are sacred cows. We need to substantially reduce our footprints in Iraq and Afghanistan immediately, and have a full plan for the withdrawal of the American military from both countries within the next two years. Almost half of our tax receipts are spent on the military. We need to look at how to fix our entitlement programs, including substantially reducing the growth curve on all programs. This may be the wrong thing to mention politically, but it is the right thing to discuss. We need to repeal ObamaCare and put in measures that will truly reduce medical costs in the future, such as tort reform and portability of insurance policies across state lines. We also need to balance the federal budget. We should put a law in place that prevents income-tax hikes unless spending is cut by a margin of at least three to one. We also need to implement a VAT or national sales tax so we can begin the process of debt reduction. This VAT tax provision will have a "poison pill" attached which will make the tax void if the additional taxes are used for additional spending. All of these items have been spelled out in my plan for fixing America. The key is there can't be any sacred cows—all ideas are open for discussion. I am looking forward to seeing the specific plans of each of my fellow candidates on stage.

John King asked each of the other candidates what their specific plans were for fixing the economy. Since none of them had specific plans, they rambled though their responses. Michele Bachmann and Newt Gingrich questioned some of the initiatives in the entitlement-reform portion of John's Nine-Point Plan. John said his specific ideas would be further disclosed in the future. He did, however, mention he looked forward to reading Congresswoman Bachmann's and former Speaker Gingrich's ideas when they were available. As a final comment, John stated:

If any politicians come to you and say they can balance the federal budget without entitlement-program reforms, they are lying directly to your face. Don't let them do that to you.

This drew a massive applause from the crowd.

The rest of the debate dealt with other issues. The majority of the responses were from the candidates' stump speeches with nothing new added. As William expected, Michele Bachmann announced her intention of running for president. At the end of the debate, John King allowed each of the candidates an opportunity to speak directly to the American people. John's response was as follows:

I love America. America has provided many opportunities for me, my incredible wife Jenny, our two beautiful children and their spouses and many promises for our grandchildren. America has allowed me to have a comfortable life. All I had to do was work hard, keep my nose clean, and work for the benefit of the company that employed me. America has always been the greatest example of liberty, freedom, and capitalism, for the entire world to see. Over the last four years, the American Dream, with its corresponding hope, has been put to the biggest test that it has seen in a long time. The housing bust, the financial meltdown, high and constant unemployment, runaway federal spending, projected massive deficits as far as you can see, and a president and Congress more worried about passing socialized medicine than helping the American people. I have put forth a Nine-Point Plan I believe will fix America. I am not willing to be elected to go on and continue the same policies of the past, whether the policies were Republican or Democrat. I want to thoroughly transform America by first fixing America. After we stop the bleeding, we can start the healing process and get America growing again.

I see a chance for Americans to work together to fix our problems. No one group caused the problems and no one president or session of Congress allowed the problems to fester. Someone needs to be the adult and be honest with the American people about the problems facing America. The problems are not easy, and the answers to the problems will not be easy either. It will take sacrifice from every American—the rich, the poor, the educated, the less educated, black, white, male, and female—every American will be called on to help fix America.

America has a history of rallying to solve big problems. During World War II, the American people did without many basic necessities so those resources could be used by our troops in Europe and in the Pacific. During 9/11, every American came together to provide not only financial support, but moral support to those who lost loved ones.

Hurricane Katrina, the Mississippi floods; the American people have a gene in their makeup allowing them to forget themselves and focus on their fellow Americans and the collective good. This gene is not found in the government but in ourselves. My plan will require this gene to come to life again so we can fix America.

The American Dream is still alive; it is just buried under massive spending, high unemployment, and unsustainable amounts of debt. The hope of America is the collective hope of its people. America's greatest days are ahead of her; I believe this with all of my heart and soul.

I thank you for listening to us tonight; I thank each of the candidates on stage, and ask that God continue to bless you, your families, and our magnificent country. Thank you.

Jenny joined John onstage after the debate. They both shook hands with the other candidates and their families. John also shook the hands of many Republican leaders who were in the crowd. As the Randolph campaign exited the building, John found himself shaking hands with the people backstage—the camera operators, the stage hands, and the security personnel. As they walked outside the building, a small group of people cheered as they saw John. John stopped, shook their hands, and talked to several of them. Most of them congratulated him on a great debate. As soon as Hank could pull John away, they loaded into the car and sped off to the airport. Once inside the car, Hank let out a massive yell. He said John had decisively won the debate, during which, he had continued to point out his opponents did not have a plan to fix America. This allowed John's Nine-Point Plan to be the center focus of the discussion, and it effectively won the debate for him. William and Debbie called Hank from campaign headquarters, and Hank put the call on his cell phone's speaker. They announced they were watching Fox News, and the independent panel had chosen John as the clear winner. Everyone was celebrating the momentous victory.

When they got to the airport, John, Jenny, and Hank walked up the stairs of the airplane and continued to the back. As the airplane took off, John looked at Jenny and said for the first time since the campaign had begun, he felt like he might just have a chance on winning. Jenny nodded in agreement. The flight home was entertaining, as Hank was practically jumping around the cabin. Hank imitated John's responses, verbatim in some instances. John was told on the flight back to Virginia that he was booked on Wednesday night's "Sean Hannity Show." Tomorrow, he would need to fly to New York for the show. On Thursday, John would meet with New York Republican leaders. On Friday, the campaign would return to New Hampshire to take a victory lap around the state. In some ways, the campaign was just beginning. Up to now, John's mission had been introducing himself to the electorate. Now, his goal was to convince America he was the right choice as their next president.

Chapter 7

John spent the next two weeks flying between Iowa, New Hampshire, South Carolina, and Virginia meeting with donors and field operation personnel. Daily, John was on a news show, whether it was regular radio, Patriot Radio, or television. Hank hired Charles Crawford as a "body man" for John. His primary job was to keep John on track and to feed information from campaign headquarters. Polling data showed the campaign was moving in the right direction after the successful June 7, 2011 New Hampshire debate.

Poll	Rasmussen	NBC/WSJ	PPP (D)	Gallup	CNN
Date	6/14/2011	6/13/2011	6/12/2011	6/11/2011	5/26/2011
Romney	30%	30%	22%	24%	15%
Palin	0%	14%	15%	16%	13%
Cain	10%	12%	17%	9%	10%
Gingrich	9%	6%	9%	5%	8%
Paul	7%	7%	7%	7%	12%
Bachmann	12%	3%	8%	5%	7%
Pawlenty	6%	4%	9%	6%	5%
Santorum	6%	4%	0%	6%	2%
Randolph	20%	14%	13%	12%	8%

In the most recent Rasmussen poll, the Randolph campaign had broken the 20 percent mark and only trailed Mitt Romney. The climb had been steady, which is exactly what a previously unknown candidate wanted. Of course, William reminded John that Palin was not in the latest poll, and she could have a considerable impact on the entire field. Hank and William believed some of the contenders would drop out after the Iowa straw poll in August. By the time Super Tuesday came in February, only three or four candidates would remain in the field. Of course, that was a long time in the future.

John and the team (William, Hank, and Debbie) met with Thomas Philpot, the campaign Finance Director. After the debate, contributions had really been heavy, and the following showed the status of campaign funds:

(000s)	Total Contributions	Total Loans from JR	Total Expenditures	Cash On Hand
5/31/2011	9,500.0	2,000.0	(2,300.0)	9,200.0
6/15/2011	4,125.0	-	(1,250.0)	12,075.0
Total	13,625.0	2,000.0	(3,550.0)	12,075.0

At this rate, John and Jenny would not need to contribute their $100 million to the campaign. The campaign was firing on all cylinders. The next critical event was the Iowa debate on August 11, 2011. On August 13, 2011, the most prominent poll to date would be held and issued. It was the Ames (Iowa) straw poll, and it would tell the candidates in what position they were in Iowa, the first state to vote during the primary/caucus season. It has always been critical to show well in the early states to keep contributions flowing to the campaign, even though the number of electoral votes would be relatively small.

Over the last two weeks, William and Hank had spent the majority of their time developing a new strategy focusing on the Nine-Point Plan. The new plan called for more details to be shared with the American public. Since the debates, Romney, Bachmann, Santorum, and Pawlenty had communicated their own fix-America plans. Romney's plan was called Five Ways to Address the Economy; Bachmann's was called Six Points to Transform America, Santorum's was Four Suggestions on Revitalizing America, and Pawlenty' s plan was Seven Guidelines to Transform America. Each of these "new" plans had aspects of the Randolph campaign's Nine-Point Plan, but all were short on specifics. Cain had presented his "Nine-Nine-Nine" plan which called for a 9 percent corporate tax, a 9 percent individual tax, and a 9 percent national sales tax. William and Hank decided to continue pressing the gas pedal and keep driving the discussion by providing further details on the Randolph campaign's Nine-Point Plan.

On Saturday, June 18th, John, William, Hank, and Debbie met at campaign headquarters to discuss the new strategy. The ultimate goal was to continue the upward momentum of the campaign and to focus on the Iowa debate and Ames straw poll. Over the next seven weeks, the campaign was going to adhere to the following agenda:

Week of	Message of the Week
June 20th	How to Fix the Economy
June 27th	How to Address The Entitlement Programs
July 4th	Going After Congress (Term Limits/Earmarks)
July 11th	Going After ObamaCare
July 18th	Department of Education
July 25th	Public Unions
August 1st	Getting Ready for Iowa Debates

For the first week, John would stay focused on how to fix the economy. Whatever question was asked, John needed to redirect the discussion back to fixing the economy. The discussion was to be 25 percent on Obama's failures and 75 percent on the campaign's plan to fix it. A heavy emphasis on balancing the federal budget also needed to be addressed. The second week needed to focus on fixing entitlement programs. The first 25 percent needed to preach about what will happen if nothing is done, and the remaining 75 percent needed to focus on remediation plans. If nothing else was heard in the discussion, the fact that current retirees would see no changes in their benefits must be the most remembered tagline of the message. The third week would start with John giving a speech at the Lincoln Memorial. He would introduce either legislation from Congress or a grassroots campaign. The grassroots effort would initiate a special constitutional convention in the state legislatures, in hopes of getting congressional term limits. William was still working with a few senators and representatives in Congress that would possibly take on the fight. The fourth week would be about repealing ObamaCare. This would be 50 percent bashing the truly heinous parts of the enacted bill and 50 percent discussing specifics of the campaign's plan to fix health care. The fifth week would be discussing the elimination of the Department of Education. All press conferences would be at schools or colleges. The sixth week would focus on eliminating public unions. Finally, in the seventh week, the campaign would prepare for the Iowa debate. This entire plan was to ensure John would perform well in the Ames straw poll which would be conducted a couple of days after the Iowa debate.

The new strategy also included details on where John and the campaign were going to spend their time. The following denotes the travel portion of the new strategy:

Tier	State	Primary/Caucas Date	# of Visits
Tier 1	Iowa	1/16/2012	4
	New Hampshire	1/14/2012	2
	Nevada	1/28/2012	2
	South Carolina	1/28/2012	2
	Florida	1/31/2012	2
Tier 2	Alabama	2/7/2012	1
Super	Arkansas	2/7/2012	1
Tuesday	California	2/7/2012	1
	Connecticut	2/7/2012	1
	Delaware	2/7/2012	0
	Georgia	2/7/2012	1
	Illinois	2/7/2012	1
	Missouri	2/7/2012	1
	Montana	2/7/2012	0
	New Jersey	2/7/2012	1
	New York	2/7/2012	1
	Oklahoma	2/7/2012	1
	Tennessee	2/7/2012	1
	Utah	2/7/2012	1
Tier 3	Michigan	2/28/2012	1
Big States	Ohio	3/6/2012	1
	Texas	3/6/2012	1
	Pennsylvania	4/24/2012	1
	North Carolina	5/8/2012	1

This part of the strategy was to break up the states into four different buckets. Tier 1 states would include the first five states having caucuses and primaries. If a candidate did not do well in these contests, campaign funds would dry up quickly. With the exception of Florida, there were actually very few electoral votes in play from the Tier 1 states. The Tier 2 states would be Super-Tuesday states. On Super Tuesday, fourteen states would hold their contests. It is crucial the candidate does well in these states and hopefully starts building a comfortable lead. The Tier 3 states would include the remaining big states. Finally, Tier 4 states would include all other states. The plan called for John to visit each of the Tier 1 through Tier 3 states at least once between the week of June 20th and August 1st, with the exception of Delaware and Montana. George Jenkins, the Press Secretary, and Charles Crawford, the "Body Man," would accompany John on all of these trips. Hank and Debbie would take turns and would accompany the travel squad on most of the trips. William said the only thing that was not in the strategic plan was intangibles. Intangibles would include mistakes made, questions from reporters needing immediate answers, events that needed comment, etc. William said these items needed to be addressed by George and never by the candidate. The group continued talking about the new strategy for the next several hours.

John arrived home to The Willows and noticed Jenny had invited the children and grandchildren over for dinner. John walked over to Jenny and showed her his schedule for the next seven weeks. She looked at him with her mouth open in amazement. John hoped she would go on some of the trips. It would be a bonus if the children and grandchildren were able to travel as well. The family spent dinner and the rest of the evening discussing plans.

Everyone seemed excited about going on the campaign trail, especially about flying on a private airplane. It was decided everyone would accompany John on the weeks of July 4th (Washington, DC, Iowa, Nevada, California, and Texas) and July 25th (South Carolina, Florida, Arkansas, and Tennessee). John called Debbie and told her about the new revelations. Debbie was thrilled the entire family was going. It would be beneficial to present John as first and foremost a family man to the American people. Debbie called Jen Harrison, Director of Scheduling and Advance, to make the appropriate arrangements.

On Sunday morning, John drove to Richmond for a Fox Sunday interview (broadcast nationally), and he got back to Williamsburg in time to go to church with the family. The afternoon was enjoyable but seemed hectic as John packed for the next week. It was the final day before the seven-week onslaught.

Chapter 8

Before John knew it, it was Monday morning. He walked out of his door at The Willows and was startled by Charles Crawford who was waiting near a car in front of the house. Even though he was surprised to see Charles standing there, he got in the car with him and rode to the Newport News airport. Waiting by the campaign's airplane were four reporters (one each from Fox News, CNN, NBC, and ABC) and George Jenkins. John and Charles greeted George and boarded the airplane. It departed at precisely 6:00 a.m. This would be the sequence of events repeating itself over the next six weeks on Monday mornings.

The first week was to begin in Iowa where Jen had scheduled meetings in the three largest cities—Des Moines, Cedar Rapids, and Davenport. The message of the week was "How to Fix the Economy." John was going to talk about reducing the corporate tax rate from 35 percent to 20 percent, reducing the size and scope of business regulations, an R&D tax credit for businesses, his plan for eliminating the deficit, and his plan for implementing a value-added tax to be used exclusively for debt reduction. On the flight to Des Moines, George held a press conference to communicate the events of the day to the press pool. John walked into that part of the airplane as George was finishing his remarks. The press asked John what he thought about the events in Libya. John did not answer the question and started talking about the pitiful state of the economy. He talked about how high the unemployment numbers were and how little the economy was growing. He talked about how he had a plan to fix the economy. The reporters asked John questions about the economy and his proposals to fix it. John answered every one of their economic-based questions. Afterwards, he walked back to the private cabin and called in to campaign headquarters. Charles jotted down notes on the day's events. When the airplane landed, John, George, and Charles loaded into a Ford Expedition. The reporters piled into a van and followed behind them. The events ranged from speeches to meetings with business leaders, to fundraisers, to meeting with field operation personnel and with Republican political leaders. At 8:00 p.m., the caravan returned to the airport, and the group boarded the airplane and departed for New Hampshire. By the time they got to the hotel at around 11:00 p.m., everyone was exhausted.

On Tuesday, the group spent the day in New Hampshire visiting Manchester, Nashua, and Concord. The message of the week was "Fixing the Economy," and it was the only subject discussed by the campaign. At 3:30 p.m., John had a phone interview with Sean Hannity, and at 6:35 p.m., he had a telephone call with Bret Baier. At 9:00 p.m. the group departed Manchester and flew the short trip to Buffalo, New York.

On Wednesday, the group spent the day in the northern part of the Empire State. The group visited Buffalo, Rochester, and Syracuse. John participated in his first "reverse town hall," and George thought the results were exceedingly positive. On Wednesday night, the team arrived at Kennedy International airport in New York City. They spent Thursday on Long Island visiting Republican strongholds. On Thursday night, they crossed the river by caravan and went to a fundraiser in Newark, New Jersey. On Friday, the group visited Jersey City and Paterson. John gave speeches at several events sponsored by civic organizations. By 6:00 p.m., John and the group arrived back at Kennedy airport. As soon as John and the group boarded the airplane, he took part in a radio interview by telephone with Mark Levine. After the airplane was airborne and the interview was concluded, he asked George to pull the reporters together. John took their questions on any subject. He stated that the president should have gotten approval from Congress before committing troops to Libya, and personally he did not see any imminent danger to America's interests. One reporter asked whether he thought Sarah Palin was going to run for president. John did not know. They asked about his former job as a CEO, and John explained the situation again. Finally, they asked additional questions about his plan for fixing the economy. After about twenty minutes of Q&A, John said he would play straight with them and hoped they would play straight with him. These press conferences would continue on each return trip to Newport News. When the airplane arrived at its destination, John was exhausted. Charles drove him to The Willows, and shortly thereafter, John was asleep.

On Saturday morning, John went to campaign headquarters and met with Hank, William, and Debbie. William told John all of the Republican candidates had spent the majority of the week on the economy, which was a telling sign: the Randolph campaign was dictating the weekly discussion. Hank said new polls would be released next week that would give them some information on how the message was being received. William and Hank did not approve of John's impromptu press conference on the airplane back from New York on Friday night. John said he wanted to show the reporters he was a straight shooter, and he hoped they would follow suit. William and Hank urged him to discontinue the Friday night "pressers." John had already made up his mind, and the Friday night pressers ("FNPs") would continue. Debbie told John that ABC News would be at campaign headquarters the next morning for a satellite interview with George Stephanopoulos. The entire team would meet at campaign headquarters at 7:30 a.m. John left the office around 2:00 p.m. and went to the Golden Horseshoe golf course. He played golf with William, his son, and his son-in-law. Afterwards, the children and grandchildren came to The Willows for dinner and a movie. It was a truly relaxing evening.

On Sunday morning, John drove to campaign headquarters and noticed an extremely large ABC News truck in the parking lot. John walked in, and Debbie met him at the front entrance. She rushed him into a small conference room where some makeup artists were waiting. After applying makeup, Debbie hurried John into the main conference room where a camera was pointed towards a chair and a poster displaying "We Can Fix America." John sat down, implanted an earpiece, and waited for the red light to illuminate. At 9:01 a.m., the red light on the camera came on, and the interview with ABC News began. Several topics were covered—the economy, Libya, Afghanistan, Iraq, the federal debt, and entitlement reforms. The interview lasted approximately twenty minutes. John shook the hands of the camera crew, who seemed surprised a political candidate would shake their hands. John drove to The Willows to get Jenny for church. After church, John and Jenny spent the day together discussing the future events of the campaign.

During the week of June 27th, the campaign visited South Carolina on Monday (both Columbia and Greenville). On Tuesday and Wednesday, the campaign was in Florida (Miami and Fort Lauderdale on Tuesday, Jacksonville and Tampa on Wednesday). On Thursday, it visited Alabama (Birmingham and Montgomery). On Friday, the campaign spent the day in Atlanta, Georgia. The message of the week was entitlement reform. The primary talking points for the week included:

1. The entitlement programs are going bankrupt faster than anyone expected.
2. Entitlement programs can and must be fixed so that they can be available in the future.

3. Social Security – **No changes to existing recipients.** There will be graduated reductions in benefit payments based on age. Of course, younger people will pay less into the trust fund. The program will have to be means tested.

4. Medicare – **No changes to existing recipients.** Repeal ObamaCare and the heinous impacts on Medicare ($650 billion abduction).

5. Welfare – Move the program to the states. The federal government has created a generational dependence.

6. Medicaid – Move the program to the states.

7. Unemployment Insurance – Change the total available weeks back to thirty weeks as opposed to the ninety-nine weeks currently in place.

8. "Don't believe the politician who says that we can balance our budget and fix our economy without reforming entitlements."

The week started particularly well with enthusiastic crowds in both Columbia and Greenville, South Carolina. A fundraiser in Greenville produced a standing-room-only crowd. In Miami, John saw the ugly head of the Progressive Movement when some people in the crowd claimed his entitlement reforms wanted to kick grandfathers and grandmothers into the street. After security escorted the protesters out of the convention center, John stood quietly on the stage. He looked out across the audience, decided to "go off-message" which he knew would draw the wrath of William, and talk directly to the crowd, consisting mostly of senior citizens. He said the following:

People of Florida. Let's cut through the mess, the untruths, and the lies, and talk about one of the differences between the current political establishment and what I am proposing. Even most of my GOP competitors are part of the political establishment. President Obama and his liberal friends in Congress are undeniably part of the existing establishment. I am not. I have never held political office in my life. I have not been part of the establishment that created this economic mess that we are in today. I know my brother, who is my main political advisor, is going to chastise me for what I am saying, but I need to get this off of my chest. How many of you remember Bernie Madoff?

John looked around the crowd and noticed that people were either raising their hands or nodding their heads in agreement.

Bernie Madoff was put in jail for the creation of a $50 billion Ponzi scheme, and he deserved to put in jail. He cheated many of the people that trusted him with their money. How are the schemes that FDR created with Social Security and LBJ created with Medicare any different than what Madoff did? Both schemes essentially pay people with funds received from others. The theory behind both was that there would always be enough future funds to offset those receiving funds. Madoff's scheme ran out of money in 2008 as the stock market went south. The Social Security and Medicare schemes are scheduled to meet their doom in the next ten years, as the number of people receiving benefits will be greater than the number contributing to the programs. These entitlement programs comprise over one-third of the total expenditures of the federal government, and they will continue to increase over the next ten years. Soon they will be at 100 percent.

I am not here to scare you. I am here to tell you the truth. The president, Congress, and even some of my GOP competitors have been unwilling to tell you the truth for fear of losing their positions or losing their chances of serving you. I will tell you now—none of them is willing to be an adult and tell the American people the truth. The American economy needs adults at the table, and I am willing to be at the head of that table. We need to have an honest dialogue about the state of our economic situation and tell the truth to the American public. The American people are the best, most resilient people in the world. During World War II, they did without to support the military cause. During Hurricane Katrina, the American people went to the Gulf Coast to help out in any way they could. If they could not go, they contributed monetarily to the cause. The Japanese earthquakes, the Haitian earthquakes, the tornados in the south this past spring— the American people always step up and come together to fix the problem, even if it is at their own personal expense. I honestly believe once the American people are given the *absolute truth about the state of our entitlement programs and how they are inherently taking money from our children and grandchildren, they will step up and make the necessary sacrifices.*

Over the last two months since I announced my candidacy, I have been the only candidate to come out with a comprehensive plan for fixing America. The other GOP contenders have attacked me behind my back as my polling numbers have improved, and of course President Obama and his minions have attacked me on every front. While my plan is highly specific and documented, they have lied, and I use the word "lied" because their deceit is willful and intentional, especially on my positions on entitlement reform. Why, you may ask? Because they do not have a plan of their own, and their only plan is to attack me. As I have stated on many occasions—If you are a retiree today or over the age of sixty, your Social Security and Medicare benefits will not change. Let me repeat that again—If you are a retiree today or over the age of sixty, your Social Security and Medicare benefits will not change. You have my promise on that. For people between fifty and fifty-nine, there will be a reduction by approximately 15 percent of today's current benefits. They will continue to decrease until today's grade-school children will not receive any benefits. For any people truly in need, benefits will be available. That is my promise to you.

This election is about more than Obama, and any one of my competitors. It is about fixing America. Please take note, I am not promising hope—I am promising to fix America with your help. The current political establishment has put this country on a crash course with ultimate bankruptcy. I am here to rescue America and the America people from this calamity. I do not need this position, and I am not looking for power. I am looking to fix America, because I feel like I owe America and the American people for the many blessings that I have been given. Please help me to succeed in this effort. I cannot do this without your support. Once we fix America, we can resuscitate the renowned American hope that currently seems so far away. God bless you and God bless your families and God bless America.

John stepped back from the podium and stood perfectly still in front of the crowd which was estimated to be over five hundred. A single clap started and then another. In a matter of seconds, the entire crowd was cheering uncontrollably about the speech John had just given. People started a chant of "Randolph!" John smiled, waved for a few moments, and walked off the stage. George and Charles met him as he walked off the stage. Both were standing there, utterly dumbfounded. John smiled as he walked by them. He continued walking past security personnel and the stagehands that were also clapping and smiling. George and Charles caught up to John as they walked toward the car. George asked what had just happened. All three were silent as they got in the car and sped off to the next event. George's cell phone started to ring, and John started to worry about who was calling—he was sure it was William. George answered the phone, and John could hear William faintly in the background, but could not pick up the entire conversation. George finally told John that William wanted to talk to him. John took a deep breath and said hello. William said the speech was incredible. The telephones were ringing off the hook, and the volume of Internet inquiries had shut down the website. All of the news outlets were running the speech in its entirety. William asked what had happened. John said a couple of liberal knuckleheads had caused a ruckus, and John essentially went from the heart on what he thought. William said even the liberal media were reacting positively to the speech. Keith Olbermann stated the entire situation was a stunt created by the Randolph campaign so John could give the speech. William told John not to say another word to the press until tomorrow. John handed the cell phone back to George. After a few minutes, George told the driver to head back to the airport.

Charles looked at John and said he was extremely proud to be working for him during this campaign. John smiled at Charles and patted him on the leg. George's cell phone rang again; he immediately handed it to John and mouthed it was Jenny. John answered, and Jenny said that was the best speech she had ever heard. She asked why he had given it. John explained the entire story again.

80

She said she was proud he had not lost his temper while dealing with the liberal hecklers. As soon as he hung up the telephone with Jenny, Hank was on the cell phone congratulating John on the speech. John thanked him for the compliment and said he needed to get off the telephone. When the convoy reached the airport, the reporters jumped out of the van and tried to get John to answer some questions. John smiled, waved, and boarded the airplane. John was following William's orders. He went back to the private quarters of the airplane and contemplated what just happened. John had gone on complete impulse, and it appeared to have worked. How could he possibly do that again?

The rest of the week consisted of John answering questions about his speech on Tuesday in Miami. The campaign was being asked to speak to nearly every political news show. The campaign did as many as possible, but some were still asking. Even the traditionally liberal organizations—MSNBC, ABC, NBC, CBS, and CNN— were all asking for John to appear. There simply was not enough time. The campaign did have time for Fox News and several of the conservative commentators who had provided an outlet for the campaign before the speech. By the time the week was over, John's speech was still being aired on every news channel on each news cycle. The speech went "viral" on YouTube.

In the Friday night presser on the way back to Newport News, John was asked his opinion of the speech that President Obama had given imploring the GOP House to start leading and come up with a solution on the debt ceiling. John stated:

President Obama had another chance to lead, and again, he has basically shunned his responsibilities. In the health-care debates, he asked Nancy Pelosi and Harry Reid to come up with a bill so he could sign it. Obama has not taken his leadership responsibility very seriously. He consistently waits for others to lead, and he swoops in and takes credit. The president must lead the country, not passively expect others to do so. The main problem is the president does not have a solution to the debt ceiling question—or he doesn't have a favorable political solution. He has only mentioned he wants to tax millionaires and billionaires more. He said they could afford more. What kind of thinking is that? Paying taxes is not a luxury! It is not something people want to do with their hard-earned money. It is a requirement imposed at the barrel of the IRS's gun. It is time for the president to give America a solution instead of more hollow talk.

On Saturday morning, John was interviewed by CBS, ABC, NBC, CNN, and Fox for their Saturday morning news shows. John announced during each of the interviews that he was going to be in Washington, at the Lincoln Memorial, on Sunday, July 3rd at 10:00 a.m. for an important announcement. He invited all the people to please join him at the Lincoln Memorial around the reflecting pool for the announcement.

On Saturday night, John, Jenny, the children, and grandchildren boarded the campaign's airplane and departed for Washington, DC. The family stayed at the Churchill Hotel on DuPont Circle. William, Hank, and Debbie joined the group for the trip to Washington. When everyone had checked in to the hotel, William met with John on the speech for the next day. William felt it necessary to coach John on how to give a speech, even though John was getting proficient at it. It was going to be an exciting event.

Chapter 9

John woke up looking at Jenny. It was about 7:00 a.m. and John did not want to wake her, but he wanted to get her advice on something. She was the smartest person John knew when it came to knowing him. He nudged her, and she awoke. John apologized for waking her up, but said he wanted her opinion on the speech that was to be given today. They talked about the speech and what it meant. She said he should poke out his chest and deliver the speech the same way he had given the one in Miami on Tuesday. John did not know if he could generate the same amount of passion.

Promptly at 7:30 a.m., Charles knocked on the door. Jenny hurried into the bathroom, and John opened the door. The room was a suite, but it still seemed small when Charles came in followed by Hank, William, George, and Debbie. By the time Jenny came out of the bathroom fully dressed, the room was buzzing about the day's event. John went into the bathroom, took a shower, and dressed for the event. When he came out, someone had ordered room service. John nibbled on a piece of toast and had a couple of cups of coffee, but was too far too nervous to eat a lot. At around 9:30 a.m., Charles told John it was time to leave. John motioned to Jenny to get the children and grandchildren for the limousine ride over to the Lincoln Memorial. As everyone loaded into the car, Jenny kissed John and said he was going to be great today. When they arrived at the Lincoln Memorial, John got out of the car and noticed there was an extremely large crowd already assembled. John and the family walked into a pseudo holding area to the left of Lincoln's chair. They waited until 10:00 a.m. John positively despised waiting to give a speech. Finally, he led his entire family out to the front of the Lincoln Memorial facing the reflecting pool and the US Capitol. John waved to the crowd which appeared to be in the thousands. He walked up to the podium with a sign on the front saying "We Can Fix America." The crowd applauded wildly. John motioned to Jenny and his family, which drew louder applause. He signaled for the crowd to quiet down and gave the following speech:

Thank you! Thank you! Thank you for coming out today to celebrate with my family and me on one of the most momentous days in our nation's future. Tomorrow, all of us will celebrate our nation's Independence Day. This is the day, 235 years ago, that fifty six people signed a document called the Declaration of Independence. This document basically stated liberty is a gift from God. God had decided America would be given that gift. That all men were created equal. It was the beginning point for the creation of the greatest nation in the history of the world. God allowed this to happen. I believe this with all of my heart and soul.

While God allowed this magnificent nation to be created, He allowed it to be filled with imperfect people; people that did not do His will. I am confident God never wanted war. I am sure God never wanted any American person to suffer from poverty, sickness, or affliction. I am sure God also never wanted able-bodied American people to rely on the successes of other people because of laziness or inappropriate moral decisions. God has blessed this nation, and we only needed to accept the blessing.

Instead, greed, lust for power, and unholy ambitions have clouded the future possibilities of this republic. However, this time and this moment have been set aside for us to start the process of "righting the American ship" and fix the cancers inflicted on America for far too long. Today, I am honored and pleased to introduce the following members of the state legislatures of all fifty states of our magnificent union.

From behind the podium, approximately 150 people walked out and stood behind John as he continued his speech.

These people have agreed to initiate legislation in their respective state legislatures around the country. This legislation calls for a special constitutional convention in which, hopefully, a constitutional amendment will be added to our Constitution. This new amendment will provide term limits for members of Congress.

There was massive applause as people started to cheer this announcement.

House members will be limited to two two-year terms or a maximum of five years and senators will be limited to one six-year term or no more than eight years. Considerable efforts were made to convince current members to introduce this constitutional amendment in Congress, but not enough of them wanted the amendment. They were more interested in their own self-preservation than in what was best for America. Shame on them! Any congressman or congresswoman that did not agree to term limits should be voted out of office. If you want to know which members did not agree to this measure, our campaign will disclose this information, which will be posted on the campaign's website. It is my hope that you will vote them out of office in the next election—Republicans or Democrats. It is time for this government to be run by Americans instead of the power brokers who have run this country into the ground over the last one hundred years. It is time for Americans to reclaim what has gradually been stolen from us.

I am not a politician. I am not wise on what is politically correct or what the best political strategy is. I am, however, confident I can fix what is ailing America. If we can eliminate the entitlement state encompassing Congress, we can start on the road to fixing America. We need this now. Congress is not prepared to monitor or regulate itself. We have seen instances where Congress members do not pay their income taxes and get by with a slap on the wrist. If you or I did the same, we would be thrown in jail. If we rotate people who are in Congress, we can ensure that proper regulation happens. Please, please help me get the process of healing started for this great country. It is a complete travesty for anyone to serve in Congress for more than eight years, much less the thirty, forty, or fifty years that certain members are currently serving. There is certainly no way these members of Congress are still beholden to the voters who allowed them to represent them. They are beholden to lobbyists and special interest groups whose objectives are based on what they want and not what is right for America. If you do not believe me, look at the financial disclosures that congressmen and congresswomen have made and how much money is being contributed to re-election committees and PACs and other forms of legalized bribery funds.

I am sure some, if not most, media sources will downplay this announcement made today. In the history of America, the method by which we are proposing to create a constitutional amendment has never been used. However, I believe the American people are sick and tired of watching our president and congressmen act on political motivations, as opposed to what is best for America. I am ready, and I hope you are ready, for the American people to take back this country from the federal government; to take away control from governmental agencies; to take away power and access from the special interest groups and lobbyists. This country was founded on the premise of the individual and its corresponding liberties. It is time for individuals to stand up and take this country back.

Congress and the president need to be beholden to the American people instead of to special interest groups and contributors. Once we get term limits for congressmen, we can get campaign finance reform and lobbyist reform. Then and only then can we truly fix America.

I am not here to lecture to you. I am here to announce a grassroots effort has begun to limit terms for congressmen. We need to pass this legislation so a special constitutional convention can be convened. Afterwards, a vote can be taken by every state legislature to require congressional term limits. The goal is to have the special constitutional convention the day after the general election—Wednesday, November 7, 2012. Once the convention passes this proposal, it will be sent back to each state legislature in the country for final approval. Hopefully, this can be accomplished in January 2013. It is not going to be easy. Congressmen and special-interest groups will do whatever they have to do to maintain the status quo. It will take all of us working together, debunking the untruths that will be coming forth shortly, and working with our state legislatures to get this new amendment. We can do this, and it will be the starting point of taking back this country.

Thank you for coming out today. I am not going to bore you for two hours, telling you that I know more than the next guy. I have a plan to fix America, and I know they do not. President Obama and my GOP competitors—none of them has a plan to fix America. They have either copycat plans that have not worked in the past or worse; they have absolutely no plan to fix America. We need to fix America, and I am willing and able to get this done. Please research my plan and let me know what you think. Do not listen to the sound bites and slogans that Obama and my GOP competitors are introducing. They do not have solutions. They have insulted my plan. Let's give them a message to either put up or shut up. What are your plans for fixing America? What do you think?

There was massive applause. The crowd started to chant—"We Can Fix America."

Thank you again for coming out today on the eve of Independence Day. I thank you for listening to what I had to say. I ask between now and the end of tomorrow that you take a minute and think back to the many people who have sacrificed everything for this country. Their sacrifice was necessary for us to be standing here today discussing congressional term limits. Their sacrifice made it possible for news outlets to push progressive agendas and attack people who think differently. It made it possible for me to be able to stand in front of you and ask for your vote. Let's work together to make sure the country they sacrificed for does not wither away and die. Let's work together to make sure our children and our grandchildren have an America that can fulfill their dreams, their hopes, and their promise. Let's work to make sure America continues to be a beacon on the hill, showing the world how freedom and liberty works. Let's work together to fix America.

Personally, I am going to thank God for the many blessings that our country has received over the last 235 years. I am also going to plead for continued blessings for this great country, its people, and its future. God bless you, God bless your families and may God continue to bless America. Thank you!

The crowd became very vocal. John noticed signs in the crowd saying "We Can Fix America" and "America Needs Fixing." After a few minutes of waving, Charles went up and told John that they needed to leave. John, Jenny, the children, and grandchildren continued waving as they walked through the Lincoln Memorial opening and down the back steps. They all got in the waiting Ford Expeditions and sped off. They drove down the road facing the south portico of the White House and onto Constitution Avenue toward the Capitol Building. The caravan passed the National Archive where a copy of the Declaration of Independence was preserved. The caravan made a right turn at the back-left corner of the Capitol Building, with the US Supreme Court building on the left. They drove past the Library of Congress which is right beside the Supreme Court. The Randolph campaign had just passed the three branches of United States government within a five-minute period. It had also passed the building where the Declaration of Independence and the Constitution were stored. The caravan continued to Dulles airport where they would depart for California. On the trip to the airport, William, Hank, and Debbie all telephoned John, as they were in another automobile. They complimented John on the speech, and William added it was going to be the story of the week. When John got off the telephone, he looked at Jenny who smiled approvingly; the same smile that John was always looking for from her. The children were also saying how marvelous it was—they were shocked at how many people had been there. As they pulled up to the airplane, John noticed the press pool standing at the bottom of the steps. As he walked by them, they started yelling questions to him. John wanted to answer their questions—every single one of them. However, he could hear William fussing at him about "leaving meat on the bone." He smiled and walked up the stairs to the airplane. John, Jenny, the children, the grandchildren, and Charles walked back to the private chambers of the airplane and shut the door. Charles had become one of the children in John's and Jenny's minds. William, Hank, and Debbie walked on the airplane and went into the private chambers too. John sat down in one of the chairs and looked out of the airplane. Everyone was talking about how powerful the speech had been and what the press, Obama, and the GOP competitors were going to say. They believed the opposition would spin the speech and the grassroots effort as a political ploy. They discussed how the campaign would be belittled for not acting presidential. John was sitting silently, thinking about the speech he had just given. He considered what it would mean to be president and what the job would mean for Jenny and him. He wondered if he truly could make the changes needed to fix this great republic. He wondered how much ill will he was creating by going after Congress. One of his grandchildren, Savannah, ran up and jumped into his lap. He smiled and kissed her gently on the forehead. He thought about the possibilities for her future—one in which she would never own a home if the country's economic path was not altered. He thought about the massive debt this generation was leaving for hers and how her income tax rates would need to be 50 percent to pay for the entitlement programs currently in place. John's stomach started to ache. In the next ten minutes, the pilot would come on the intercom and announce that Randolph One, the new name for the campaign's airplane, was ready for takeoff. John thought, how prophetic. He and his campaign had banked the entire process of fixing America on term limits for Congress, cutting spending to balance the budget, and raising taxes to pay back the debt. None of the other campaigns had stuck their necks out with detailed plans. Most importantly, Barack Obama did not have a plan, other than to blame George Bush. John was more convinced than ever Obama liked the idea of being president, but was not able to lead or be an effective leader. This utterly scared John to death, because he was fully aware of the power of the presidency.

As the airplane taxied down the runway, John was more convinced than ever he needed to win this election. He needed to give America the wake-up call it desperately needed. He needed to fix America so his grandchildren could have a future. John wished the airplane was already in California so he could start talking to the American people.

Chapter 10

On the trip to California, William, Hank, Debbie, and John called Thomas Philpot, the campaign's Finance Director. The following information was presented during the conference call:

(000s)	Total Contributions	Total Loans from JR	Total Expenditures	Cash On Hand
5/31/2011	9,500.0	2,000.0	(2,300.0)	9,200.0
6/15/2011	4,125.0	-	(1,250.0)	12,075.0
6/30/2011	10,256.0		(2,250.0)	20,081.0
Total	23,881.0	2,000.0	(5,800.0)	20,081.0

Thomas reported that contributions had continued to be exceedingly strong over the last two weeks and to be greater than expenditures. Thomas also reported all Tier 1-to-Tier 3 state campaign offices were established. John thanked Thomas for the report and asked him to keep up the fabulous work. William reminded John that Mitt Romney had brought in $20 million in June. The campaign needed to spend more time on fundraising.

William, Hank, Debbie, and John discussed the messages of the week, which were congressional term limits and the debt ceiling. The logistical schedule for the week was going to be extremely hectic. On Monday, the campaign was going to be in San Diego and then Los Angeles. On Tuesday, the campaign would be in San Jose and Sacramento. On Wednesday, it would be in Las Vegas and then on to Texas in the afternoon. On Wednesday night, it would be in Dallas. On Thursday, the group would be in San Antonio and then Houston. On Friday, the campaign would swing by Iowa on the way back to Newport News. There would be many air miles accumulated during the week. Jenny was planning on taking the children and grandchildren to Disney World on Tuesday and catching up with the campaign in Texas on Wednesday.

Originally, the week's message was going to focus only on congressional term limits. The debt-ceiling discussion was added because of the massive amount of coverage it was generating in news outlets. Congress needed to increase the debt limit, but the Democrats would not agree to massive spending cuts. The Republicans could not increase taxes without losing the support of the Republican base, including the Tea Party. This was actually working out remarkably well for the Randolph campaign. William stated if there were term limits, both parties could come up with a resolution.

On the flight to California, John walked by the press-pool section of the aircraft. One of the reporters asked what he thought of the debt-ceiling impasse gripping the White House and Congress. John responded that he saw President Obama's speech being about getting something done before the July 4th holiday. Senate Majority Leader Harry Reid had held the Senate over to discuss options. John said he thought it was strange for Congress to still be in Washington working on a solution when the president was on vacation in Cape Cod. In addition, he could not believe both parties were discussing cuts of $1 trillion over ten years. That small a figure would not balance the current-year budget shortfall of $1.4 to $1.6 trillion. Any discussions not involving considerable spending cuts were completely political. Any tax increases to fund bloated spending were a complete cop-out by Obama and the Democrats, because they lacked the will and conviction to make spending choices. The only tax increases that were appropriate were those needed to reduce the massive federal debt. Anything else would mean the current leadership was incapable of managing the economy and the country. These comments were meant for both parties. This situation showed why the country needed congressional term limits.

William, of course, was not a fan of the impromptu speech and told John of his dissatisfaction. John said he could not help himself. The country was nearing a massive financial crisis, and Congress was fighting over $100 billion a year in spending cuts versus the $1.4 trillion projected deficit, and the chief executive of the United States was on holiday in Cape Cod. John could not believe the American people were not protesting in the streets to throw all of them out of office.

Randolph One landed in San Diego at about 4:00 p.m. PST. Several Ford Expeditions were waiting on the tarmac. The group loaded into the SUVs and went to a rally near Balboa Park. The speech was on congressional term limits, and the crowd enthusiastically agreed with the proposal. John introduced several people who were spearheading the grassroots effort in Southern California. Interestingly, one of the people was a known Democrat, and one was an equally known Republican. John made sure this fact was presented to the crowd. That night, John went to a fundraising dinner to talk about the debt ceiling. Afterward, Randolph One departed for Los Angeles. Upon arriving at LAX airport, the entire group loaded into awaiting Ford Expeditions and went to a hotel in Pasadena. John met privately for drinks with some Republican donors shortly after arriving at the hotel.

On Tuesday morning, the campaign met with Republican leaders in Los Angeles and with people in the Los Angeles field office. At noon, it flew to San Jose for a meeting with local Republican leaders, and afterwards to Sacramento for a fundraising dinner, including a speech on congressional term limits. Jenny and the children and grandchildren, however, stayed behind and visited Disneyland near Los Angeles on Tuesday. When Randolph One landed in Las Vegas on Tuesday night, the Ford Expedition caravan had a couple of people from the Nevada field office in John's car so he could meet them as they drove to the hotel.

On Wednesday morning, the campaign held a fundraising breakfast meeting in which John gave the congressional term limits speech again. On the way to the airport, the campaign stopped by the local Republican

Party's offices for meetings with its leaders. At noon, Randolph One was en route to Dallas, Texas. The campaign went to the Dallas field office, and John spent time getting to know the staff. At 4:00 p.m., he met with local Republican Party leaders and at 7:00 p.m., there was another fundraising event. John continued to stay on message about congressional term limits and, at opportune times, discussed how poorly Congress was functioning vis-à-vis the debt-ceiling debate. Jenny and the family flew to Dallas that night and rejoined the group.

Early Thursday morning, the campaign flew to San Antonio for a meeting with Republican leaders and a campaign rally at the Alamo. Jenny and the family joined the campaign for the rally. The congressional term-limits speech was given yet again. At noon, the campaign left for Houston, where John met with local Republican leaders and had a dinner fundraiser at 7:00 p.m. After dinner, John met with Houston field office personnel to discuss local strategies.

Early Friday morning, the campaign held a breakfast fundraiser at the hotel. After the meal, it flew to Des Moines, Iowa for a rally at 1:30 p.m. Jenny and the family also attended this rally. Afterwards, the campaign loaded onto Randolph One and departed for Newport News. The airplane touched down at 7:00 p.m. at the Newport News airport. Everyone on the airplane was tired from the week. When John and Jenny arrived at The

Willows at about 8:00 p.m., they sat down in the living room and fell asleep in their chairs. They finally gained enough strength to walk upstairs to go to bed around 11:00 p.m.

The next morning, John went to campaign headquarters to meet with William, Hank, and Debbie about the upcoming week. The campaign would visit Michigan, Ohio, Pennsylvania, and North Carolina. Its main message was to criticize ObamaCare, both in how it was passed by then Democrat-controlled Congress and the heinous parts of the legislation. Collectively, they reviewed the stump speech on ObamaCare, including the campaign's position of repealing the law and what changes were necessary to fix the health-care system in America. They discussed the logistical schedule for the week which included several television interviews. On Sunday, John had been invited as a guest on "Meet the Press" for the second time. It would be held, via satellite, at campaign headquarters.

After the morning meeting, John had a one-on-one meeting with William. William wanted to discuss one of the future topics that would be discussed on the campaign trail and one they were in disagreement about—eliminating the Department of Education. William argued the campaign's policy should be revamping the department, not eliminating it. Without a central source for mandatory educational requirements, William stated, less advantaged locales would fall further behind more affluent ones. John argued the department had been a complete failure. Since Jimmy Carter founded the Department of Education, test scores have continued to drop, as America continues to pour more and more money into a bottomless pit. John stated an unpaid congress of educators from each state, that was not federally run, would meet to set curriculum standards for the entire country. William asked what would happen if a state elected not to take part. John said that would be within their mandate. John and William continued to discuss the topic for the rest of the morning. Finally, William gave up and said the speech would be written as John requested. At noon, John returned to The Willows. In the afternoon, he read correspondence from the campaign, and he also signed letters of thanks to many supporters and donors. At 6:00 p.m., John fixed dinner for Jenny and himself. They both were asleep by 9:00 p.m.

The next morning, Jenny accompanied John to campaign headquarters for his appearance on "Meet the Press." The interview was focused on congressional term limits and the debt ceiling fiasco. John used most of the points from the previous week's stump speech, but he did take the analysis further. He criticized both parties for politicizing this issue. He stated that going after $100 billion per year in spending cuts while the deficit was $1.4 trillion was almost comical. He equated the effort to paddling a boat with a spoon. John also discussed how congressional term limits would have allowed Congress to fix this problem, as opposed to pushing it to the future.

The host tried to insinuate John was criticizing Congress for not fulfilling its duties, but he would not take the bait.

After the interview, John and Jenny went to church and had lunch with the children and grandchildren. Afterwards, they went back to The Willows, packed their suitcases, and went to the Newport News airport for the flight to Michigan. The wheels were up on Randolph One at 3:30 p.m.

Chapter 11

Randolph One touched down at the Detroit Metropolitan Wayne County airport at 5:30 p.m. The airplane taxied over to the private aircraft hangers where several Ford Expeditions were waiting. John, Jenny, Charles, and George jumped in one car, and five reporters hopped in the second car. They sped off to a rally being held at the Greater Detroit Chamber of Commerce. When they arrived, they were met by several chamber members. Jenny, Charles, and George were whisked away to seats in the front row, and John was led to an entrance that emptied onto a stage. As he walked onto the stage, he shook the hands of several people including the president of the Greater Detroit Chamber of Commerce. John walked up to the podium and looked out over the crowd. He estimated there were at least four hundred people in attendance. John gave the following speech:

Thank you! My wife Jenny and I are honored to be in Detroit tonight to discuss my plan to fix America. America is in extremely difficult financial shape—one that Barack Obama might not have totally caused, but one that he surely has not been able to fix. One of the most heinous pieces of legislation in our country's history was passed by Nancy Pelosi and Harry Reid behind closed doors in the middle of the night and was enthusiastically signed by Barack Obama: ObamaCare. This 2,700-page bill was passed without most of the members of Congress even reading it. Nancy Pelosi said we needed to pass the bill so we could find out what was in it. Well, I am here tonight to tell you what is in the bill, and most importantly, I am putting forth a case that repealing the bill is one of the most crucial requirements for fixing America.

Before revealing to you what is in the bill, I think it is necessary to know why the president and the Democratic-controlled Congress was willing to "bet it all" on this one issue. They knew the bill was extremely unpopular with the America people, and it would probably cause them to lose some seats in the 2010 mid-term elections. President Obama even suggested he was willing to be a one-term president as long as the bill was passed. Why did they want this bill passed? The answer is simpler than you would think. It all goes back to control. The far left of the Democratic Party, the Progressives, want the federal government to be all things to all people. They want the federal government to control every aspect of their lives. After they make the American people beholden to them for every aspect of their lives, they will control them. Barack Obama, Nancy Pelosi, and Harry Reid are part of this far-left portion of the Democratic Party. It did not start with them—it started with Woodrow Wilson and the creation of massive federal bureaucracies, including the Federal Reserve. It was continued by the progressive policies of FDR and LBJ. Do not be fooled—ObamaCare was a means to an end. It was one more step to control every part of our lives. It has already been proven by the congressional budget office that ObamaCare will cost more in the long run. It will cost the taxpayers trillions of dollars more than if nothing is done. Does this make sense? The US health-care system is the best in the world—that is why people from other countries come here for complicated surgeries. ObamaCare wants to throw all of this away. They want America's health-care system to mirror those in Canada and Europe. They want Americans to spend more of their time waiting for medical care, which will happen when ObamaCare is fully implemented.

How dreadful is this bill? It states it will steal $650 billion out of Medicare to partially fund this program. Medicare is already facing an uncertain future—by taking $650 billion out of it, you have probably put Medicare into intensive care. It will increase health-care costs for everyone, because the bill has new taxes for medical-device manufacturers and drug companies. They will pass those additional costs directly onto us, the users of the devices and the drug-takers. All investment income to American taxpayers will be subject to 3.8 percent Social Security and Medicare taxes. This includes the sale of your home. If you choose not to have health insurance, you will be assessed an excise tax of 2.5 percent of your income. Did you know the new bill nationalizes student loans? Private lenders will not be able to lend money to parents wanting to send their children to college. Instead, the federal government will create another massive bureaucracy to administer this program. Businesses that cannot afford health insurance will be assessed a $2,000 penalty per worker. Do you think businesses will simply eat that cost? No, they will pass those cost along to you.

The federal government, under ObamaCare, will be able to fund abortions. Finally, the biggest problem with ObamaCare was found by Democratic Senator Baucus of Montana. He stated the real increase to the deficit over the next ten years would be $2.5 trillion. Are these solutions what we expect from our elected officials in Washington?

There is only one way to fix this bill. We must repeal it. That will not happen until Barack Obama has been relieved of his duties as president and both the House and Senate are under Republican control. Then, and only then, can we fix our health-care system.

Now the real question is how **do** we fix the health-care system? There is no question that increases in health-care costs have exceeded inflation over the last twenty years. What has been the biggest single culprit in increases in medical costs? Malpractice insurance. The medical tort lawyers have made a killing over the last twenty years suing doctors, hospitals, and even nurses for every single thing they can find. The payouts of large settlements have increased health-care costs for everyone. However, the hidden costs are insurance companies requiring doctors to administer multiple tests for things they know will not detect or fix the medical issue. These tests are necessary to avoid an unfavorable settlement in a lawsuit. If you want to decrease healthcare costs, implement medical tort reform immediately. If you bring a lawsuit against a doctor or hospital and you lose, you pay. Before attorneys or plaintiffs bring a case, they must prove they will be able to pay if they lose. Our legal system is set up for greedy, medical tort lawyers to roll the dice. If they roll craps, there is no skin off their backs. If they hit lucky number seven, they win. Let's stop them from increasing costs for everyone by making the health-care system a slot machine.

We need portability of insurance products across state lines. Currently, insurance companies are regulated on a state-by-state basis. This is causing the natural progression of supply-and-demand economics not to work as it is intended. If insurance companies are allowed to quote medical insurance rates without the silly state regulators managing them, the price of insurance will go down. Now, some will say that I am being hypocritical here. In most cases, some will say that I want the states to handle their own affairs. I consistently have wanted less federal-government interference and have wanted decision making at the state level. In this case, I am proposing less state government and letting the people dictate insurance-policy pricing. I am willing to bet you that people will force the prices of medical insurance down in the long run.

We also need to change our definition of what insurance is. If you own a car and you have an accident, does your insurance pay for damages to your car? Of course. When you need an oil change, does your auto insurance pay for it? How about when you get a flat tire? How about a broken taillight? For those who own a home, does your home-insurance policy pay for a lawn service to cut your grass? How about paying for your utility bills? A lot of people believe our medical insurance should pay for 100 percent of all of medical costs, but we do not think that way about our automobile and home-insurance policies. Medical insurance should work the same way. Some people will say we pay a lot more for medical insurance than for auto and home insurance. They would be right. If you took away the costs of office visits, it would cut medical-insurance premiums by 20 percent. If you continue to go through the medical procedures that are done and take out the ones that are normal maintenance, the reduction in medical insurance premiums would be over 50 percent. We should only have insurance for major medical events like surgeries. This would force medical insurance costs down.

We must also eliminate the burdensome and unnecessary red tape our doctors and hospitals have to endure, primarily from the federal government. We need doctors and hospitals to see and help patients and not fill out a bunch of papers and read ever-changing regulations.

We need to massively reform and potentially eliminate the Federal Drug Administration. America's current drug-approval system is the slowest in the world. The delays in releasing drugs are not for consumer safety. The burdensome approval process by the Federal Drug

Administration is the real culprit. It is too big and too massive to be effective.

Finally, we need to allow drug companies to write off the costs of their drugs faster. This will reduce the time before these drugs can be generically produced. These are several substantial changes in the health-care system that would lower costs, provide more access to everyone, and still allow us to maintain the best health-care system in the world.

Barack Obama and even some of my Republican opponents will criticize my plan. That is okay with me. Where are their solutions? ObamaCare is not and will never be the solution. There are lawsuits currently in the court system from twenty states arguing the unconstitutionality of ObamaCare. I agree the bill was unconstitutional and for many reasons not even spelled out in the lawsuits. I find it rather insulting the Obama administration's best argument to ObamaCare's being constitutional is the commerce clause of the Constitution. Mr. President, please do not insult us. This is one of the most ridiculous arguments ever perpetrated on the American people and its court system. "Man up" and admit your true intentions and let the American people decide. In my opinion, any judge accepting that argument needs to take a long look at whether he or she is interpreting the law or trying to make laws. Those judges should resign from their posts and start working for the Obama re-election committee.

I want to thank you for taking time out of your weekend. I know you work harder today than you did yesterday and continue to have little to show for it. I know Michigan has been hurt by the poor economy. I am here to tell you that, for the first time in a long time, America has a truly different choice for president. I am not, nor will I ever consider myself a politician. I was a businessman, and I am now a retired businessman. It is time for America to fix itself. It is time for the American people to take back their country from the massive political machine that has driven it into the ground. It is time for each of us to say "enough is enough." I have a comprehensive plan to fix America. I cannot do it by myself. I need you. I need your help. I need your support. I need your vote. Please help me fix America for ourselves, our children, and our grandchildren. God bless you, your families, and God bless America.

The crowd erupted in applause. Jenny joined John onstage and waved to the crowd. They exited stage right and were greeted by George and Charles. They walked out of the building into awaiting Ford Expeditions. The caravan went to the Detroit Hyatt Hotel where John and Jenny had dinner with some local high-dollar contributors. After dinner, they retired to their hotel room.

On Monday morning, John had the 7:00 a.m. morning phone call with William, Hank, and Debbie. Hank reported the news outlets were positive about the speech. William reminded John to stay on message this week, as he had done each week. John had started to make faces when William "reminded" him each week. At 7:30 a.m., Charles knocked on the door, and John and Jenny followed him out to the waiting Ford Expeditions. George was already in the car. This morning, the campaign was holding a fundraising breakfast meeting at the Hilton Hotel. George told John what to expect when he got there. After the breakfast meeting, George was going to introduce him to some generous contributors, who would be backstage. Afterwards, they would visit the local campaign office in Detroit to meet the staff. At lunch, John would speak to a group of health-care professionals. At 3:00 p.m., John would visit the Michigan GOP offices. At 5:30 p.m., the campaign would conduct an interview with the local ABC affiliate. At 6:15 p.m., John would have a dinner fundraiser, speaking to members of the automotive industry. At 8:00 p.m., Randolph One would depart Detroit for Ohio. The day was rather uneventful except for meeting the campaign staff at the field office. John was surprised most of the staff looked remarkably young—perhaps just out of college. John asked several of them why they had come to work for the campaign. The answers were almost the same—they did not see a bright future for America with the other candidates. John discussed this with Jenny and George on the airplane. John said he would mention this revelation to William in the next morning's briefing meeting. The flight landed in Columbus, Ohio at 10:15 p.m. There were two Ford Expeditions waiting for the group, and they carried them to a Sheraton Suites hotel. John and Jenny finally got to bed around 11:30 p.m. They were both very tired.

On the Tuesday 7:00 a.m. telephone call with William, Hank, and Debbie, John mentioned the discussion with the field staff members in Detroit. They were surprised by the comment. William told John they would work with those comments in next week's stump speech, but he needed to stay focused on ObamaCare this week. Promptly at 7:30 a.m., Charles knocked on the door. Jenny let him into the room, and shortly thereafter, they left for that day's events. John gave the ObamaCare speech to the local chamber of commerce in Columbus. After the speech, John talked to several of the attendees about local economic issues. Charles pulled John away, because they were running late for their next appointment—with Ohio's GOP chairman. John spent approximately one hour with the GOP chairman discussing a host of issues. John could sense he did not agree with the campaign's position on congressional term limits. After this meeting, John gave the ObamaCare speech again at a lunch fundraiser in a private conference room at a local hotel. Afterwards, the caravan traveled back to the Port Columbus international airport for a short flight to Cincinnati. At 3:30 p.m., John met with several members of the Cincinnati GOP office to discuss field operations and fundraising. As John's popularity continued to rise, the GOP was actively asking him to campaign for other Republican candidates. At 5:00 p.m., John was interviewed by the local CBS affiliate. John found these local interviews to be friendlier than the national ones. At 6:15 p.m., John joined the local chamber of commerce for dinner and gave the ObamaCare speech yet again. At 8:30 p.m., Randolph One departed Cincinnati and travelled to Cleveland. John met with some large donors at 10:30 p.m. in the lobby of the airport's Hilton Hotel. By 11:30 p.m., John was exhausted. He walked into the hotel room; the lights were still on, but Jenny was asleep. John turned off the lights, went into the bathroom, and got ready for bed. He fell asleep as soon as his head hit the pillow.

On Wednesday morning, the schedule was similar to the previous two mornings. A breakfast meeting with GOP leaders in Cleveland and a quick visit to the campaign field office to meet the staff started the day. At around 10:30 a.m., Randolph One departed Cleveland and flew to Pittsburgh, Pennsylvania. John met GOP leaders for lunch, and the campaign held an outdoor rally near PNC Park at 1:30 p.m. John estimated the crowd to be at least one hundred in size. At 3:30 p.m., John had a television interview with the local NBC affiliate. At 6:00 p.m., the campaign held a fundraiser dinner at the airport Hilton. At 8:00 p.m., Randolph One departed Pittsburgh for a short flight to Philadelphia. By 10:30 p.m., John and Jenny were in their hotel room, ready for bed. William instructed Charles to ensure John returned his telephone call that night. John returned the call. William said they needed to talk since he would be visiting the Philadelphia Chamber of Commerce early the next morning, so the morning meeting was cancelled. William said he had a terrific idea for the bright future comments from the staffers in Detroit. William said next week's message would be on education. What better way to speak of education than how it relates to a bright future? William said Hank was personally working on the stump speech for next week and was incorporating that image. John liked the idea. William told him that contributions were still coming in very strongly, and they would have a new report by Saturday. He also told John that he would need to fly to New York on Saturday night for a Fox News in-person interview on Sunday morning. John moaned. Finally, William said new polling numbers would be out tomorrow, and he would pass him the information through Charles. They said good night, and John went to sleep.

On Thursday morning, Charles knocked on John's door at 6:50 a.m. John and Jenny followed Charles and George out to waiting Ford Expeditions. The Philadelphia Chamber of Commerce breakfast meeting started at 7:00 a.m. John had breakfast with the members and presented the ObamaCare speech. Since they were running a little ahead of schedule, John answered questions for about thirty minutes. Most of the questions were about the economy—very typical for chamber members. Afterwards, John met with some donors at a Marriott Hotel in downtown Philadelphia. At noon, Randolph One was "wheels-up" and on the way to Charlotte, North Carolina. At 2:30 p.m., John met with GOP leaders in

Charlotte. John also met briefly with Charlotte's mayor, Pat McCrory, who was highly influential in North Carolina. At 4:30 p.m., he visited the Campaign's Charlotte field office. John enjoyed talking to the staff members in these offices. He thought they all looked very young, but he liked their bright ideas and thoughts. At 6:30 p.m., the campaign held a dinner fundraiser, and John gave the ObamaCare stump speech again. In an effort to amuse himself, John tried to give the speech entirely from memory. At this time in the week and having given the speech at least ten times, he was just about successful. At 8:00 p.m., Randolph One departed Charlotte on its way to Raleigh. They landed at 9:00 p.m. and arrived at the hotel at 9:45 p.m. John met with GOP leaders in the lobby of the Hilton near the airport. He was in bed by 11:00 p.m. This was the first trip that Jenny had accompanied John step by step, and she was really tired. She said emphatically she would stay in Virginia next week. Silently, John wished he could join her.

On Friday morning, John got on the 7:00 a.m. conference call. William said Fox News had agreed for John to be on the show remotely—which meant he could do the interview from campaign headquarters. John was elated. He could stay in Williamsburg on Saturday. John asked William to get tee times at the Golden Horseshoe golf course for Saturday afternoon. The conference call, as usual, consisted of a discussion of the day's events. William also mentioned some information about the upcoming week. William said Hank would be the "handler" next week, and George was going to stay in Williamsburg. Finally, William said the contributions report and the polling data would be discussed on Saturday morning at campaign headquarters. At precisely 7:30 a.m., Charles knocked on the door, and they were on their way to WRAL TV5 for an interview. At 9:00 a.m. John met with GOP leaders and at 10:30 a.m., he visited the campaign's field office in Raleigh. At noon, there was an outdoor rally near the state fairgrounds. George estimated there were over six hundred people in attendance. At 1:30 p.m., the campaign stopped at the Angus Barn restaurant for lunch with some donors. At 4:00 p.m., John had a photo session with the mayor of Raleigh. At 5:00 p.m., Randolph One departed Raleigh for Newport News. The flight touched down at 6:30 p.m., and John and Jenny walked into the door of The Willows at 7:15 p.m. John grilled a couple of steaks, and he and Jenny were in bed by 10:00 p.m. This completed another week in the exhausting life of a candidate.

Chapter 12

On Saturday morning, John drove to campaign headquarters. As usual, the cars of William, Hank, and Debbie were already in the parking lot. John walked into the office and noticed a lot more people buzzing around than usual. The office was humming with people on telephones or clicking away on computers. As William walked into the conference room, he noticed John standing in the doorway. He motioned John to the conference room. John smiled politely and nodded at several people as he walked by them. As he walked into the conference room, he asked William who were all the new people. William said these additions were only a beginning. There would be a great many more people hired in the next couple of weeks. Hank would introduce John to some of the new people as soon as they were finished with today's agenda.

William started the meeting by introducing a new overall campaign slogan. Instead of "We Can Fix America," the new slogan would be "We Can Fix America **Together**." The campaign would also begin producing posters, buttons, pamphlets, etc. with "Randolph – The **Only** Way for A Bright Future for America." William, Hank, and Debbie all looked at John for his reaction. He absolutely loved it. Hank left the conference room to get the printers started. He wanted a background message board for the Fox News interview in the morning, and he also wanted the first shipment of campaign literature on the airplane on Sunday night.

William and Debbie talked to John about the message of the week—education. They showed John a copy of the stump speech. John read it and made more than a few changes. William and John argued about a couple of the changes, but finally William acquiesced. Debbie took the marked-up speech back to her desk and started to make revisions. William told John that there would potentially be some negative reaction to eliminating the Department of Education. He reminded him not to get defensive or angry at any reactions, and most importantly, to stay on message. John agreed. William said one of the reasons Hank was going on this trip was to help out in sticky situations. John agreed with William's decision. He believed America was ready for what he was going to say. The evidence was surely in the campaign's favor. William hoped John was right.

Hank walked back in the conference room and led John around the office, introducing him to fourteen new people. John thought most of them were either college kids or just out of college. John thanked each of them for helping out with the campaign. He also told them that he would never be able to repay them for their support. As John was leaving, he asked Hank and Debbie if they wanted to join William and him for golf today, his treat. Both said they had too much work to do, but thanked him for the invitation.

John and William met at the Golden Horseshoe golf course at 1:30 p.m. and started their round. They were paired up with two local businessmen who happened to recognize John. Very little golf was discussed, as the local businessmen were more interested in John's plans for fixing the economy. Both gentlemen were highly frustrated at the fragile economy and ObamaCare. John enjoyed talking directly with these businessmen and getting to know more about them. It was obvious their businesses had struggled since the financial meltdown, as they both complained about the lack of available credit. The businessmen asked John and William to join them for a post-round drink, and they graciously accepted. John spent the time asking questions of the businessmen, in particular what *they* thought the answers were. William was impressed at how John could get these strangers to open up and give their opinions on how to fix the economy. After drinks, the businessmen thanked John and William for the round of golf, and they left. William was absolutely sure that the Randolph Campaign had just picked up two votes for the Virginia primary. During the round, Jenny had called and told John that William and Sarah were coming for dinner. John and William left the golf course for the short ride to The Willows. It was an enjoyable afternoon and evening.

The next morning, John awoke very early and was at campaign headquarters by 7:30 a.m. William, Hank, and Debbie were already there. Moreover, a Fox News truck, with the long communications boom, was already there. John walked in and said hello to everyone. At precisely 8:03 a.m., John was interviewed by one of the anchors on the weekend national broadcast. The questions were about the status of the campaign, the campaign trail, and of course the Nine-Point Plan. It was a rather easy interview compared to some of the others. After the interview, John drove to The Willows to collect Jenny for church. As usual after church, John and Jenny took the children and grandchildren out for lunch. One of the younger grandchildren asked John, when he became president would he be able to go to lunch after church. Everyone at the table laughed. John told her if he was fortunate enough to be elected president, some things would have to change. One of the things that would not change would be his love for his grandchildren. She smiled and continued eating her lunch.

At 7:00 p.m., John, Hank, and Charles boarded Randolph One for New Hampshire. John felt like Iowa and New Hampshire were becoming as familiar as Virginia. They arrived in Manchester around 9:00 p.m. and were at the hotel by 10:00 p.m. John suspected this week was going to be a bit different from prior weeks.

Chapter 13

John woke up alone, because Jenny needed a week in Virginia. It was 6:00 a.m., and John decided to watch the morning news. Obama and Congress still had not come up with a solution to the debt-limit crisis, and a potential time bomb was ticking. At 6:30 a.m., John took a shower and got ready for the day. At 7:00 a.m., he called in for the morning conference call. Debbie said the campaign would be in New Hampshire for the day only; on Tuesday and Wednesday, the campaign would be in Illinois; on Thursday, Randolph One would fly to Missouri; and on Friday, the campaign would make a return trip to Iowa. It would be an extremely busy week with nonstop speeches, visiting many GOP leaders, several fundraisers, and a lot of air miles. William stated John would need to give the education stump speech at each event during the week. William said to expect some less-than-enthusiastic responses to the speech. On Friday night, John was not to give the weekly presser on the trip home to Williamsburg. The campaign would have said enough during the week already. John agreed to each of the instructions.

At 7:30 a.m., Charles knocked on his door, and John followed him out to the awaiting Ford Expeditions. He got in and noticed Hank was already in the car. Hank had not taken part in the morning call as he was still working on the schedule for the week. He said they were going to a chamber-of-commerce breakfast and speech event. Hank said it was crucial to show the failures in the current

121

educational system. Hank felt the chamber members would agree with the campaign's position since they had seen firsthand how ill-equipped the children in this country were for the rigors of business. As they drove to the event, John was starting to get a little worried he might get booed based on what William and Hank had said. Finally, he concluded they did not know what they were talking about. When they got to the hotel where the breakfast meeting was being held, John was hurried to the front of the banquet hall. He saw a few familiar faces as he walked up and shook the hands of several people he met on previous trips. Finally, John sat down at the head table in the room. As usual, the eggs were overcooked, and the bacon was undercooked. He ate a little of it not to be rude. Eventually, the chairman of the Manchester Chamber of Commerce got up and introduced him. He arose from his chair and gave the following speech:

Thank you!! Thank you! I am so glad to be here again in the great state of New Hampshire. I have spent the last several weeks traveling around this country meeting the most phenomenal people. I have been in awe of the resiliency of the American people, even in this poor economy. They continue to do whatever they need to do to make ends meet—to make a better life for their families. I will tell you it does not need to be this way. President Obama and Congress have failed to provide a means for this economy to get healthy. They have made it impossible for us to get out of the economic funk that we are in. I have provided a Nine-Point Plan to fix America, but I cannot do it without you. As you can see by our new slogan—We Can Fix America Together—I need your help to provide a better future for America. None of the other candidates or the president can do it. I sometimes wonder if they even understand the problems, much less know how to fix them. I do understand, and with your help we can fix America.

I want to talk to you about another part of my Nine-Point Plan. It is on education. We need to eliminate the federal Department of Education, today! I know a lot of people will question this observation. I have several numbers for you.

America is 12th in the world in Grade 4 testing out of 26 countries. America is 28th out of 41 countries in Grade 8 testing. America is 19th out of 21 countries in Grade 12 testing. However, America spends five times more than any country in the world per student. How did the greatest country in the world get into this predicament? Is it the teachers' unions? I think teachers' unions have had a significantly negative impact on the quality of education. However, I think that is only one of the many problems facing our educational system today. I think we have relied on the federal government to provide leadership in making our education system the best in the world. Based on the numbers that I provided, I would say the Department of Education has failed in its duty to make the American educational system the best in the world. We

are 19ᵗʰ out of 21 countries for Grade 12 students, for
goodness sakes!

I am proposing we disband the Department of Education.
It has failed to do what we have deeply and abundantly
funded it to do. Last year, we appropriated $180 billion for
the Department of Education. Based on the test scores, I
would venture that was the biggest waste of money in the
history of the world—other than the stimulus package
that Obama spent over the last two years.

In Atlanta public schools, it has been reported teachers
are getting together and changing students' test scores so
they can meet federal guidelines. They have even put on
parties called "Fit Parties," and at one school, the vice
principal comes in with surgical gloves so no fingerprints
can be found. When Barack Obama was asked about this,
his answer was "we" decided a long time ago to have a
federally run school system as our economy went from
agricultural to industrial so that our workforce could be
more educated. Guess what Mr. President— "We" failed.
The federal part of our education system became a reality
when Jimmy Carter was in office. The president makes it
sound as if the federal government has been involved in
the educational system since the early 1900s. It simply is
not true.

We have failed our children, and we have failed our
promise to provide hope to our children. Our educational
system is ill-equipped to meet the rigors of the new world

economy. We are teaching our children to pass a test, as opposed to teaching them how to maximize their intellect to succeed in this economy. We are trying to act as if we are maximizing the potential of our children, but we are failing them. We all need to wake up to this reality.

The Democrats have consistently pointed out that over the last ten-to-twenty years the rich have gotten richer while everyone else stayed about the same or got poorer. Is it possible the not-rich people's performance on wage growth is in direct relation with our poor public-education system? Ask yourself, where do most graduates of Harvard and the other Ivy League schools go to high school? Generally those students go to private schools. Private schools provide much different educational opportunities than are being offered in public schools. Of course the enhanced education opportunities come with an extremely expensive price tag.

My solution is remarkably straightforward. We need to move the responsibility of educating our children back to the people who know best—parents, local school board leaders, and state governments. They know what is best for the economic requirements of their states. My plan calls for the creation of a non-compensated board of educators from each state in the union. These people would create an overall national agenda for all school systems to meet. We would put school choice in place. Schools that do not make the grade would be eliminated and replaced by schools that succeed. It would be at the mandate of the states—not the federal behemoth we are stuck with today.

I know a lot of people will disagree with me on this subject. I understand why. Anytime a sweeping change is made, the most common impulse is to worry the change has gone too far. We need to fix America, and it will take sweeping changes like this. We have failed our children on education, because we failed to see the problems that are facing us. It is time to fix the educational system in this country. Together, we can fix this problem.

Some of the other candidates and President Obama will criticize this call for action. They will say my plan will make America weaker, and our children will not be prepared for the future. I do not care. The current system has failed. One of the most fundamental characteristics of a leader is to recognize when something is not working and make necessary changes in direction. We are there. We have been there for over twenty-five years. The educational system should have been changed years ago. We have to fix our education system, and it needs fixing now. Please help me do this. Our children need this. Our collective future needs this. America's future is desperate for this change. We can fix America together. God bless you and your families, and God bless America.

The crowd sat quietly for a minute. Suddenly one person started clapping, then two, and then the entire crowd started cheering. John stood back from the podium and waved to the crowd. A chant started of "Randolph!" Hank motioned John to walk out of the room. John gave one additional wave and walked out. As soon as he walked off, Charles handed him a cell phone and mouthed it was William. John said hello, and William said the speech was being played on every one of the news outlets. The "talking heads" were saying it was a gutsy move, but it appeared to be working. As William was talking, John, Hank, and Charles reached the Ford Expeditions. John said he needed to go and would call back later. The group left the chamber building and travelled to the offices of the state GOP. When they arrived, John walked into the building and met with the chairman of the New Hampshire Republican Party. He had already heard about the speech and asked several questions about the proposal. John continued to discuss his proposals for fixing the educational system, including the elimination of the Department of Education. The proposals were favorably received by the chairman.

At 11:30 a.m., the campaign held a luncheon fundraiser in which John gave the speech again. The people enthusiastically applauded the speech. After the fundraiser, they were met by a huge bus with "We Can Fix America Together" written on the side. Hank introduced John to the campaign's new mobile office. John got on, and they departed for the relatively quick ride to Nashua. The bus was very roomy with a large office in the back. John sat at the desk and called William on his cell phone to continue their discussion. The education speech was the only thing being talked about on the news shows. The White House had already released a statement criticizing the proposal. They stated disbanding the Department of Education was too extreme. They agreed, however, that some changes were needed and would propose some changes in the near future. William suggested bringing this up in the speech that night in Nashua.

At 5:30 p.m. the bus arrived at the Hilton which was the site of the dinner speech. John walked into the hotel and was greeted by several local GOP leaders. John thanked them for the invitation, and they walked into a holding room. Charles walked in, and handed John the cell phone. It was William again. He said John would be interviewed on ABC's "Good Morning America" in the morning, at 7:10 a.m. EST. William advised him to start hammering the message home during tonight's speech. John walked out and gave the same speech as before; however, he used a more forceful tone in the delivery. As with the previous times, it was favorably received. After the speech, John shook hands with many of the people in the audience until Hank motioned for John to leave. The bus left Nashua at 6:30 p.m. and drove back to the airport in Manchester. Wheels were up on Randolph One by 9:00 p.m. They arrived in Chicago at 9:30 p.m. CST. It was almost 11:00 p.m. when they finally got to the hotel.

On Tuesday morning, Charles knocked on the door at 5:15 a.m. John was already dressed and ready to go. They went down to the awaiting Ford Expeditions which whisked them away to the local ABC affiliate. John walked into the studio, went to makeup, and at 6:05 a.m. was being wired for the interview. The studio manager gave final instructions to John and precisely at 6:10 a.m., which was 7:10 a.m. EST, the red light illuminated. The exchange was predictable. There was a growing list of "haters" of the Randolph educational proposals. John kept hammering away at the poor performance of the educational system and the continued increase in spending. John also criticized the White House for belittling his plan without having one of its own. Moreover, John said the president needed to lead on something. Why not something as important as our children's education. The interview was about six minutes long. Afterwards, Charles collected John, and they left for a breakfast fundraiser. The education speech was given again with a few modifications criticizing the White House's response from the previous day.

After the fundraiser, John, Hank, and Charles left for a meeting with the Illinois GOP chairman. It was a lively meeting, and the chairman was concerned the education speech would cause some issues with the teachers' union in Illinois. John told him that he was against public unions of any type. This revelation seemed to worry the chairman. John went into considerable detail about his thoughts on public unions. After the discussion, the chairman had a better understanding of John's position, but John could tell he was not convinced. After the meeting, the campaign visited the local field office, and John spoke to most of the people working there. Again, the office consisted mostly of young people. After this meeting, John was driven to a chamber-of-commerce luncheon where the speech was given again. The afternoon consisted of donor meetings in a conference room at the Hilton. John enjoyed meeting with individual donors and discussing the country's state of affairs, but he did have a tendency to converse too long with each donor. Hank was constantly pushing John to wrap up the discussions. At 5:00 p.m., John gave an interview to the local NBC affiliate. At 6:00 p.m., he was in front of a group of business executives discussing the status of the educational system in America. At 8:00 p.m., John took part in a town-hall meeting. Most of the questions were related to John's proposed changes in education. The majority of the people in the meeting were positive about John's proposals for fixing the educational system. For the first time, however, there were a few negative comments. One in particular was highly negative and mean-spirited. The question related to John's previous job as CEO of an investment banking firm. The questioner asked whether he felt guilty stealing money from the common man and now lecturing America on what was wrong. John respectfully said he had not stolen money from anyone, and the majority of the money was not from bonuses, but from selling his stock when he retired. John also pointed out he was educated in public schools including at a public university. However, the Department of Education was still in its infancy when he finished high school. Therefore, the education afforded him was handled at the state and local levels; not by an office in Washington. The people in the crowd applauded his response. The town-hall meeting was about one and one-half hours long. Afterwards, John, Hank, and Charles returned to the hotel and went to sleep.

On Wednesday morning, Charles knocked on the door at 5:30 a.m., and they walked downstairs to the campaign bus, which had made its way from New Hampshire. Hank was already seated on the bus, and soon after, they departed for Peoria, Illinois, which was about three hours away. At 6:00 a.m. CST, John and Hank joined William and Debbie for the morning conference call. William said to stay on message—it was working well and beyond his wildest dreams. At 8:30 a.m., the bus pulled into the local NBC affiliate; John walked in and was interviewed by the local news staff. At 9:30 a.m., he met with the chamber of commerce, and at noon, he gave the speech to the Peoria rotary club. Afterwards, the team loaded back onto the bus for the trip to Springfield, Illinois, which was about one hour away. At 4:30 p.m., John met with several local GOP leaders. At 5:30 p.m., he took part in an interview with the local CBS affiliate. At 6:30 p.m., he gave the education speech at a fundraiser. Overall, it was a good day as John got to talk directly with a lot of people specifically about their concerns for America.

On Thursday morning, Charles knocked on the hotel door in Springfield at 5:30 a.m. John was ready and followed him out to the bus. Hank, as usual, was already onboard. They left for St Louis, Missouri which was about two hours away. John and Hank had the morning conference call at 6:00 a.m. CST. William told John that several of the GOP candidates had started criticizing the campaign's educational proposals. A couple of them had proposed some ideas that were not as drastic as those of the Randolph campaign. William instructed John to keep giving the speech and talking about his education proposals. John knew this advice was a bitter pill for William, who had always favored a federally led educational system, and they had several disagreements about this part of the Nine-Point Plan. John also knew William was decidedly pragmatic and knew deep down that a complete elimination of the Department of Education was probably the only workable solution. While William was going to take criticism from the liberal establishment, including very close friends, John was proud to know and be related to a liberal who cared more about the country than his own political party and its political agenda. John knew liberals, in particular Progressives, were more interested in cause than effect. They did not care if someone's reputation was destroyed as long as their agenda moved forward. The means did not matter as long as the ends were met. John thought what a pitiful group of people it was whose values and principles were that warped.

At 8:00 a.m., John gave the education speech to the St. Louis Chamber of Commerce. At 10:00 a.m., John met with local field-office personnel. At noon, John presented the message of the week at a luncheon fundraiser. At 1:00 p.m., the bus left for Kansas City which was four hours away on I-70. John spent the entire time on the telephone with potential donors and William. When they arrived in Kansas City at 5:00 p.m., John was interviewed by the local ABC affiliate. At 6:30 p.m., he gave the education speech to the Kansas City Chamber of Commerce. When the campaign arrived at the Hilton Hotel that night, John met with some potential campaign donors for drinks. At 11:00 p.m. CST, John was finally in his room, and he called Jenny. She had kept up with the news and said the campaign's education proposals were the only topic being discussed. All of the liberal news stations (ABC, CBS, NBC, and MSNBC) were lukewarm to negative about the education proposals. This fact did not surprise John. The liberal establishment was clearly backing President Obama in the next election. It was obvious to anyone who was willing to notice. John finally went to sleep at 11:30 p.m.

At 5:30 a.m., Charles woke John up for the trip to Des Moines, Iowa about three hours away. John and Hank had the 7:00 a.m. conference call with William and Debbie from the bus. William said nearly all political commentators and blogs were still discussing the education proposals. Some of the blogs heavily criticized the White House's response and lack of detailed plans to fix education. Some of the liberal commentators were even repeating John's speculation that the poor education system probably caused some of the rich/poor divide. Debbie stated they would start the day at a Firestone tire plant where the visit would include a tour and a speech. At noon, the campaign would have a luncheon fundraiser. At 2:30 p.m., they would have an interview with the local FOX station. At 3:00 p.m., the campaign would visit the local field office. At 5:00 p.m., they would meet with some donors on the ride to the airport. Two of the donors would accompany them on the airplane back to Newport News.

The day went just as Debbie had planned it. At 5:00 p.m., John, Hank, and Charles met with some donors who accompanied them back to the airport in a very large limousine. John explained to the donors the importance of moving education from a national level to the state level. The donors asked John about the campaign's money situation. John stated the campaign was doing well bringing in contributions. However, both Obama and Romney were still setting the pace. When they got to the airport, two of the donors, a husband and his wife, boarded Randolph One with John, Hank, and Charles. Wheels were up at 6:15 p.m. CST.

The airplane arrived in Newport News at 9:15 p.m. EST. After John had said goodbye to the donors, Charles drove him to The Willows. They said goodbye, and he walked into the house. Jenny was downstairs in the parlor reading a book. John greeted her, and they discussed the many events that had occurred that day. Jenny had continued to watch several of the political news shows, and people were generally pleased with John's proposals for fixing the education system. Of course, the Progressives and the unions were dead against his proposals and had started some television advertisements criticizing them. They talked until 11:00 p.m. about the status of the campaign, the children, and grandchildren.

Chapter 14

On Saturday morning, John awoke at 7:00 a.m. and after breakfast went to campaign headquarters. It was July 23rd, his wedding anniversary, and he wanted to return home as soon as possible. John had already planned out the evening. He had made reservations at Christiana Campbell's Tavern. It is one of the restaurants on Duke of Gloucester Street in Williamsburg and was their favorite place to dine. Afterward, they would probably take a ride in their boat on the James River. It would be an enjoyable night.

John walked into the offices and noticed a lot of people were already there including William and Debbie. Last night as they left the Newport News airport, Hank had told John that he would not get to the office until around 9:00 a.m. William started talking about the impact of last week's education speech. William admitted he had never thought it would go over so positively. John smiled. He said it was time for a wholesale change in the American education system, and this plan was the first one ever proposed. He was sure the other campaigns, including Obama's, were coming up with their own education-reform plans, but was doubtful there would be any substantial changes.

William stated the campaign would focus on public unions during the upcoming week. Debbie said her team had prepared the stump speech on public unions as she handed it out in the conference room. Both John and William read the document and made some changes. Debbie took notes of their changes and left the conference room to alter the speech. William said there might be some union protests after the speech, for the first time. John agreed. However, he stressed to William that public unions have caused much more harm than good since their inception in the early 1960s. Today, public workers are compensated almost twice as much as workers in private industry. Typically private company workers work more hours as well. William reminded him they had already argued these points. Jen Harrison, the Scheduling Director, walked into the conference room to discuss the schedule for the upcoming week. She said the campaign would be in Arkansas on Monday, Tennessee on Tuesday, Florida on Wednesday and Thursday, and South Carolina on Friday. John groaned. Moreover, Jen said, the original scheduling plan was changing and would be discussed after the Iowa debate, which was the week after next. She also reminded John that the entire campaign staff would join him in Iowa for debate preparation. Space had been rented at the Gateway Hotel in downtown Ames, Iowa. They would check out on the morning of the debate to give Iowans an opportunity to use the same hotel. John was not looking forward to more quality time with the debate hounds.

William stated the new polls had just come out:

Poll	Quinnipiac	Fox News	Rasmussen	NBC/WSJ
Date	7/11/2011	6/28/2011	6/14/2011	6/13/2011
Romney	19%	18%	30%	30%
Palin	10%	8%	0%	14%
Cain	6%	5%	10%	12%
Gingrich	5%	3%	9%	6%
Paul	5%	7%	7%	7%
Bachmann	12%	11%	12%	3%
Pawlenty	3%	3%	6%	4%
Perry	10%	13%		
Santorum	1%	2%	6%	4%
Randolph	25%	25%	20%	14%

The good news was the Randolph campaign had maintained its frontrunner position and was showing the best momentum. William said that from Sunday through Monday, the campaign would be in Ames to meet people. Hopefully these steps, along with the other trips, would allow John to win the Ames straw poll.

Thomas Philpot, the Finance Director, brought in the financial report, encompassing the first fifteen days of July and the corresponding expenditures:

(000s)	Total Contributions	Total Loans from JR	Total Expenditures	Cash On Hand
5/31/2011	9,500.0	2,000.0	(2,300.0)	9,200.0
6/15/2011	4,125.0	-	(1,250.0)	12,075.0
6/30/2011	10,256.0		(2,250.0)	20,081.0
7/15/2011	18,566.0		(4,575.0)	34,072.0
Total	42,447.0	2,000.0	(10,375.0)	34,072.0

John asked how this analysis compared to the other candidates' finances. Thomas stated Romney would be around $22 million to $30 million for the quarter. This would put the Randolph campaign as the second highest among the Republicans. Obama would probably report $60 million for the quarter. Thomas stated the Randolph campaign was doing remarkably well considering they had been unknowns at the beginning of the quarter. It was an impressive start. Thomas also stated Romney had brought in $44 million in the second quarter of 2007 when he was the front-runner. Everyone around the table was happy with the news, but they knew it was just a starting point.

John mentioned his wedding anniversary that day and his need to leave. Before he departed, Debbie said George would be travelling with him next week. Of course, Charles would also be on the trip. George would bring the final draft of the speech on the airplane on Sunday. John said goodbye to the entire group and wished them a good weekend.

John went back to The Willows. Jenny was on the patio beside the pool. He noticed several of the grandchildren were there jumping and swimming in the pool. John walked out and sat down beside Jenny. He told her about the national polls and about the finance report. She was amazed at the amounts contributed until John told her that Obama probably would report $60 million in contributions.

Around 5:00 p.m., all of the children showed up for a celebratory anniversary dinner. William and his wife also joined in the festivities. John later told Jenny about the dinner reservations. She said she was sorry, but he knew this was the celebration she wanted—around the children and grandchildren. John was happy too. The children made dinner and decorated while John, Jenny, William, and Sarah were on the boat ride. Around 7:00 p.m., they docked the boat and returned to the house. The pool area and the dining area had been decorated, and dinner was ready. It was a delightful evening with the entire family. John and William, as usual, talked about the campaign.

By the time everything had been cleaned up, it was almost 10:00 p.m. Everyone said goodbye. John and Jenny walked upstairs and talked about next week. The week of July 25th was the second week that the entire family would be going with John on the campaign trail. The plan was for the family to be with John through Wednesday. On Wednesday, Jenny would take the children and grandchildren to Disney World in Orlando for five days. They would take a commercial flight back to Newport News on Monday. On the following Wednesday, Jenny would fly to Ames, Iowa for the Thursday-night debate. They finally fell asleep at 11:00 p.m.

On Sunday morning, John and Jenny went to church and afterward to lunch with the children and grandchildren. It was a quick lunch, because they needed to leave by 4:30 p.m. for Little Rock, Arkansas. John and Jenny had completed some packing that morning and had just a few remaining things to do. At 3:50 p.m., Charles arrived at The Willows, loaded their bags into the car, and they left for the airport. John looked at the airplane and noticed the words on the side "We Can Fix America Together." This would be a very great week to see that in action. As John and Jenny were walking up the stairs to the airplane, they noticed the children and grandchildren were being shuttled over to it. John went into the airplane, and saw George was already there. George handed a copy of the revised speech to John, who walked to the back of the airplane where his private chambers were. A few minutes later, several of the grandchildren came running to the back of the airplane and started scurrying around John in his office. Jenny and the children walked in next; she shooed them into the cabin directly in front of the back cabin and got everyone buckled into their seats. Jenny returned to the back cabin and sat with John as the captain announced their immediate departure. Wheels were up at 4:30 p.m.

Chapter 15

Randolph One landed in Little Rock, Arkansas at about 5:15 p.m. CST. At the bottom of the stairs, there were three Ford Expeditions waiting on them. John, Jenny, George, and Charles got in the first one, and the children and grandchildren got in the second and third SUVs. There was also a van to transport the news-media personnel. This group had continually grown, from the original five people to nine people now. Hank said if the campaign continued to do well, there would be over thirty news personnel. The caravan left the airport and went to a nearby Comfort Inn. It had a swimming pool, which appealed to the grandchildren. John, George, and Charles left the hotel and went to a dinner meeting with some prospective donors. The rest of the group ordered pizza and went swimming. John arrived back at the hotel around 9:30 p.m. and wished the grandchildren a pleasant night's rest as they were getting tucked into bed. Afterwards, he went to his room and discussed the dinner meeting with Jenny. It was with some of the Walton family—the family that founded Wal-Mart. Tomorrow, John's speech on public unions would be given at Wal-Mart headquarters. Wal-Mart had always been against unions. While John's speech was not deriding all unions per se, it would be critical of public unions specifically and the problems they had caused. Jenny, the children, and grandchildren were not attending this speech, because William felt there might be some heckling. John and Jenny went to sleep about 10:30 p.m.

John awoke uncommonly early, and went downstairs to find some coffee. He spoke to several other early risers about the problems facing the country, including the debt-limit impasse still going on in Washington. He found these people were extremely knowledgeable about the subject and were terribly concerned about the political gridlock in Washington. Some believed new taxes were needed, but nearly all thought spending needed to be slashed. Most of the people recognized John and were complimentary of what they knew about him. John urged each person to learn more about his Nine-Point Plan and to get more involved in the process. John told them that he needed their personal help to fix America, should he be fortunate enough to be elected.

At 6:00 a.m., John got on the conference call with William, Hank, and Debbie. John noted the revised speech was good. He also told them that the meeting with several members of the Walton family had gone well. Debbie told John that at 9:30 a.m., he would give the public-union speech at Wal-Mart headquarters. Afterwards, he would go to the local ABC affiliate for an interview about the speech. At 12:30 p.m., he would give the stump speech at a luncheon of the chamber of commerce. At 2:30 p.m., he would meet with local GOP leaders. At 5:00 p.m., he would take part in an interview with the local Fox affiliate. At 6:05 p.m., he would be on the radio program, the "Mark Levin Show" by telephone. At 6:30 p.m., John and Jenny would be guests of honor at a business leaders' forum. At 8:15 p.m., John would be on the "Sean Hannity Show" broadcast from the local Fox affiliate. The flight out of Arkansas would be at 6:30 a.m. CST on Tuesday. Jenny listened in the background and shrugged.

Charles knocked on the door at 8:00 a.m. and gathered John for the trip to Bentonville, Arkansas. Since Bentonville was over three hours away by car, the campaign travelled by a small private airplane which took about an hour. The flight arrived at 9:00 a.m., and a Ford Expedition met John, George, and Charles to transport them to Wal-Mart's corporate headquarters. They arrived a few minutes before 9:30 a.m. and John met with several of the executives. Promptly at 9:30 a.m., he was introduced by George and walked onto a makeshift stage. Around five hundred people were estimated to be in attendance, and they politely applauded as John made his way to the podium. The following speech was given:

Thank you! Thank you! I want to thank Wal-Mart's directors, officers, managers, supervisors, and employees for allowing me to come to your beautiful headquarters and be with you this morning. Some of you may not know me that well, but I hope you will have an opportunity to read my Nine-Point Plan for Fixing America. My campaign slogan is "We Can Fix America Together," and I truly believe we can. America has over its 235-year history shown itself to be a resilient country. A country able to make corrections once issues or challenges are put in front of its people—whether it was fighting for independence in 1775-1782, abolishing slavery in the war between the states, stopping madmen dictators in both world wars, or working together to help each other out after Hurricane Katrina, and recently the terrible tornados that swept through the southern states this past spring. The ability of America to fix itself is one of its greatest God-given gifts.

Since the beginning of the industrial revolution, the federal government saw fit to take part in America's growth. This included regulating how companies could work, how they could hire and fire their employees, how products had to meet certain governmental standards and how much to pay their employees. The federal government writes one law to prevent unfair trade—to keep one company from having too much power over an industry sector or a competitor. Then the government passes laws that allow workers to unionize and have monopolistic power over that employer. It also allows different unions to combine to form super unions over a whole industry like the United Auto Workers union.

I am not here to discuss all unions because, at their inception, there were many positives that came out of them. Worker safety, better working conditions, and child labor laws were all positives that came from collective bargaining. I am here to discuss a serious and much more harmful derivative of the union movement—public unions. What is a public union? It is when government workers join together to have collective bargain rights against *their employer—the taxpayer. How does this make sense? Federal workers should do the taxpayers' bidding. How can they do this when they are against the taxpayer in collective bargaining? It is one of the biggest contradictions in the history of the American political system.*

Don't believe me? There are two people in American history who loved the very idea of unions and collective bargaining, and they thought public unions were wrong:

George Meany, the former president of the AFL-CIO stated, "It is impossible to bargain collectively with the government" [www.askheritage.org]. FDR, one of America's most progressive presidents stated: "The process of collective bargaining, as usually understood, cannot be transplanted into the public service" [www.realclearpolitics.com]. With these two pioneering union representatives boldly stating unions should not be in public sectors, how did it happen? Greed and power. It is shocking to me that President Obama does not point out greed and power exist in other things besides "rich people" and corporations, like your esteemed company, Wal-Mart.

In the early 1950s, private union members peaked and then started to drop by the end of the decade. In an effort to keep the union dues coming in to the greedy union bosses, a massive push was made to expand union membership to other areas, including public sector jobs.

Beginning in the 1960s, union bosses starting recruiting government workers for union membership. Of course, the promises made were for better wages, benefits, and job security. To anyone listening, this sounded very good— almost too good to be true. Today, private-company union membership is around 8 percent of all private workers, but public union membership has swelled to 37 percent. Union participation in the overall labor pool is around 12 percent.

If you remember a minute ago, I said better wages, benefits, and job security were too good to be true. They are. Over the last ten years, government pay including benefits has grown by almost 37 percent while private workers' comparables have increased by only 9 percent. How is this fair? What do federal, state, and local governments have to show for this? Massive budget deficits will require either massive tax increases or bailouts from the federal government. If there is one thing in America that needs fixing, it is the elimination of public-sector unions. They should be deemed unconstitutional.

Compensation is just one of the problems. Additional costs of 34 percent are levied on federal workers' salaries for pensions, health-care programs, post-retiree medical programs, etc. For private workers, employers contribute around 22 percent. Most private companies do not provide defined-benefit pension plans. The only place that you will see them is in private union-based companies and the government. This needs to be fixed now. Why should a *government worker receive more pay and benefits than a non-government worker? The straightforward answer is they should not.*

The crowd in attendance cheered loudly at this point. The speech was effective in playing a new kind of class warfare. Instead of rich vs. poor, or white vs. black, John had just put a divide between government workers and private workers.

This problem would have been fixed already if Congress had term limits in place. Members of Congress would have stopped stealing from private-sector workers to give the bounty to public-sector workers. You want to talk about the biggest transfer of wealth in a generation. While the individual transactions have been small, the aggregate wealth transfer from the private sector to the public sector has been enormous in the past ten years. Have any of you been around Washington, DC in the last five years? New roads, new housing, and new buildings are springing up everywhere, while the rest of the country is suffering. Everyone in Washington needs a reality check on what the rest of America is going through. Without stopping public unions and Congress, this wealth transfer will continue. It is not right for an average federal government worker to make $123 thousand per year plus benefits when an average private worker makes $61k. That is more than twice as much! It needs to stop now!

The crowd erupted again. It was unbelievable how much hatred there was for Washington in the country. John felt even more assured of congressional term limits.

I beg of you. Please help me fix America. America has some serious trouble ahead. It has a president and Congress unwilling to be adults and get things fixed. This country has serious spending problems—it does not know how to live within its means. It has a crippling amount of debt, including a large portion held by China. We have to fix America so our children and grandchildren can have the same opportunities we had. We have to make shared sacrifices for the good of the country. Most, if not all, Americans believe the country spends too much money. Some Americans are perfectly agreeable to taxing another group of people, or taking away benefits from those people. They get upset when additional taxes are imposed on them, or when some of the federal goodies will no longer be given to them. Did our parents think that way? Mine surely did not. It took more than the last one-hundred years to get us into this mess, and it will take all of us working together to fix this mess. It did not happen overnight. We have become overly reliant on the government, and it will be extremely difficult to stop the gravy train. They will fight us every step of the way. I am not talking about just Democrats. I am talking about both parties that have accepted this is the way it is. I am here to tell you there is another way. The current way is not the best way for America. We must fix America now!

I want to thank you again for taking time out of your busy day to come and listen to me. I do not have all of the answers, but I am the only candidate who has compiled a comprehensive plan for fixing America. We can't simply continue racking up $1.4 trillion to $1.6 trillion deficits and hope the problem goes away. We need to get working, and it needs to start today. We can't wait any longer. We need to have adults at the table to fix our country's problems. I can't fix them without you, and I mean every single one of you. I ask that you read my Nine-Point Plan— before you leave today, you will be given an opportunity to take a copy for yourself. After reading my plan, I ask you to decide if you agree with it. It is okay to disagree with me and my plan. However, I challenge you, just as I have and will continue to challenge President Obama and my Republican opponents—if you do not like my plan, develop one yourself. The key is to get started fixing America. Together, we can fix America.

God bless each of you. I ask God to bless your families. And I beg God to have mercy and show His grace on the United States of America. Thank you!

The crowd started cheering before John could finish the speech. A loud chant of "Randolph!" started. John waved heartily to the crowd. As he walked off the stage, he was met by several Wal-Mart executives who enthusiastically shook his hand. George also walked up to John, smiled, and shook his hand. Charles led the group back to the airplane for the return trip to Little Rock. As the Ford

Expedition pulled off, John could still hear the crowd. George was rambling on about how well the speech had been received. Charles' cell phone rang, and he gave it to John. It was William. The speech was being shown on Fox News, *live!* William could not think of another candidate who had received live coverage this early in the presidential nomination process. William said the speech was impressive; however, he did point out that John went off message a couple of times. John said he could not help himself; he had gotten caught up in the moment. After hanging up with William, John received a call from Jenny, who said the speech was the best one that he had ever given. John thanked her for the compliment and said he would see her shortly. The caravan was approaching the airport for the quick flight back to Little Rock.

The rest of the day went just as Debbie had described that morning. The campaign had successfully made the message of the week about public unions in that one thirty-minute speech. All of the interviews given that day focused on the destruction that public unions caused and the campaign's corrective actions. As expected, some of the unions, in particular those in the public sector, were responding negatively to the speech. As these unions put out their press releases, members of the campaign's press pool were asking for counter-responses. After one extremely mean-spirited press release, George responded that union bosses were more interested in saving their own jobs than doing what was in the best interests of the American taxpayer or even the union membership. George was berated by William and Hank for his response. John secretly liked the response, because the union bosses would not be able to refute what was said. John noticed George on a cell phone, taking a tongue lashing. He looked at George after the terse phone call, presumably from either William or Hank or both, and said he agreed with what George had said. George smiled.

At a dinner where John and Jenny were the guests of honor, several business leaders urged John to engage not only public unions, but also private unions. John reminded them that Rome was not built in a day. He persuaded the business leaders to go after the fastest growth areas first, those being the public unions. Once these groups were dismantled, the private unions would be unwound next. At dinner, John gave a condensed version of the public-union speech. He put some humor into his remarks, but made sure to keep the message as serious as possible. After dinner, John went to the Fox studio and was interviewed by Sean Hannity. Sean stated he loved the speech and hoped it would continue to be discussed by all of the other candidates. Finally at 10:30 p.m., John and Jenny walked into their hotel room. The grandchildren were already asleep. They finally went to bed at 11:00 p.m., knowing tomorrow was going to be an event-filled day.

Everyone was awake by 5:30 a.m., including the grandchildren, who were walking around with their eyes still closed. Charles knocked on all of the doors at 6:00 a.m. to gather people for the waiting SUVs. The caravan arrived at the airport at around 6:15 a.m. After everyone was onboard, Randolph One departed Little Rock at 6:30 a.m., right on time. The flight to Memphis would be less than one hour. As soon as the flight was airborne, John started the morning conference call with William, Hank, and Debbie. Since the call was going to be abbreviated, Debbie started with the day's agenda. They would land in Memphis and go to the local GOP office to "meet and greet." Next, they would have a campaign rally at Mud Island on the Mississippi River where the union speech would be given again. Over lunch, they would meet with the local chamber of commerce and give the union speech once again. After that, the campaign would fly to Nashville, which was about one hour away by airplane. At 3:00 p.m., John would meet with some potential donors. At 4:30 p.m., he would be at the local CBS affiliate for an interview. At 5:30 p.m., John would visit the local campaign field office for a "meet and greet." At 6:30 p.m., John and Jenny were guests of honor at the Nashville business leaders' forum. At 8:30 p.m., John was to meet with some additional potential donors. At 6:30 a.m. on Wednesday, they would depart Nashville for Florida on Randolph One. William congratulated John again for the speech at Wal-Mart the day before, and they concluded the conference call.

The day again went as expected. John did notice some picketers outside the hotel where the business leaders' forum was being held. He was convinced they were protesting his stance on public unions, but he was not too worried. By the time he got to the hotel room later that night, he was exhausted. He washed up, said good night, and was asleep by 10:00 p.m.

Everyone was ready by 5:45 the next morning, and the group left for the airport by 6:00 a.m. Randolph One was ready for departure to Florida at 6:30 a.m. The airplane landed in Tallahassee, Florida at 7:30 a.m. John met with GOP leaders for a breakfast meeting at one of the airport hotels, and with some potential donors at 8:30 a.m. At 9:15 a.m., the airplane left Tallahassee for Orlando which was about a one-hour flight. Jenny, the children, and grandchildren left on a minibus to Disney World while John, George, and Charles left the airport for meetings with potential donors. At noon, John had a luncheon with the Orlando Chamber of Commerce, which included a short Q&A session. At 1:30 p.m., John was interviewed by the local ABC affiliate. At 2:00 p.m., the campaign bus was on its way to Tampa/St. Petersburg about one and one-half hours away. At 3:30 p.m., John met with the local Tampa/St. Petersburg GOP leaders. At 5:00 p.m., he was interviewed by the local NBC affiliate. At 6:30 p.m., he was the keynote speaker for a business leaders' forum. John gave the public-union speech again, and it was positively received by the crowd. At 8:30 p.m., John was back in the bus on the way to Port St. Lucie which was two hours away. During the trip, John spoke to several national GOP leaders by telephone. They were not as positive on the public-union speech as the general populace, but they did admit it was gaining a lot of positive national attention. At 10:30 p.m., John arrived at the hotel and was asleep by 11:00 p.m.

At 7:00 the next morning, John met with local GOP leaders for a discussion, and at 8:00 a.m. he was asked to speak at the Port St. Lucie Chamber of Commerce breakfast. At 9:00 a.m., the bus was on its way to Ft. Lauderdale which was two hours away. During this time, John spoke to William, Hank, and Debbie about the rest of the day. They would have an interview with the local Fox affiliate at 11:30 a.m. and lunch with several potential donors. They would leave Ft. Lauderdale for a rally in Boca Raton, thirty minutes north of Ft. Lauderdale. At 3:00 p.m., they needed to be on the road for Port St. Lucie one and one-half hours away. At 5:00 p.m., there would be an interview with the local ABC affiliate. At 6:00 p.m., John was to be the honored guest of the local chamber of commerce. At 7:30 p.m., they needed to be on the bus heading back to Orlando. At 8:00 p.m., John was going to be a guest on Bill O'Reilly's show via satellite phone. At 9:30 p.m., Randolph One would be heading for Charleston, South Carolina which was about one and one-half hours from Orlando.

The day progressed just as expected. George was surprised by the turnout at the rally in Boca Raton. He estimated there were over one thousand people. John was not so sure. On "The O'Reilly Factor," the host pressed him about negative feedback on the campaign's position on public unions. John said that public unions have created an unbalanced system that needed fixing. He pointed out even FDR could not see any possible way there could be public-sector unions. At 9:30 p.m., the bus pulled into the Orlando airport. The travel-weary group got on the airplane and departed for Charleston, South Carolina. When they finally arrived at the airport, it was almost midnight. They went to sleep shortly after arriving at the hotel.

On the 7:00 a.m. morning call, Debbie started with the agenda for Friday. At 8:00 a.m., John would be interviewed at the hotel by ABC's "Good Morning America." At 8:30 a.m., he would have a breakfast meeting with some potential donors. At 10:00 a.m., there would be a rally near Church Street in downtown Old Charleston. At noon, John would have a luncheon with the local chamber of commerce. At 2:00 p.m., he would meet with some local GOP leaders, including some people driving down from Columbia. At 4:30 p.m., the campaign would take part in a festival near Patriots' Point. At 6:30 p.m., John would be the keynote speaker at a business leaders' dinner. At 8:30 p.m., he was to meet with some potential donors. At 10:00 p.m., Randolph One would depart Charleston for the trip back to Newport News. Debbie told him that happily there would not be a Saturday-morning meeting. Instead, they would have a meeting on the airplane ride to Des Moines on Sunday morning. John invited William, Hank, George, Debbie,

Charles, and their spouses and significant others over to The Willows for cocktails and dinner on Saturday. He apologized for the last minute-invitation, but everyone agreed enthusiastically.

The day proceeded just as Debbie and her team had envisioned. Randolph One arrived at the Newport News airport at 11:30 p.m. Charles drove John to The Willows, and bid him adieu until the following night. John walked into The Willows, went upstairs, and went to bed. Another long and tiring week had mercifully ended without any blood being shed. The campaign was still driving the discussion among Obama and the other Republican candidates. The model created by William and Hank was working. Next week's poll in Ames, Iowa would be the most prominent one to date in the campaign.

Chapter 16

Charles knocked on the door of The Willows at 9:00 a.m. on Sunday. On the way to the airport, he told John how much he and his girlfriend had enjoyed dinner the previous night. John had invited the campaign staff for cocktails and dinner. Everyone had arrived at 5:30 p.m. for cocktails and promptly at 6:30 p.m., John had steaks and chicken prepared with baked potatoes and a fresh salad. For dessert, John had prepared a fresh Key lime pie. Everyone seemed to enjoy the meal and each other's company. Campaign matters were discussed—much to the chagrin of the spouses and significant others. At 10:00 p.m. the party broke up, and John cleaned the kitchen. He did not want to incur the wrath of Jenny with an untidy kitchen on her return on Monday.

John and Charles arrived at the airport at 9:30 a.m. William, Hank, Debbie, and George were already onboard the airplane. Randolph One took off shortly afterward for Des Moines, Iowa. John was starting to feel like Iowa was a second home as this was his fifth trip there since announcing his candidacy for president. The flight was about two hours long, and the campaign would gain an hour on the way due to the change in time zones. The entire senior campaign staff would be together for almost a week. John doubted they would be on speaking terms afterwards. The flight landed in Des Moines at 10:30 a.m. CST. There were two Ford Expeditions waiting on the tarmac to take the group to Ames. The caravan left for the forty mile trip north to Ames. On arrival, the group checked in to the Gateway Hotel. Hank had inspected the hotel several weeks before to ensure the campaign would have a proper war room for debate preparations. Hank showed the team the hotel and its amenities. The campaign had rented two of the conference rooms. One had already been set up for debate preparations and the other was outfitted with desks and a large conference table. They were located in the very back of the conference center. Hank had heard a couple of the other candidates would be there later in the week. Hank had also arranged a special surprise—he had booked the Atanasoff Suite for John. John was obviously very impressed with the room.

At noon, the campaign traveled to a "meet and greet" near a local college eatery on the campus of Iowa State University. John introduced himself to the people as they went into the restaurant for lunch. Some appeared to know him judging by the expressions on their faces. Others did not know who he was. That afternoon, Debbie had set up a rally for John to speak to the townspeople of Ames. George estimated there were four hundred people at the rally. John spoke to the gathering about his Nine-Point Plan on how to fix America. He also discussed his hope there would be term limits for congressmen. The crowd was loud and vocal, and John was honestly glad to be there. Hank had asked Stephen Curtis Chapman to come and perform, and he got the crowd going after John's speech. Chapman was one of John's favorite musicians. That night, the campaign had a team dinner meeting to discuss the next week's schedule. It would be a terribly long, tension-filled week getting ready for the debate on Thursday night. Everyone retired to their rooms by 8:00 p.m. In the morning, they would meet at 9:00 in the conference center. John called Jenny shortly after getting to his room. Jenny and the children had their hands full getting the grandchildren ready for bed and getting packed for the trip back to Williamsburg on Monday; therefore, the telephone conversation was unusually short. John tried to watch some television, but nothing caught his attention. John looked at his watch and saw it was 9:30 p.m. He finally decided to shut his eyes.

John woke up at 5:30 the next morning and worked out in the hotel's exercise facility. Afterwards, he went upstairs, showered, and got ready for the day. At 8:00 a.m., he walked down and had breakfast in the hotel's restaurant. He ate a very small breakfast, figuring there would be plenty of food in the conference center. At 9:00 a.m., John walked into the conference center. He said a little prayer as he walked into the room. William, Hank, Debbie, George, and Charles were already there. Hank introduced John to several people including some "experts" on debating. There were tape-recording machines already set up. It looked a lot like a television studio.

William sat down with John and talked about the upcoming debate. He explained the debate would be on the campus of Iowa State University. It was being sponsored by Fox News, *The Washington Examiner*, and the Republican Party of Iowa. Iowa has always been a very "red state," and has always been highly conservative in its social attitudes. John's own social beliefs were also extremely conservative. He did not believe homosexuals should be legally married; he believed legalizing abortion was one of the most unforgivable decisions ever made by the Supreme Court; and he believed the breakdown of the family unit was behind a lot of the problems facing America. John also believed political correctness was unquestionably killing the ability of America to judge between right and wrong; and John believed there were absolute rights and wrongs. However, he did not want the campaign to focus on these matters. He wanted it to stay focused on fixing America. He knew these questions would probably be asked in the Iowa debate. William said they would work on getting John's beliefs across without negatively impacting the overall message.

William stated Mitt Romney, Michelle Bachmann, Herman Cain, Ron Paul, Tim Pawlenty, and Newt Gingrich were all scheduled to be there along with some of the lesser-known candidates. William wanted John to focus on Bachmann and Romney, because they had been number one and three respectively in the last Ames, Iowa poll. John also needed to be ready for a "Hail Mary" by some of the other candidates, especially Tim Pawlenty who had spent over $200,000 on radio and media advertising over the last several weeks. William was also worried about Herman Cain and Ron Paul who were known to vocalize "zingers." It was going to be a tough debate with a lot of potential pitfalls.

Debate preparations began with a series of questions on the economy, the debt ceiling, the education system, and public unions. William had set up a mock debate platform with hot lights. On the right side of John was Debbie, acting as Michelle Bachmann and on the left side, George, who would play Mitt Romney. Hank gave answers for Tim Pawlenty, Herman Cain, and Ron Paul. The primary purpose of today's debate session was to find problems with John's presentation and mannerisms. William and Hank were sure John was immensely knowledgeable on this subject matter, but the Kennedy/Nixon debates showed substance was not the deciding factor. Catchphrases were significant. The candidate needed to make a connection with the American people. In Iowa, it was critical for the candidate to live out his or her principles.

Finally at 10:00 a.m., the debate "experts" started firing questions at each of the people behind the podiums. It was obvious both Debbie and George were well prepared, and their answers were straight out of their respective candidate's stump speeches. John agreed, disagreed, and stated his positions on each of the asked items. William had coached John that whenever he got stuck in response to a question he should refer to a previous stump speech, or in the most extreme case, start talking about the Nine-Point-Plan. After about one hour of "back and forth" between the questioners and the "candidates," William stopped the proceedings and asked everyone to take a break. John noticed William and Hank walked over and started talking with the "debate experts" who were asking the questions. During the break, John called Jenny, but he did not reach her on her cell phone. He was convinced she and the family were still en route from Orlando. After about fifteen minutes, William walked over to John and discussed the comments from the experts. Some of the news was good, and some of it was not. The most useful comment was not to be overanxious about rebutting an opponent's response. He needed to stand there looking at the person talking, and when he or she was finished, start his rebuttal.

At 11:30 a.m., the second session started. It was similar to the first session until Hank started answering questions the way Herman Cain, Ron Paul, and Tim Pawlenty would. It seemed every exchange became more testy and over-the-top. At one point, John felt he was losing his temper. He pulled it back in, and the session concluded around 12:30 p.m. William and Hank walked over to the experts again. Later, John found out one of them had asked if he was getting mad at one point. He could not believe he had figured that out. The experts did not know him. He admitted to William that he was getting angry at one point. William already knew. The third session would begin at 2:00 p.m. after lunch.

John walked out of the room with William on his tail. William told him that he was either the front runner or at a minimum, in the top three of the GOP candidates. He could not afford to lose his temper. He could not look too stoic either. John walked away from William utterly confused. He went to his room and sat down on the bed. He wondered why these debates were so vital to the electoral process of America. He knew there would be two more sessions in the afternoon. John actually felt nervous, something he had not felt for some time. He did not want to embarrass himself or let Jenny, the children, and grandchildren down. He did not want to let down William, Hank, Debbie, George, Charles, and the entire campaign staff who had already worked so hard. John did not want to disappoint any of the people who had donated to the campaign. There were going to be many more debates including, potentially, debates against President Obama who was known for being very cool and collected. John sat on the bed and prayed. It was not going to come from him to get through this.

At 2:00 p.m., John walked back to the conference center, and the questioning started again. He tried to keep his emotions in check and at the same time passionately articulate a way to fix America. He hammered points that were crucial. He stressed the major differences between himself and the other candidates. He criticized the failed policies of the Obama administration. After an hour, William called for another break and William, Hank, and Debbie returned to the experts. After a very short time, William walked up to John and said the session had gone exceedingly well. John was stunned. What had happened? The only thing he felt was different was a massive pity party upstairs and his prayer. Maybe God was searching for some humility in him. It had worked. During the fourth session, Hank started again with answers from Herman Cain, Ron Paul, and Tim Pawlenty. After about an hour, William stopped the session and went back to the experts. A short time later, William came out and said John had done much better in the afternoon sessions.

At 4:30 p.m., John was scheduled to be on Sean Hannity's radio show and at 6:00 p.m., he had dinner with several potential donors. He enjoyed dining separately from his campaign staff. When he finished dinner, Charles took him back to the hotel. Instead of going upstairs, he decided to go back down the hallway where Team Randolph had held its "beat-down" that day. John noticed the lights were still illuminated. He opened the door and to his surprise, William, Hank, Debbie, and the experts were watching the tapes from that day's debate preparations. It appeared they had been there for a while, as evidenced by the empty pizza boxes, and they were heavy in discussion. As soon as William saw John, he stopped the tape recording and met him at the door. William asked how dinner was. John knew William was trying to get him to leave the room. John asked what was going on. Hank jumped up and said they were assembling a game plan for tomorrow's debate preparations. John noticed all eyes in the room were on him. John asked whether he needed to worry. Collectively, the team said absolutely not. William told John to go upstairs and get some rest, because there was a lot to do tomorrow.

As John walked up the hallway leading away from the conference center, he started to have doubts again. He had left the conference room many hours ago, but his senior campaign staff and the debate experts were still in the room discussing something. What did they see and why wasn't William telling him about it? John started to think back to the sessions that day. What wasn't he doing correctly? He went upstairs to his room, sat down on the sofa, and thought about it. After two hours, he was thoroughly frustrated. He could not help fix the problem if he did not know what it was. John decided he could not take it any longer. He called William's cell phone to find out what the experts were saying. William picked up the call, and said he would come to John's room.

William knocked on the door, and John opened it. Hank was standing behind William, and they both walked into the room. John was fearful of a "tag team" now. John said he needed to know what the problem was. William said the experts had noticed John's verbal delivery, and his mannerisms were not like any politician they had ever coached. The experts had shown them examples of how career politicians answer questions and how those responses compared. There were significant differences. Politicians tend to hold things back; they tend to use generalities and never show their complete hand. John, on the other hand, tended to "let the cat out of the bag" immediately and to spend the remaining time justifying the point. He used specifics, and he rarely left anything off the table. It was tremendously different from how other politicians work. John stood there quietly, taking in the critique. After a couple of tension-filled moments, he said he was not a politician and would never be one. He thought the American people were sick of politicians and how they have bent the truth for their own self-interest. He thought the American people were ready for someone who was plainspoken and truthful, even if it was to a fault. William looked at him and said they agreed, and that they had just dismissed the experts who would not be back in the morning; tomorrow would be a new day. The team would refocus on the issues and the many challenges facing America. There would be less time spent on fluff. As William and Hank were leaving, John told them he appreciated them not wanting to change him into another cardboard politician. William said he did want to change him except on some issues. They all laughed. John had no problem sleeping that night.

Over the next two days, John was put through four sessions a day. Questions were asked and answered, and John made sure everyone knew he was not a career politician. He pounded home the answers and made sure his Nine-Point Plan was in the debate discussion. At one point, Hank, who was playing Ron Paul, tried to zing John on a response. John, who was extremely quick-witted, fired back a retort that made even William chuckle. By the end of Wednesday, William, Hank, and Debbie were convinced John was ready. John was even starting to feel pretty confident about Thursday's debate. When he got to his room, Jenny was already there. He told her about the week and the firing of the debate experts. They discussed the strategy of debating the issues and not window dressing. Jenny asked what the schedule was for the next day. He said debate preparations were finished. He would visit the campus in the daylight hours and meet as many people as he could. Jenny asked if the other candidates were going to do the same. He was not sure, but he was not going to be another politician. He was going to trust his gut and speak plainly to the American people.

The next morning, John got up, worked out, had breakfast, and went with Charles down to the campus. There was a lot of activity around the auditorium where the debate was to be held. John started introducing himself to people, many of whom were busy putting the stage together and getting the sound system up. Most seemed a little surprised John was speaking to them. John asked them about their thoughts of the economy, their own personal situations, and what they thought the right answers might be for fixing America. Most had never been asked those questions. John and Charles stood out near the auditorium for over four hours talking to different people. John enjoyed it. At 2:30 p.m., he went back to his room and took a two-hour nap. It was the first time in a long time that he had done that. At 4:30 p.m.,

John and Jenny went and had a very light dinner. At 6:30 p.m., he took a shower and got dressed for the event. At 7:15 p.m., Charles knocked on the door as it was time to leave for the debate. When they arrived, John was escorted to a makeshift makeup room where his makeup was applied. After that, he was ferried to a holding room with his name on the door. When he walked in, William and Hank were already there. They both looked at him and said he would be great. At 7:55 p.m., one of the stage managers came and collected John and took him to the stage. John walked up and shook the hands of Michelle Bachmann, Mitt Romney, Ron Paul, Tim Pawlenty, Herman Cain, and Newt Gingrich. At 8:00 p.m., the red light came on; it was time for the Ames Republican debate.

Chapter 17

Chris Wallace welcomed the television audience and those in attendance at the Iowa State University Center to the Iowa GOP debates. The panel consisted of Wallace and two members from *The Washington Examiner*. The format of the debate would be one and one-half minute answers and a response from one or two of the other candidates. The host introduced the candidates, and the debate started.

The first set of questions dealt with the economy and the debt ceiling. The first question went to Michelle Bachmann. What do you think is the most critical problem facing America today? Michelle Bachmann stated unemployment was the most pressing matter facing America today. She stated the unemployment matter had been disregarded by President Obama, and his policies have prolonged the unemployment situation. John was asked for his answer to this question. John remarked:

A complete lack of leadership is the most critical problem facing America today. Over the last six years, the country has faced a housing bubble bust, a complete credit meltdown, unemployment rates not seen since the early 1980s and lasting a lot longer, massive and uncontrolled spending, bailouts for anyone and everyone, and a brand new set of federal bureaucracies that will burden our economy and future generations at levels that are unprecedented. Our leaders, and I mean both parties, have failed to see the obvious signs that terrible times were coming and failed to make the appropriate changes when needed. Instead, both parties have been content to let things stay as is as long as they stay in power. The Federal Reserve is still stuck in a Keynesian economic model when it obviously has become a relic. Our educational system has failed our children and our society. Our president has continually shown his inability and inexperience in leading this country. He consistently presses others to make the hard decisions and to lead. He is more interested in acting as the president of the United States than being the president of the United States.

I am here to tell you that America needs someone who can fix America. No one person can fix it alone. It will take every single one of us working and sacrificing together for us to fix America. We need leadership. We need someone willing to make decisions. Not all of the decisions will be right. I will make the decision, and when it is necessary, will make changes to move the country forward. I will never make decisions for political reasons. The decisions I make will be made for the betterment of this great country. Thank you.

The crowd started to cheer. The host had to remind the audience that the applause would come at the end of the debate.

The questions continued through the debate. The candidates spent a considerable amount of time criticizing

President Obama and his failed policies. During one of the questions, Ron Paul criticized John's position on congressional term limits, his position related to the Constitution and the freedoms guaranteed to the people of the country to choose who they wanted to represent them in Congress. John was given an opportunity to respond:

Congressman Paul. You are correct the founding fathers put forth this powerful document, the Constitution, to be the master document of the American progression. I believe, as you do, the document was perfect in how it was written at the time. However, the founders also put forth a process in which this Constitution could be changed from time to time. America has successfully changed the Constitution, including the original Bill of Rights, on sixteen occasions. I will tell you that the founders would have never imagined the corruption, the deceit, the complete disregard for responsibility of many members of Congress. They would have never been able to fathom the sums of money that are passed around at the drop of a hat in Washington. I believe they would have fully supported term limits for Congress.

In the South Carolina debate, you mentioned you thought it was perfectly acceptable for the legalization of drugs, including the real addictive drugs. I did not speak up at that time, because quite frankly, I really did not have a voice. But I will tell you, Congressman Paul, you are wrong. The Constitution was not set up to allow unlimited freedoms for every American. It was established to provide the guaranteed liberties and freedoms given by Almighty God. The freedom to do drugs is not guaranteed by the Constitution. Your ability to claim that there is such a right IS protected by the Constitution. The problem with drug use is its aftermath—potential damage to life, liberty, and the pursuit of happiness of others. And with our current federal system, the additional cost of curing and fixing the effects of drugs, which will have a negative impact on the overall American experience. The damage it causes families, friends, and others makes it something that should be prevented in our society.

Congressman Paul, I commend you for your never-ending efforts to have our society and government live within the confines of our Constitution. But I will tell you: your interpretation of both congressional term limits and unfettered drug use are contrary to the Constitution that I know. Thank you.

The crowd broke out in loud applause. William and Hank even shouted in reaction to John's response.

Finally, the panel was asked what their positions were on homosexual marriage. Each of the candidates gave his or her opinion. Most were against recognizing homosexual marriages. Congressman Paul, as expected, had no real problem with the legalization of homosexual marriage. John was finally asked his opinion which was:

I am a Christian. I will never hide this fact regardless of the political impact. Being a Christian and understanding what the Holy Bible says, I think homosexual unions are against God's plans for men and women. Nothing I can say or do will ever change what I believe. Nor will I ever lie to you and say something other than what I believe. However, I understand people are people. People are individuals who make choices. Those choices may or may not agree with my own personal belief system. While I will never condone or perhaps understand some of the decisions made by people, I will always try to find a way to make a connection with every person. We, as Americans, are the melting pot of the world, looking for freedom and liberty. At the end of the human process, all people want to feel hope; they want to feel accepted; they want to feel that they matter. I will never intentionally make them feel different because of the choices they make or the lifestyle they have chosen. Hopefully our commonalities and love for this country will trump any disagreements that we have.

The crowd erupted again, and the host again admonished them.

The host gave each candidate an opportunity to give a one and one-half minute closing statement. Each of the other candidates gave a rehash of their various stump speeches. John, since he was in second place going into the debate, was given the final closing statement. He said:

I want to thank Fox News, The Washington Examiner, and the Iowa Republican Party for hosting this event tonight. I want to thank each of my fellow Republicans for their involvement in the debate tonight. And I want to thank each and every one of you in the audience and at home for taking time out of your busy schedules to listen to us tonight. I know a lot of you are struggling. You are struggling from an economic point of view; from worrying about your future; from worrying about your children's and grandchildren's futures; and from worrying about our beloved country's future. I understand.

I am not a politician. I truly respect each of the people on this stage and the dedication they have given our country, and our state and local governments over their careers. I have never run or been in political office. I am a retired businessman. Over the last year, I was given an opportunity to teach at my alma mater—The College of William and Mary. As I instructed the class, I found a new and unexpected love for my country. At the same time, I watched my country fall into an abyss in which bad decision after bad decision was being made. I watched as ObamaCare passed; I watched as new bureaucracies were created; I watched as massive and uncontrolled spending took place; and I watched as bailouts were doled out like candy. I watched as America's influence in the world went from worried to laughable. The more I watched, the more I felt a responsibility to give back to this great nation.

I have been blessed! I am Saved! I have the best wife and family in the history of the world. I have been given opportunities to succeed, and with hard work I exceeded even my own high expectations. Now it is time for me to give back to my country. We can fix America, together. I have a Nine-Point Plan which will fix America. I need your help. I can't do this alone. Together we can fix America not just for ourselves, but for our children and grandchildren. We can have hope in America's future. Thank you.

The crowd erupted again and didn't bother to listen to the host as he closed the debates. Jenny walked onto the stage and held John's hand as they waved to the crowd. As John walked off the stage, he shook the hands of all of his fellow GOP competitors. He told Congressman Paul that he hoped his response hadn't offended him. Congressman Paul said he was not offended as they shook hands. John walked into the hallway by the auditorium and saw both William and Hank. They walked quickly out to the bus waiting for them. They loaded onto the bus and left for the short ride to Des Moines. Hank could barely talk. He was so excited about the results of the debate. William was simply sitting across from John, smiling. Jenny even joined in the excitement of the celebration. John smiled, but was somewhat reserved in his enjoyment. He knew he had won the debate, but he had won it at the expense of another candidate. The real opponent was Obama and the Progressives who were running the country into the ground. This was only a practice game moving toward the regular season. The World Series, to use a baseball analogy, was still a long way away. John knew the fighting among the Republicans needed to end so all energies could be spent on defeating Obama.

The campaign bus arrived at the airport and pulled alongside the airplane. John, Jenny, William, Hank, Debbie, George, and Charles all got out and walked up the stairs. Randolph One departed about fifteen minutes later on its flight to Virginia, getting back to Newport News around 1:00 a.m. Debbie had been on the telephone the entire way to Virginia. John was to be interviewed by NBC's "Today Show" at 7:10 a.m. At 11:00 a.m., there would be a rally on the steps of the J. Christopher Wren building on the campus of the College of William and Mary. At 3:00 p.m., John would be a guest on the Sean Hannity radio show. The success of the debate was making Friday extremely busy.

Chapter 18

John and Jenny arrived at The Willows at 1:30 a.m. and were in bed shortly thereafter. John awoke at 5:30 a.m., took a shower, dressed, and drove to the NBC affiliate in Portsmouth about an hour away. John was interviewed and was on his way back to Williamsburg by 7:30 a.m. He went to campaign headquarters, which was already humming with people. Hank motioned John over to the conference room and said every political commentator had pronounced that he had hit a home run at last night's debate. None of the other candidates was mentioned in the same breath. Moreover, the White House had even criticized some of the things John had said the previous night. If the White House was making negative comments, they felt threatened by the Randolph campaign. Debbie walked over and handed John a copy of the speech he would give at 11:00 a.m. He sat down and started reading it. He made some changes and gave it back to her for modification.

William walked into the conference room and stated last night's debate was the best debate he had ever seen. William and Hank had remapped the entire strategy for the next three months. William said they could discuss the details on the airplane that night back to Ames, Iowa.

Thomas Philpot, the campaign's Finance Manager, came in with the July second-half report. The following information was shared:

(000s)	Total Contributions	Total Loans from JR	Total Expenditures	Cash On Hand
5/31/2011	9,500.0	2,000.0	(2,300.0)	9,200.0
6/15/2011	4,125.0	-	(1,250.0)	12,075.0
6/30/2011	10,256.0		(2,250.0)	20,081.0
7/15/2011	18,566.0		(4,575.0)	34,072.0
7/31/2011	14,250.0		(6,875.0)	41,447.0
Total	56,697.0	2,000.0	(17,250.0)	41,447.0

Thomas said contributions were still exceptionally strong. He suspected they would assuredly increase after last night's Iowa debate. John asked whether they were being careful as to not waste money. Thomas said that all expenditures were being very carefully monitored and a proper accounting would be made. At 10:30 a.m., Jenny, the children, and grandchildren walked into campaign headquarters. They left together for the J. Christopher Wren Building at the college, arriving about ten minutes before the speech. A makeshift stage was set up with the sign "We Can Fix America Together" draped on it. John walked over and shook the hand of the College President, Dr. Thornton Smith. Dr. Smith told John how proud he and the entire college were of John's success so far in the presidential campaign.

Precisely at 11:00 a.m., Dr. Smith walked up to the podium and introduced John. Dr. Smith spoke of John's teaching at the college during the previous semester. He also spoke of his own personal experiences with John and Jenny. John stood there uncomfortably, listening to the flattering introduction. Finally, Dr. Smith finished, and John walked up to the podium. There must have been about one thousand people on the lawn of the Wren Building and spilling down Duke of Gloucester Street. John gave the following speech:

Thank you! Thank you! I always love being back at the college in Williamsburg, Virginia. I grew up in Virginia, and went to college at William and Mary. Even though Jenny and I moved away for quite a while, we always missed Virginia. When the opportunity arose for us to move back, we jumped at the chance. As most of you may know, our children and grandchildren all live in the Williamsburg area. It has been great to be closer to them.

I would like to thank Dr. Smith for his kind remarks and for allowing me to be here today to talk to you about something extremely important. Over the past five years, our country has seen many challenges. Our leaders have had many opportunities to make changes and to fix the problems facing America. However, the decisions made were incorrect in practice and rarely done in time to make a difference. These decisions included forcing banks to merge, a $700 billion bank bailout package, bailing out car and insurance companies, an $861 billion stimulus package, spoken intentions of raising taxes, and passing the biggest entitlement program in the history of America—ObamaCare. Look where we are today— unemployment is stuck over 9 percent and the accuracy of that number is very suspect; an economy that is extremely fragile; a massive fight over increasing the debt limit which could threaten the bond rating of our debt; massive and *uncontrolled spending; deficits that are the largest in the history of America and the world; and a political system that is more interested in self-preservation than in helping Americans. The problems and challenges seem to be overwhelming, and finding a starting place seems like an impossible task.*

I am here to tell you there is a starting point. I am here to tell you the American people have always faced challenges head-on, and they refuse to lose. I am here to tell you that our best days as Americans are still ahead of us. I am here to tell you that "We Can Fix America Together." The starting point involves us recognizing there are problems. Once we come to that conclusion, we, as Americans, will pull up our boots and get ready to tackle the problems head-on.

Last night was a terrific night for many obvious reasons and not so favorable for other reasons. The debate in Ames, Iowa went remarkably well for the Randolph campaign. The political pundits and the after-polls were highly complementary. It showed that my Nine-Point Plan is starting to be embraced by the American people. While the other Republican candidates have some plans for dealing with some of the issues, the debate showed I am the only candidate with a comprehensive plan. The biggest revelation from last night's debate was my Nine-Point Plan is moving the discussion from the current broken system to one that will fix America. What was not good about the debate was the tearing down of people. Why, in our society, is it so critical for one person to be built up on the backs of others? Why can't we just keep the monologue civil and debate the various points of view? At the end of the day, the ultimate goal is to defeat Obama and his progressive agenda.

We, as Republicans, must come together, instead of insulting and tearing each other apart. We have a real challenge in front of us. The extremely progressive agenda that Obama, Pelosi, and Reid put forth from 2007 until 2010 has made the needed economic recovery much harder to achieve. They gave us the auto and insurance bailouts and called them necessary. They gave us the $861 billion bailout, saying that it would prevent unemployment from increasing to greater than 8 percent. They gave us political divisiveness and called it political correctness. They gave us massive and unfettered spending, and said that it was necessary to prevent economic hardship. They gave us ObamaCare, which will saddle this country with massive debts, and said it was humane. They said the rich need to pay more taxes and called it fair. We need to recognize the extremely smooth words of Obama, and the Progressive Movement is for change—from the freedoms espoused by our founders to a socialist society. This socialist society does not allow Americans to succeed on their own work and efforts. It does not allow children to work hard and succeed by their own efforts. It does not allow businessmen and women the ability to make a better way of life for their families through working hard. Instead, a socialist society simply takes all of the money from every *single person and divides it based on what the socialist government says is fair. I will tell you that our founders never imagined such a government, and I can't either. We need to stand up together and say enough is enough. We want opportunities and the ability to succeed. We do not want the government to rule over our lives and tell us what we can and can't do. We need to tell Obama and the Progressives that we are for freedom, and we do not want the socialist society that you are trying to push down our throats. We, as Republicans, need to come together right here and right now to start the tremendously hard fight against the Progressive Movement.*

I have a Nine-Point Plan for Fixing America and stopping the Progressive and Socialist Movements in this country. The first three steps must be put into place before the rest of the corrections can be done. Step 1 – We must have congressional term limits. As I have said before, there is no way in which people who spend their entire working lives in Washington can have any responsibility to the people who put them in office. The American people showed considerable wisdom when they put forth an amendment for presidential term limits. Now it is time for us to have the same thing for Congress. Step 2 – We must have campaign finance reform. President Obama raised and spent over $700 million in the last presidential election cycle. Remember, this job pays $450 thousand a year. A rational person has to assume that kind of money is buying influence, or in some cases, massive paybacks in the form of special governmental loans or massive government *project awards. Step 3 – We must have comprehensive lobbyist reform. Lobbyists pay exorbitant amounts of money so they can discuss topics with congressmen and the president. This type of influence is keeping politicians from always working for the best interest of the American people.*

The next six steps are what can be done when we get the first three out of the way. The first three are essential. In other words, once we get the American political landscape back to where it was envisioned, we can start the process of fixing America.

Step 4 – Reform our entitlement programs. During the debt ceiling debates, I watched as our president and certain members of Congress used Social Security as a tool to get their way. I watched Obama say, without an increase in the debt ceiling, the Social Security checks would not go out on August 3rd. My fellow Americans—That was a lie. I am not going to try to be politically correct on this statement because quite frankly, I would be committing the same offensive our president spewed on all of us. The president and most members of the progressive caucus have said restructuring and reforming entitlement programs are not necessary for us to get spending under control. That, also, is a lie. We need to force our leaders to either tell the truth or get out of office. We need honesty, not politics. We need someone to be an adult and not act as if they were adults. Mr. President, either tell the truth to the American people and lead the effort or get out of the way.

Step 5 – We need to repeal ObamaCare now! We need to replace it with true health-care reforms. This involves tort reform, portability of insurance across state lines, and finally, changing the way we think of insurance. All of these can be done and done rather quickly as long as the politics are taken out of the discussion. ObamaCare was a means for Progressives to nationalize our health-care system. It has been the intent and desire of every Progressive since Woodrow Wilson to have socialized health-care. The president, Pelosi, and Reid took the economic meltdown as an impetus to force this law on us. Losing the 2010 mid-term elections was perfectly acceptable, because they got what they wanted. Let's keep voting members of Congress out of office who are in favor of ObamaCare until we get representatives who care about what we think.

Step 6 – We need to eliminate the use of earmarks and have substantial reductions in spending. As long as Congress continues to show no restraint and willingness to balance our budget, we must push for the passage of a constitutional balanced budget amendment. While I dislike putting this measure in place, it is necessary to prevent Congress and the president from overspending. They simply do not know when to say "enough."

Step 7 – We need to disband the Department of Education and push the responsibility back to the states. Our *spending for federal education continues to increase, and children's test scores continue to decline. The Department of Education has proven to be a complete failure. Instead of continuing to fund a failing effort, let's change course and make modifications to fix the problem.*

Step 8 – We need to make unions for public employees a thing of the past. Public employees should not continue to be enriched at levels greater than the private sector, based on monopolistic negotiation powers. We need to disband these unlawful organizations and make public employees advocates of the taxpayer and not the other way around.

And finally, Step 9 –We need to modify and simplify the tax code. Tax loopholes should be eliminated. Tax deductions should also be eliminated. Once this is done, the tax rates should be reduced. This will not only make the system fair, but it will also take away lobbyists' efforts to get certain deductions for their causes.

These are the nine steps that I envision as a means to fix America.

I am not a politician. I have never been a politician, nor do I aspire to be one. I am a retired businessman with a desire to help America regain its position as the world's greatest country. Over the last two and one-half years, our President has made it his goal to minimize America's role in the world. By apologizing for military acts that were done to keep America safe; by using our military in non-constitutional acts of aggression; by pitting one group against another; by continuing to print and spend money and mortgage the futures of our children and grandchildren, the president has not shown the willingness or ability to lead in any situation. Where is his plan for fixing America? Either he does not think there are problems or he does not know where to start. I believe we should help him figure out where we should start—help me to put him and his Progressive friends in Congress on the unemployment line. They need to feel how over 9 percent of Americans feel. Then and only then can we fix America together.

Thank you again for coming out today. I love this country. I love the promise of a better future. I love the idea that if you work very hard, you can succeed in this country. I love the idea that America is still the best example of liberty and freedom in a world wanting it to fail. Let's show the world what America is all about. Let's show the world there are no problems too large for America to fix. Let's show the world when the American people are confronted with enormous problems, we can work together and fix those problems. Let's show the world what the American spirit is all about.

Thank you! God bless you! God bless your families and loved ones. God bless America!

The crowd's response was overwhelmingly positive and extremely loud. A chant of "Randolph!" started. Jenny walked up the steps of the Wren Building and waved to the crowd with John. After a couple of minutes, John and Jenny walked down the steps and followed Charles to some cars waiting near Blair Hall. The caravan turned left on Richmond Road and travelled to campaign headquarters. When John and Jenny walked into the offices, they saw William, Hank, and Debbie smiling. The entire office started to clap. John tried to quiet them down, but they kept cheering. He walked back to the conference room and shook most of the hands on the way. Only when the conference room doors were shut did the staff return to their jobs. William said the speech went remarkably well. He thought the keys—uniting the Republican Party and showing the progressives' true intent—were met.

Even though William said he would explain the new campaign strategy on the airplane that night, he was too excited to wait and started revealing it in the conference room. The first part of the strategy was that the campaign would take part in only four more GOP debates. These would include one in California and one in Florida, both in the month of September. In addition, there would be a debate in Iowa in December 2011 and one in New Hampshire in January 2012. He did not think it was necessary for any additional debates. In terms of campaign travel, they would need to make some changes in the schedule. Starting this week, the schedule would extend into Saturdays to take advantage of fairs, carnivals, ball games, etc. so the work week would be Tuesday to Saturday. The campaign would focus less on the other

Republican candidates' positions and more on the failed policies of the Obama administration. The campaign would visit two states per week and would try to use the bus as much as possible. Finally with its continued upward movement in the polls, there would be bodyguards hired immediately. John did not like that idea, but William did not give him a choice.

Later on Friday afternoon, John was a guest on the Sean Hannity show. Afterwards, John left campaign headquarters and returned to The Willows to pack for the trip back to Ames, Iowa. Charles arrived at The Willows at 5:25 p.m. and drove John to the Newport News airport. Randolph One was airborne shortly after 6:00pm. They arrived in Des Moines at 7:15 p.m. CST and drove north for thirty minutes to Ames. The campaign checked back into the Gateway Hotel for the night. Tomorrow would be the Ames straw polling event.

Chapter 19

The Ames, Iowa straw poll is a very interesting event. It is held at the Hilton Coliseum on the campus of Iowa State University. The event is an extended daylong fundraiser for the Iowa Republican Party whereby paying customers have an opportunity to talk to the candidates and to vote in the straw poll. Each of the candidates is given an opportunity to speak before the voting takes place. Charles knocked on John's door about 11:30 a.m., and they walked over to the coliseum. The Randolph campaign had bid and paid for a booth near the entrance. Those slots are typically pricey. John saw George there already talking with several Republican Iowans. There were about ten "Randolph" people at the booth.

John spent the day talking to dozens of Iowans about the problems affecting their state. John asked a lot of questions and what people thought about the problems facing America. Most agreed with his idea of congressional term limits. They also agreed on disbanding the Department of Education and the elimination of public unions. John ate extremely well—he had barbeque, fried corn on the cob, and corn muffins.

Later in the afternoon, each of the candidates was given an opportunity to speak to Iowans in the coliseum. John's speech was a variation of the one given at the College of William and Mary the day before. As soon as the candidates were finished, the voting began. Each paying person had the opportunity to vote. According to George, several busloads of people backing both Paul and Bachmann were in attendance. John asked George if their campaign had done anything like that. George was not aware of any voter manipulations funded by the Randolph campaign. At the end of the voting, the following results were announced:

	Votes	%
Romney	1,858	15.0%
Palin	-	
Cain	619	5.0%
Gingrich	372	3.0%
Paul	743	6.0%
Bachmann	2,477	20.0%
Pawlenty	1,362	11.0%
Perry	1,486	12.0%
Santorum	124	1.0%
Randolph	3,220	26.0%

The Randolph Campaign won the Ames straw poll by 6 percent. John's debate performance had been the deciding factor in the straw-poll results. Michelle Bachmann, the expected winner, had come in a distant second behind the Randolph campaign. Obviously the entire campaign staff was elated by the results. John walked back to the hotel and was asleep by 9:00 p.m. The entire three days were a complete blur and had utterly gassed him.

On Sunday morning, John woke up and went downstairs to work out in the hotel gym. Afterwards, he had breakfast in the restaurant. Finally, he went upstairs to his room, took a shower, got dressed, and was ready to leave just as Charles knocked on the door at 9:30 a.m. The Ford Expeditions took John, George, and Charles to the airport in Des Moines for the two-hour trip to Manchester, New Hampshire. It was now time to put the new strategy into place.

On the airplane, John was on a conference call with William, Hank, and Debbie regarding the message of the week. The message would include simplifying the individual tax code and reducing corporate federal-income-tax rates. However, the new strategy called for every message to include the following tenets: (1) congressional term limits, (2) unifying the Republican Party, (3) never mentioning the other GOP candidates, (4) distinguishing John as the only non-politician, (5), continually discussing the failed policies of the Obama administration, and (6) start referring to Obama as Barack Obama and not the president. This would be the new formula going forward. Debbie sent a copy of the stump speech over the Internet. John read it and made changes online. The speech was printed on the airplane. Technology is great.

Randolph One touched down in Manchester around noon on Sunday. The campaign checked into a hotel near the airport. John spent the afternoon on the telephone with William, Hank, and Debbie discussing the new strategy. On Sunday night, John had dinner with potential donors in Manchester.

On Monday morning, John had breakfast with local GOP officials in Manchester. At 9:30 a.m., he was interviewed by the local FOX affiliate. At 10:30 a.m., there was a rally near city hall. John was introduced by George, who estimated there were about one thousand people at the rally. John gave the following speech:

Thank you Manchester! Thank you! I am glad to be here with you this morning. Over the last several days, the Republican presidential decision has begun to become much clearer. There is only one Republican candidate that has a plan to fix America. There is only one Republican candidate that can take back this country from the far-left Progressives that have put us on a destination to the poor house. There is only one Republican who can put Barack Obama on the unemployment line. The Randolph campaign is that group, and I am John Randolph, Republican candidate for president of the United States.

Barack Obama and his far-left-wing Progressives have hurt this country. Barack Obama increased discretionary spending by over 24 percent since he has been in office. Barack Obama has taken on over $4 trillion of new debt. Barack Obama has signed ObamaCare into law which will further add to the debt and will not solve the health-care problems in this country. Barack Obama has increased spending at the Department of Education and test scores continue to drop. Barack Obama spent $862 billion, which he called a stimulus bill, but it did not stimulate anything other than the bank accounts of people getting him elected. Barack Obama bailed out banks, automobile companies, and insurance companies. What do we have to show for all of these things? We have an unemployment rate over 9.2 percent. We have a weak US dollar compared with other currencies around the world. We have a very weak economy that could fall back into a second recession. We have continuing declines in housing prices. We have more divisiveness in this country as Barack Obama likes to pit one group against another. We have more crime. Never in the history of the world has one person been given so much latitude to govern and have so little to show for it afterwards. Barack Obama's 2008 campaign slogan was "Change We Can Believe In." Mr. Obama, we do not believe anymore.

It is time for this country to be taken back by Americans. It is time for regular Americans to say "enough is enough." We need to make sure our leaders are working for us as opposed to their own self-interests and self-preservation. We need to hold them accountable for the decisions that they make. We need congressional term limits, and we need them now!

Once we get term limits, we can fix what ails this country.

Today, I am here to talk to you about Point Nine in my Nine-Point Plan for Fixing America. Point Nine calls for the modification and simplification of our federal tax code. Our current tax system is a progressive income-based tax system. The US tax code is made up of a series of rules, with exceptions to the general rule and exceptions to the exceptions to the general rule. There are loopholes, tax sweeteners, tax deductions, tax credits, earned income tax credits, tax refunds for those who pay taxes and for those who do not pay taxes, and tax rebates. Billions and billions of dollars are spent by lobbyists each year to get new tax laws written so they will get favorable treatment, and additional billions and billions are spent preparing and enforcing tax laws. I have a better way. I have a way in which we can lower tax rates and still generate enough revenues to run the country.

First, we need to lower the corporate income tax rate from 35 percent to 20 percent. Now I know most of you will say that will reduce tax receipts and add to the deficit and you are correct. To reduce the corporate tax rate from 35 percent to 20 percent will reduce tax receipts by $95 billion. However, if we can keep more jobs and investment opportunities in America, we can increase employment and at the same time increase the tax base. The United States has the highest corporate tax rate of the G-20 nations. Is it any wonder why companies are leaving America and finding cheaper places to do business abroad? In addition, I will directly pay for this reduction by immediately selling land-lease rights for oil companies to drill on federal lands. We must become energy independent, and I will start us on that path within one month of taking office.

Second, we need to rewrite the individual tax code. I would limit tax deductions to home-mortgage interest, state income taxes and charitable contributions. Then I would reduce the tax rates to where the maximum tax rate would be around 20–to–22 percent. The tax-rate structure would stay progressive. The income-tax rates would generate revenues of around 18–to–20 percent of gross domestic product. I would eliminate FICA, FUTA, SUTA, and Medicare taxes because to say they are trust funds is simply a lie. I want to make the tax code only three pages long. We could reduce the size of the IRS and save money. Every American will pay taxes. It might only be $50, but every person will contribute to running this country.

Third, I want to implement a national VAT tax of around 4 percent to be applied on every aspect of economic transactions. These receipts can only be used to pay down our debt. This fund cannot and will not be used for general-fund expenditures. A provision in the VAT law must include that any attempt to use it for current expenditures would render the VAT null and void. If we use these funds to pay down our debt, we could potentially be debt free in thirty-five to forty years. I know that is a long time, but we did not rack up these debts in a short time period either. We have been building debt since the final year of President Andrew Jackson's second term.

Fourth, I propose we sell a portion of the federal government's land holdings as a down payment on paying off our debt. Currently, the federal government owns over

780-million acres of land in this country. If we sold 200 million for around $10,000/acre, we could pay down $2 trillion of our $14 trillion debt. This seems to be an excellent first step in making America stronger for future generations.

Fifth, those who decide to cheat on taxes will be brought to justice. The punishment will be more financial than criminal. If you cheat on taxes, the financial penalty will be five times your liability on the first offense. On the second, the penalty will be ten times your liability. Weekly, the IRS will publish a listing of all tax cheats and distribute on the Internet. If you cheat, you will be put to shame. The IRS will immediately take your assets and sell them off to pay for unpaid liabilities. If you do not have enough assets, we will garnish your wages. If you work in the federal government and have not paid your taxes, you will be fired immediately, no questions asked.

Finally, future tax-rate changes must be approved by both Congress and the president. If the increase or decrease is more than one percent, it will require a two-thirds vote in Congress. If it is plus or minus five percent, it will require a three-fourths vote in Congress. We can no longer just cut taxes without a means for paying for them. Additionally, I would love to see a law that requires Congress to cut spending by two times for every new tax rate increase. This would keep the funny accounting practices used by some in Congress from happening.

This is what we should do to modify and simplify our tax code. These steps are logical and should not be difficult to implement.

I know tax lawyers and tax accountants may disagree with me on these proposals. I am sure progressives will disagree with cutting the corporate tax rate. I am sure many conservatives will not want to implement a VAT tax. I am sure the environmentalists will not want me to sell federal lands or start drilling on federal lands. I am most confident tax cheats do not want to see my disciplinary proposals. I have two words for each of these groups —Too bad! To fix the tax system will involve drastic changes to everything including your self-serving areas of interest. We need to fix the current tax system and this is what I know will work.

We have a lot of work to do. First we all need to admit we have serious problems. I am speaking to Democrats, Independents, and Republicans. Once we get past this revelation, we can start fixing the problems. All of the problems seem very big and almost impossible to fix. The American people that I know will not let problems beat them. The American people that I know consider problems to be opportunities. It is now time to come up with plans, put them in place, and execute on them. It is time for us to fix America together. We can do this!

God bless you! God bless your families and God Bless America. Thank you!

The crowd was wildly clapping and someone started a "Randolph!" chant. George nudged John, and they walked off the stage. The speech was obviously well received by the crowd.

At noon, John had lunch with the chamber of commerce and gave the tax stump speech again. At 2:00 p.m., John visited with some potential donors and discussed the status of the campaign. Afterward, the campaign traveled by bus to Concord, New Hampshire. At 4:30 p.m., John was interviewed by the local ABC affiliate. At 6:00 p.m., John was invited to have dinner with a local business forum and to give the tax stump speech again. At 9:30 p.m., John met with some potential donors at the hotel.

On Tuesday morning, the campaign was invited to a breakfast meeting with the Concord Chamber of Commerce. John gave the tax stump speech again. At 9:00 a.m., John was interviewed by a local radio station. During the interview, John was asked about his music-listening pleasure. John admitted to favoring late 1970s and early-1980s pop music. At 10:30 a.m., the campaign held a rally near the state capitol which over five hundred people attended. The tax stump speech was again well received. At noon, John met with a local bankers' forum to discuss the tax code. At 2:30 p.m., the bus was on its way to Nashua which is just over one hour away from Concord. At 4:00 p.m., John was interviewed by the Sean Hannity radio show by telephone. At 5:30 p.m., he was the keynote speaker at the Nashua Chamber of Commerce dinner, where he presented the stump speech again. At 8:00 p.m., he met with local Nashua GOP officials at the hotel.

On Wednesday morning, John had breakfast with some potential donors. At 9:00 a.m., the bus left for the one-hour trip to Boston. At 11:00 a.m., there was a rally at the Boston Harbor. John gave the tax stump speech again, and included references to the Boston Tea Party. At 12:30 p.m., John spoke at the Boston Chamber of Commerce's luncheon. At 2:30 p.m., John was interviewed on the local ABC affiliate. At 4:00 p.m., the campaign held a rally in Lowell, Massachusetts that included at least five hundred people. At 6:00 p.m., John was the keynote speaker at a business leaders' forum in Concord. At 8:30 p.m., John met with potential donors at the hotel.

On Thursday morning, the bus traveled one hour west to Worcester. At 8:30 a.m., John met with local GOP leaders. At 10:30 a.m., he was interviewed by the local FOX affiliate. At noon, he was the keynote speaker at the Worcester Chamber of Commerce, and on the menu was the tax stump speech. At 2:30 p.m., John met with some potential donors. At 4:00 p.m., the campaign held a rally near city hall in a park, which included the tax stump speech. At 6:00 p.m., John was the featured speaker at a local tax preparers' dinner. The tax stump speech was given. Surprisingly, there was some positive excitement on the part of the accountants in the room. At 8:00 p.m., John met with some more potential donors.

On Friday morning, the bus traveled one and one-half hours west to Springfield. The campaign held a rally at 9:30am near city hall. George estimated there were at least seven-hundred-and-fifty people in attendance. At 11:00 a.m., there was a conference call with national GOP leaders. At noon, John spoke at the Springfield Chamber of Commerce luncheon. At 2:00 p.m., he was interviewed by the local NBC affiliate. At 4:00 p.m., he met with potential donors. At 6:00 p.m., John spoke at a fundraiser. At 8:30 p.m., he met with local GOP leaders at the hotel.

On Saturday morning, John took part in a groundbreaking at a new manufacturing operation in West Springfield at 10:00 a.m. At 11:30 a.m., John had a closed-door meeting with local education leaders, the first of such meetings. There were a lot of questions about his plan to disband the Department of Education. At 2:00 p.m., the campaign went to the Springfield airport, the group boarded Randolph One, and wheels were up by 3:30 p.m. When John got back to Newport News, he was exhausted. He and Jenny had dinner at 7:00 p.m. and John went to bed at 9:00 p.m. On Sunday morning, John and Jenny went to church and took the children and grandchildren to lunch. John rested all Sunday afternoon. This was proving to be an immensely rewarding, but exhausting experience.

Chapter 20

On Monday, August 15th, John got up, worked out, had breakfast, showered, and was dressed by 7:00 a.m. At 7:15 a.m., Charles was at the door for the short trip over to campaign headquarters. John noticed one of the campaign buses was there. He also noticed the parking lot was full. He walked into the building and went up to the second floor as usual, where he noticed a lot of changes. The space that the campaign was using had more than doubled, and it appeared Hank had stuffed people into every inch available. John nodded to the receptionist and walked to the conference room in the back. William, Hank, and Debbie were in the room discussing something.

William looked up and saw John. He said they were working though the final details of the schedule for the next several weeks. First, however, the latest news was that Rick Santorum had suspended his campaign. The latest poll numbers gave the reason:

Poll	PPP (D)	NBC/WSJ	Fox News	Rasmussen	PPP (D)	Quinnipiac
Date	8/15/2011	8/10/2011	7/30/2011	7/25/2011	7/17/2011	7/11/2011
Romney	17%	17%	18%	18%	18%	19%
Palin	9%	9%	9%	10%	10%	10%
Cain	6%	6%	6%	6%	7%	6%
Gingrich	4%	4%	4%	4%	5%	5%
Paul	4%	4%	4%	4%	5%	5%
Bachmann	10%	10%	10%	11%	13%	12%
Pawlenty	2%	2%	2%	2%	3%	3%
Perry	6%	7%	8%	8%	10%	10%
Santorum	1%	1%	1%	1%	1%	1%
Randolph	36%	35%	33%	31%	28%	25%

Santorum's campaign never got going. He was having fundraising problems, and it just did not look good. William suspected Pawlenty and Gingrich were not far behind Santorum. Hank started talking about what the polls numbers meant for each of the candidates. The Randolph campaign continued to show exceptionally well. It had increased its polling numbers by 10 percent in one month. The Romney camp had seen its numbers decrease by 2 percent over the same period. Bachmann also saw a 2 percent decrease month over month. The rest of the campaigns were treading water or decreasing. William said the strategy of never mentioning the other Republican candidates was working and needed to continue.

Next on the agenda, Thomas Philpot came in the conference room. He had the August mid-month finance report:

(000s)	Total Contributions	Total Loans from JR	Total Expenditures	Cash On Hand
5/31/2011	9,500.0	2,000.0	(2,300.0)	9,200.0
6/15/2011	4,125.0	-	(1,250.0)	12,075.0
6/30/2011	10,256.0		(2,250.0)	20,081.0
7/15/2011	18,566.0		(4,575.0)	34,072.0
7/31/2011	14,250.0		(6,875.0)	41,447.0
8/15/2011	23,758.0		(8,985.0)	56,220.0
Total	80,455.0	2,000.0	(26,235.0)	56,220.0

Over the last two weeks, contributions were over $37 million. Barack Obama had brought in over $60 million during the same period. Thomas said expenditures would continue to rise to around $10–12 million every two weeks, based on the current strategy. John thanked Thomas for his report.

Next, Debbie passed out the campaign schedule for the next several weeks:

Week of	Message of the Week	States To Visit
8/8/2011	Modifying and Simplifying the Tax Code	NH and MA
8/15/2011	How to Fix the Economy	NC and SC
8/22/2011	How to Fix the Economy	NV and CA
8/29/2011	How to Fix the Economy	GA and KY
9/5/2011	How to Fix the Economy	IO and MO
9/12/2011	California Debates (Simi Valley) Reagan Library, NBC News, Politico	
9/19/2011	Florida Debates (Orlando) Fox News/FL Republican Party	

Debbie said the campaign would be in ten states over the next six weeks. During the weeks of September 12th and September 19th, it would be holed up in hotels in California and Florida, respectively, for the debates those weeks. In the four weeks prior to those debates, Hank said the campaign would focus entirely on how to fix the economy. The stump speech would be broken down into four different sections: (1) congressional term limits, (2) criticizing the failed Obama policies, (3) specifically addressing solutions to fix problems such as unemployment, runaway governmental spending, debts and deficits, the housing market, and general economic growth, and (4) uniting the Republican Party. Debbie interjected the travel schedule would be comparable to last week's—leaving on Tuesday morning and returning on Saturday night. She also said William, Hank, and George would take turns on the trips.

After the scheduling portion of the meeting was finished, William brought three people into the conference room to meet John. William told John that these gentlemen were his bodyguards. William stressed John was not to go anywhere without these bodyguards in the future. This included working out in hotel gyms, going down to breakfast, and going out to dinner in Williamsburg. William told John that he was not going to argue about this. John did not like the idea, but did not think he had much choice.

Finally, Debbie handed out the first draft of the economy stump speech. John read the speech, made several modifications, and handed it back to Debbie. He knew this speech was extremely important to his campaign. Being the one and only "true outsider," he knew his plan for fixing the economy was his biggest drawing card. In addition, he knew he would give this stump speech two-to-four times per day for the next four weeks. As they concluded the staff meeting, John went and found Charles who was talking with several people at the desks in the center of the room. John and Charles left campaign headquarters, and Charles drove John to The Willows. John packed and had a nice, quiet dinner with Jenny. The campaign would leave at 4:30 a.m. by bus on Tuesday morning for the trip to North and South Carolina. The next four weeks of campaigning and the two weeks afterward were going to be instrumental in continuing to build momentum for the campaign.

Chapter 21

The next four weeks went without a hitch. John followed the script which was to ask the American people for Congressional Term Limits, pound the Obama Administration's failed policies, give specific solutions on for how to fix the economy, and stress the importance of Republican unity without ever naming one of the other Republican candidates. At the end of the four-week period, William "allowed" John to come home early—on Friday instead of Saturday. John was truly appreciative of the additional day at home.

Since the California debate was going to be held on Wednesday, September 14th at the Reagan Library in Simi Valley, the campaign travelled to California on Sunday morning. Simi Valley is northwest of Los Angeles and extremely close to Santa Barbara. The campaign established camp at an Embassy Suites near Valencia.

On Randolph One, William scheduled a staff meeting while everyone was in close proximity to one another. The first discussion was on recent polling numbers:

Poll	Fox News	Rasmussen	PPP (D)	NBC/WSJ
Date	8/31/2011	8/25/2011	8/15/2011	8/10/2011
Romney	16%	17%	17%	17%
Palin	8%	8%	9%	9%
Cain	6%	6%	6%	6%
Gingrich	3%	4%	4%	4%
Paul	4%	4%	4%	4%
Bachmann	9%	9%	10%	10%
Pawlenty	2%	2%	2%	2%
Perry	6%	6%	6%	7%
Santorum			1%	1%
Randolph	40%	39%	36%	35%

In the last four weeks, Pawlenty and Gingrich had dropped out of the race. Hank reported the campaign's polling numbers continued to be better than those of all of the other candidates. William noted several of the other campaigns had "gone negative." In particular, both Romney and Paul were attacking John's direct involvement in the mortgage-backed securities debacle that had been a factor in the 2008 financial meltdown. William continued to advise not to negatively attack either of these candidates. William called the negative advertisements "stunts" and "Hail Marys" and said the other candidates would take part in negative campaigning in the near future.

William telephoned Thomas Philpot who gave the following end-of-August finance report:

(000s)	Total Contributions	Total Loans from JR	Total Expenditures	Cash On Hand
5/31/2011	9,500.0	2,000.0	(2,300.0)	9,200.0
6/15/2011	4,125.0	-	(1,250.0)	12,075.0
6/30/2011	10,256.0		(2,250.0)	20,081.0
7/15/2011	18,566.0		(4,575.0)	34,072.0
7/31/2011	14,250.0		(6,875.0)	41,447.0
8/15/2011	23,758.0		(8,985.0)	56,220.0
8/31/2011	25,985.0		(10,215.0)	71,990.0
Total	106,440.0	2,000.0	(36,450.0)	71,990.0

Thomas said contributions were exceedingly strong; however, expenditures were continuing to creep up. The vast majority of new contributions were coming in small denominations from websites. John thanked Thomas for the report.

For the remainder of the staff meeting, John, William, Hank, and Debbie talked about the strategy after the debates. William and Hank wanted to stay on the economy, because if the US economy remained bleak, it would the best way for John to win the Republican nomination and the general election. Debbie and John were concerned that focusing on the economy would pigeonhole the campaign. If the economy improved over the next fourteen months, the basis for choosing John would be minimized if not eliminated. They debated their points for over two hours, but came to no conclusion. William suggested tabling the discussion for the next two weeks as the two debates would engulf most of the campaign's time.

After Hank and Debbie had left the back compartment, William told John that the California debate could be very ugly. Each of the Republican candidates needed something to jump-start their campaigns, which had been in the muck since the Iowa debate. William said they would come after John with everything they had. Debate preparations would include nasty, negative comments being hurled at John, and he would need to fend them off without losing his temper. The key to the debate was to look and act presidential—above the fray, but still highly engaged. John's political upside to the debate was very small, but his downside was enormous. The other candidates were exactly the opposite.

Randolph One arrived at LAX airport at 2:00 p.m. PST. A couple of Ford Expeditions were waiting near the tarmac as the airplane came to stop. Team Randolph loaded into the SUVs and drove about one hour north to Valencia. When they arrived at the hotel, the advance team had already checked them in, and they went directly to their rooms to freshen up. Afterwards, John walked down to the first floor with one of his bodyguards in tow. The campaign had reserved two of the meeting rooms, and a debate platform had already been assembled. John walked in and noticed William and Hank already there talking quietly. In the back of the room, several cameras had been set up so debate preparations could be taped and reviewed later. As John walked into the conference room, he caught the attention of William. William walked over to him and said they needed to talk about the debate for a few moments. They sat down at a table. William said one or more of the candidates was going to "shoot the moon." This meant they would bring to light some shocking or not-yet-revealed piece of information on either the Randolph campaign or one of the other competitors. The best-case scenario for this strategy would be to force the debate to this topic. John asked who they thought might try something like that. William admitted Romney would be the most likely culprit, while Hank thought it might come from Bachmann or potentially from Paul. William told John that Hank and George were going to attempt to "shock" him on stage in anticipation of the debate. William reminded him that the most effective response to an attack was not to retaliate, but instead look as if the revelation was expected. William was worried about John in this situation, but kept this to himself.

William also said all of the candidates would treat John like Public Enemy Number One. Not only would they try to embarrass him, he thought each of the candidates would try to trap him during the debate. They would try to pick holes in his positions—in particular those that were against typical Republican positions. During debate preparations, Hank and George would not only attack him, but would try to trip him up either in one of his positions or in how he responded to questions. John would win if he didn't lose his temper, appeared to be above the fray, and acted presidential. John asked William, did one not need to be president to act presidential? William said no, as he laughed at the question. At 5:30 p.m., Charles came into the conference room and collected John. John had a dinner meeting with several potential donors. Two of the bodyguards tagged along and stayed in proximity to him.

After dinner, John walked into the hotel and was met by several reporters who were not part of his regular media group. They started asking questions about certain current events out of Washington. Charles and the bodyguards pushed through the reporters and loaded John in an elevator. When the doors shut, John asked Charles what that was about. Charles did not know. When he got back to his room, he called William and Hank and told them what had happened. Hank said this was not unexpected, but he was surprised it had started so soon. Typically, this "camping out" by reporters usually started around the Iowa caucus, not four months beforehand. Hank said he would handle it.

John called Jenny at around 9:00 p.m. PST, which was midnight EST. He apologized for the late call. They talked about the day and the conversation that John had with William. John said he was more worried about keeping his temper in check than about any of his political positions. She told him to pray about it and they said goodnight. John turned on the television and watched a baseball game on ESPN until he was tired. He fell asleep around 10:30 p.m.

On the previous evening, John had made plans with Big Fred, one of his bodyguards, to workout at 5:30 a.m.

Accordingly, Big Fred knocked on John's door at the appointed time, and they walked downstairs to the hotel gym. John started walking on the treadmill, gradually building up to a slow and steady run. He ran for about thirty minutes, working up a sweat. At 6:00 a.m., they finished their workouts and went back upstairs. John decided to order room service. He turned on the television and watched some of the morning news. After breakfast, he took a shower and got dressed for the day. At 8:30 a.m., Big Fred was at the door to escort John down to the conference center. The press was in the lobby again, but Big Fred shielded John as he walked into the conference center. The bodyguards stood at the entrance to the conference room, which prevented people from entering, in particular the press. John noticed William, Hank, Debbie, and George were already in the room. In addition, several other people were in the room providing support services.

John noticed Charles standing near the food table and motioned for him to come over. John asked for Tylenol, because he already had a headache. William came over and asked if he was ready to start. John walked on the stage, and the California debate preparations began. As the day wore on, John could not shake the headache, and he started to feel achy. By noon, he had chills. During lunch, John pulled William to the side and said he thought he had the flu. He described the symptoms, and William agreed with the diagnosis. William told Charles to escort John to his room and then procure some flu medicine from a local pharmacy. Big Fred and Charles took the patient to his room. Charles helped him get into his night clothes and into bed. Charles left in search for medicine.

John felt horrible for the rest of the day. He never vomited, but he felt extremely nauseated. That evening and into the night, he did not sleep well as the chills kept returning as soon as the medicine wore off. Surprisingly, John woke up the next morning feeling a lot better, but very tired. Charles checked on him at 9:00 a.m. and was surprised to see him feeling so much better. Obviously Charles talked to William soon after leaving John's room, because William called about fifteen minutes later. John said they should start debate preparations again after lunch. He got up and took a shower. He still did not feel like eating. He lounged around the room and watched some television until around noon. A knock at the door startled John. He opened the door and there was Jenny standing in the entrance. She asked how he felt and what was he doing out of bed. John said he felt much better, and it must have been a twenty-four-hour bug. Jenny had stopped by the store and purchased medical supplies and additional drugs. She took his temperature, and it was back to normal. Jenny said she did not like the idea of John attending debate preparations that day, and she was going along to supervise. If he started to look tired again, she was going to pull the plug. They walked downstairs with Big Fred. The press was still in the lobby, and they tried to ask questions of John. John and Jenny walked directly into the conference room where they saw William.

Debate preparations went very well that day. Hank and George tried to frustrate John with some "zingers," and tried to get the debate off the agreed-upon topics. John did not lose his temper and was able to keep the debate focused on relevant topics. At around 5:00 p.m., John said he was tired and wanted to call it a day. He and Jenny walked back upstairs. Jenny ordered room service, and John nibbled at his food but did not eat a lot. He was asleep by 8:00 p.m. and slept quite well that night.

The next morning, William called and asked how John was doing. John was feeling a lot better and had started to get back his appetite. William asked if he was ready for debate preparations that day. John said he did not need any additional debate prep. William said okay; however, John could tell he did not agree with that assessment. Later in the morning, Hank called and asked how he was doing. John knew William and Hank were probably having a nervous breakdown. They did not think their candidate was ready for the debate. John and Jenny spent the day in the hotel room just resting. At 4:30 p.m., room service was delivered and afterwards, John took a shower and got ready for the debate. At 5:00 p.m., Charles knocked on the door and led John and Jenny down the evaluator to waiting Ford Expeditions. They drove to the Reagan Library and walked into the massive building. John was amazed at how beautiful the Reagan Library was. Ronald Reagan was his absolute favorite president of the modern era. Hank led the group through the library and through some service doors on the far left side of the building. John was whisked away to a holding area while Jenny was seated near the front of the room. At 6:00 p.m. PST, the candidates were led onto the stage. Behind the stage was the hangar where Reagan's Air Force One was displayed. It was a grand sight.

MSNBC's Chris Matthews was the host of the debate. He explained the debate would focus on the economy and the debt. He further explained each candidate would be given one and one-half minutes to respond, and he would have the option to allow candidates to have a thirty-second rebuttal as he deemed necessary. John was placed in the middle position on stage—where all of the candidates could attack him verbally.

The first question was a repeat from the Iowa debate—what was the single biggest problem negatively impacting our economy. John was asked to respond:

As I said in Iowa, the biggest problem facing our economy right now is a lack of leadership coming out of the White House and Congress. Every decision, every thought, every breath is politically motivated and not based on what is best for the America people. Barack Obama has not led one discussion, has not led on one debate, and has not led one group unless you count playing golf every Sunday. Congress has been just as destructive. They have spent more time proving their correctness, as opposed to being right. There is a difference between the two. The America that people expect and deserve is much better than what they have gotten.

Once the proper leadership is in place, the task of reducing the size and breadth of government can begin. We can slash federal spending; we can fix our tax code, including the reduction of corporate income taxes; we can balance our budget; and we can start to pay off the debt that we owe. I know some of my contemporaries on this stage do not like the idea of a VAT tax, but we have to pay back our debts. We cannot hope we will derive enough revenues from traditional means. The debt cannot simply be pushed to the next generation. We need to be adults and fix the problem, as opposed to the spoiled child who expects everything to be given to him or her.

We need to reduce the massive regulation that is stifling our economy. We need to let businesses run their own destinies, as opposed to a federal monster telling them what their future is. And finally, we need to get rid of unions. I have spoken about eliminating public unions in my Nine-Point Plan for Fixing America. I am telling you now that if I had my way, all unions would be a thing of the past. Thank you.

John had decided to put forth a new proposal of eliminating all unions before any of the other candidates had a chance. William and Hank looked at each other because neither knew this was coming. John thought by introducing the concept, a portion of the debate would have to be used to discuss this. He was right, because the next two rounds of questions dealt with the elimination of all unions. John knew private union members would have little impact on his campaign and on the overall election. There were only 7 percent of working people still represented by private unions. He believed all unions were against antitrust laws. What was the difference between three widget-manufacturers conspiring to fix sales prices and a union representing the workers of all three plants and mandating what all three companies should pay their employees? It was one of the biggest contradictions in the history of American business.

After the union dialogue Chris Matthews asked, if you were president, would you have asked for the increase to the debt limit? The question was first given to Mitt Romney. Newt Gingrich was asked second. Both stated they would have asked for the debt-ceiling increase. Ron Paul was next, and John enjoyed Ron Paul's response, even though it was a little off base. Finally, John was asked. He said if his debt-reduction plan had been followed, there would have been no need to increase the debt limit. He continued:

One of the basic tenets in my plan to simplify and modify our tax code is to sell unnecessary land holdings that the federal government owns. Currently, our government owns 782 million acres of land in this country. The next largest landowner owns around two million acres. Why do we need to have this much land? I understand military bases and land for federal buildings, but I do not understand 782 million acres. Owning the land is one problem. Maintaining and tracking the land is costing the country millions upon millions of dollars each year.

If we were to sell some of the land—let's say for argument's sake around 200 million acres for $10,000 per acre—we could raise $2 trillion. This money could be used to pay down our debt. Therefore, there would be no need to raise the debt limit.

Chris Matthews followed with a rhetorical question: Suppose that option was not available; would you ask for a debt-limit increase? John responded:

Chris, if we are going to deal in abstracts and limit the available options, I would have convinced Congress and the American people about the VAT tax. Your follow-up question is one of the major problems with Congress and the White House today. They do not have any ability to think outside the box. Debt is a liability and is on one side of the balance sheet, but the current leadership does not think about the other side of the balance sheet—the assets. Federal land holdings are one of the most valuable assets of this federal government, but the government does not want to use these resources in fighting our debt problems. Our military is a vital asset of this country. The productivity of the American worker is a crucial asset of this country. Oil under the ground is a major asset of this country. We need to stop looking at problems on a micro-

level and start looking at problems on a macro-level. We need to be able to use all of our resources and options to fix our problems.

So the answer to your question is no, I would not have asked for a debt-ceiling increase. Thank you.

The next hour of the debate went as expected. During her answer to a question, Michelle Bachmann looked directly at John and noted the Randolph campaign had not spoken the name of any of the other candidates one time since the Ames straw poll. Bachmann asked whether John believed he could quiet the other Republicans so he could be named the nominee before the primaries and the convention. Chris Matthews reminded Bachmann that asking questions directly to the other candidates was against the rules. John asked if he could respond to the question, and Chris agreed.

Congresswoman Bachmann, when you or your campaign want to contribute to mine, I will mention your name as often as you want.

There was laughter in the convention center.

Seriously, we have a tremendously difficult challenge in front of us, whoever may be the Republican nominee for president. Barack Obama, while unable to lead and govern this country, is uncommonly skilled at campaigning. In the last cycle, he raised over $700 million. Most of the media are infatuated with him.

John looked directly at Chris Matthews due to his infamous tickle-up-my-leg comment back in 2008.

We, as Republicans, need to stop the cycle of bashing each other every four years during the selection of our candidate. While it may be fun for the media, it leaves our candidate bloodied and bruised when the real fight begins.

We all have differences in how we would fix America. Some believe spending and tax cuts will fix everything that ails America. I do not think these two things will fix everything, but I am here to tell you that we have one thing that unites us. We believe in liberty. We do not want big government. We do not want massive spending. We do not want ObamaCare. We do not want four more years of the most progressive president since FDR. We need to join and fight the good fight together. We do not need to beat each other up to make ourselves look better.

I am asking all Republicans including those on this stage not to fall into the old-time habit of personally attacking each other. Some of you have already done it. We can disagree and debate on the issues, but let's keep the dialogue positive and civil. Do I have your agreement?

John started looking at the other candidates. None of them knew what to do. Romney started to nod his head in agreement, then Bachmann. Finally, all of them started to nod their heads. Chris Matthews asked all the candidates whether they agreed to no negative comments or advertisements against fellow Republicans. Each of the candidates agreed verbally. William was impressed. John had used a question from Chris Matthews to get the other Republican candidates to agree not to use negative tactics. Of course, William was convinced most of the Republicans had just lied, but it was something that could be used against them in the future. It was a smart move.

At the end of the debate, Chris Matthews allowed each candidate to give a thirty-second monologue. John focused on his Nine-Point Plan, specifically, modifying the tax code. There was no blood drawn during the debate, and John had managed to look presidential. At the end of the debate, Jenny walked onstage and waved to the crowd with her husband. John shook the hands of all of the candidates and joked around with a few of the people in the crowd. Hank came out and said he needed to talk to him for a minute. When they were alone, Hank said Congresswoman Michelle Bachmann wanted to talk to him in private. John agreed and off they went.

John was led to a private room where the congresswoman was standing. When they were alone, Bachmann said she was going to suspend her campaign the next day. She said it was obvious John was going to be the Republican nominee. Bachmann said she agreed with about 85 percent of what John was proposing. She was complimentary of the Nine-Point Plan. She even agreed with congressional term limits to a degree. John thanked the congresswoman for her kind words. Bachmann said she was not going to come out and publicly support the

Randolph campaign at this time, but she knew John was the best candidate that the Republicans had. John shook her hand and left the room.

When they got in Ford Expeditions, John told Jenny, William, and Hank what was said. William was the most surprised. He did not think Bachmann would bow out until after the Iowa caucus at the earliest. The SUVs drove to LAX airport and pulled alongside Randolph One. The campaign would take a red-eye flight back to Virginia so John could have a couple of days at home before leaving for Florida on Saturday. On the ride to the airport, William and Hank told John they thought he had done great. William did ask about the private-union comment, and John laughed. He told them that they do not know everything and he would continue keeping them on their toes. They laughed together.

At 10:30 p.m. PST, Randolph One lifted its wheels; the airplane and the campaign were climbing fast.

Chapter 22

Randolph One did not arrive at the Newport News airport until 6:30 a.m. EST Thursday morning. John never slept well on airplanes and did not sleep particularly well then. Charles and one of the bodyguards took John and Jenny to The Willows. John took a nap, and Jenny called their children to let them know they were safely in Virginia. John woke up around 11:00 a.m. and telephoned campaign headquarters. Hank answered the telephone and told John about the debate results from the previous evening. Most of the commentators were saying the Republican race was over—John Randolph would be the Republican candidate for president. John was quiet as Hank went on about the positive information. Hank told John about the new NBC/WSJ poll that had just been published:

Poll	NBC/WSJ	Fox News	Rasmussen
Date	9/13/2011	8/31/2011	8/25/2011
Romney	14%	16%	17%
Palin	8%	8%	8%
Cain	6%	6%	6%
Gingrich		3%	4%
Paul	4%	4%	4%
Bachmann	9%	9%	9%
Pawlenty		2%	2%
Perry	6%	6%	6%
Randolph	45%	40%	39%

Moreover, Hank had heard Palin had decided not to run, but it was not confirmed. It was a one-horse race. It was

223

also announced Congressman Ron Paul was suspending his campaign.

John walked out onto the patio and saw Jenny sitting there. She said the children and grandchildren would be joining them for Friday-night dinner. Since John was not leaving for Florida until Saturday morning, this worked out well. The entire senior campaign-staff would make the trip to Florida on Saturday morning, because the Florida debate would take place the upcoming week.

John drove to the Golden Horseshoe golf course that afternoon. He played nine holes and went back to The Willows. John and Jenny had dinner together and took a boat ride after dinner. They were both extremely tired from the night before and were asleep by 10:00 p.m. The next morning, John called the children and asked if he could pick up the grandchildren from their respective schools. John mapped out his plan since not all of the grandchildren went to the same school. He drove Jenny's BMW X5, which could transport more people than John's Ford F-150. At 2:30 p.m., John left The Willows with Fred, went to school number one, and picked up his youngest grandchild. School number two had the second and third oldest grandchildren. At the middle school, John picked up the oldest grandchild. Each of them was surprised and excited Granddaddy John was picking them up. John took them for ice cream and begged them not tell their grandmother. They all agreed. Big Fred got a triple-scoop, Rocky Road cone, which amazed the grandchildren.

Afterwards, John took them to The Willows for dinner later that evening.

John started up the grill at 6:00 p.m. just as the children got there. He was cooking steaks for dinner, which was everyone's favorite. Jenny had been to the grocery store and had purchased rib-eye steaks, which were on sale. Earlier, John had set them on the counter so they would be at room temperature when the charcoal was ready. Jenny made baked potatoes and baked sweet potatoes. John had made a fresh iceberg-wedge salad with a homemade parmesan-cheese dressing. At 6:45 p.m., dinner was served.

After dinner, the grandchildren talked John into a movie down in the basement. They started watching the movie, and John was fast to sleep in ten minutes. After it was over, the children and grandchildren left for their own homes. John and Jenny finished cleaning up and went upstairs to bed. It was 10:00 p.m., and they were both asleep in fifteen minutes. They were leaving for Florida at 8:00 a.m. the next morning.

John woke up at 5:30 a.m. and worked out. Afterwards, he had breakfast, took a shower, and got dressed. Promptly at 7:30 a.m., Charles knocked on the front door of The Willows. John and Jenny rode to the Newport News airport with Charles and two of the bodyguards. When they got there, the car pulled up at the base of Randolph One. One of the reporters showed John a picture in the morning newspaper. It was a picture of him picking his grandchildren up at school the day before. John smiled and asked if he could keep the picture. When they got to the back of the airplane, William, Hank, Debbie, and George were already there. John also saw Big Fred in the section of the airplane between the press and the campaign's onboard office. The pilot came on the intercom and welcomed everyone onboard. Randolph One was airborne by 8:00 a.m.

During the flight to Orlando, John met with the senior campaign staff on the following week's schedule. The debate, hosted by Fox News and the Florida Republican Party, was to be held in Orlando on Thursday, September 22nd at 9:00 p.m. Debbie explained the campaign would be in New York and New Jersey the week following the Florida debate. The week after that (October 3rd), the campaign would be in Nevada and Utah. Hank stated the message of the week had not been decided, but it would be by the end of this week. John asked if the mid-month financial report was available. William showed him the report from Thomas Philpot:

(000s)	Total Contributions	Total Loans from JR	Total Expenditures	Cash On Hand
5/31/2011	9,500.0	2,000.0	(2,300.0)	9,200.0
6/15/2011	4,125.0	-	(1,250.0)	12,075.0
6/30/2011	10,256.0		(2,250.0)	20,081.0
7/15/2011	18,566.0		(4,575.0)	34,072.0
7/31/2011	14,250.0		(6,875.0)	41,447.0
8/15/2011	23,758.0		(8,985.0)	56,220.0
8/31/2011	25,985.0		(10,215.0)	71,990.0
9/15/2011	32,855.0		(12,515.0)	92,330.0
Total	139,295.0	2,000.0	(48,965.0)	92,330.0

John could not believe the campaign had raised $139 million in four months. He also could not believe there was $92 million in available cash. William stated the campaign needed to raise over $1 billion to win this election. John said, underneath his breath, America needs campaign finance reform now!

During the remainder of the flight, John and the team talked about their strategy after the debate. It would center, as before, on John's being a true outsider, the economy and debt situation, critiquing Barack Obama's policies, and unifying the Republican Party. In the weeks after the debate, the campaign would visit at least two states per week. The visits would encompass a combination of rallies and speeches on the messages of the week. There would also be a lot of fundraising activities.

At 10:30 a.m., Randolph One touched down in Orlando. The campaign staff left the airport in SUVs and went to a local-area hotel. This would serve as base operations for debate preparations. That afternoon the campaign held a rally at a park in Orlando and, that evening, John was the guest speaker at a business leaders' forum. On Monday through Wednesday, John and the team worked on debate preparations by day, and John met with potential donors for dinner and drinks each night.

The week progressed as expected, and John felt ready for the debate on Thursday night. The only candidates that were invited were John, Mitt Romney, Herman Cain, and Rick Perry. The other candidates had either suspended their campaigns or did not have enough support. John did not like that formula and thought if one was running for office, he or she should have an opportunity at the debate. On the other hand, William and Hank liked the rule from a political point of view.

The Florida debate did not offer any new revelations. The debate was primarily on foreign matters, but the economy and the debt did make cameo performances. At the end of it, most commentators thought John had won, yet again. Both William and Hank also thought John had won, but acknowledged he "held his punches." John said he was trying to stay above the fray and act presidential. In any event, John certainly did not harm his campaign.

During the week of September 26th, the Randolph campaign was in New York and New Jersey. Once

Randolph One landed in Syracuse, one of the buses was used to transport the campaign around the two states. John was joined by George, Charles, and his bodyguards. Sunday through Wednesday was spent in New York, and Thursday through Saturday was spent in New Jersey. The message of the week was the economy, debt, and runaway government spending. As with other weeks, John spent time giving speeches, meeting with potential donors, meeting with local GOP party leaders, and shaking many peoples' hands. During the week, John tried to estimate how many hands he had shaken since the beginning of the campaign. He felt like he could not come up with even an educated guess.

On the flight from Newark, New Jersey to Newport News, John took part in a conference call with William, Hank, and Debbie. The first order of business was the release of the new Fox News poll:

Poll	Fox News	Rasmussen	PPP (D)	NBC/WSJ
Date	9/30/2011	9/25/2011	9/16/2011	9/13/2011
Romney	14%	13%	13%	14%
Palin	6%	7%	7%	8%
Cain	6%	6%	6%	6%
Paul				4%
Bachmann	9%	10%	9%	9%
Perry	6%	6%	6%	6%
Randolph	50%	48%	47%	45%

Hank reported that for the first time the Randolph campaign was favored by 50 percent of registered voters. Hank also pointed out that John's favorable ratings were higher than Barack Obama's, *much* higher. Hank said he wished the November 2012 presidential vote was being held today. Everyone laughed nervously, but they silently agreed. The second item on the agenda was the September end-of-month financial report. Thomas Philpot presented the following:

(000s)	Total Contributions	Total Loans from JR	Total Expenditures	Cash On Hand
5/31/2011	9,500.0	2,000.0	(2,300.0)	9,200.0
6/15/2011	4,125.0	-	(1,250.0)	12,075.0
6/30/2011	10,256.0		(2,250.0)	20,081.0
7/15/2011	18,566.0		(4,575.0)	34,072.0
7/31/2011	14,250.0		(6,875.0)	41,447.0
8/15/2011	23,758.0		(8,985.0)	56,220.0
8/31/2011	25,985.0		(10,215.0)	71,990.0
9/15/2011	32,855.0		(12,515.0)	92,330.0
9/30/2011	29,855.0		(11,985.0)	110,200.0
Total	169,150.0	2,000.0	(60,950.0)	110,200.0

John asked where all of the money was coming from—$170 million contributed in five months and one full year away from the election. Thomas explained the money was coming from many sources, including Internet giving. While there were numerous maximum contributions of $2,500, the majority of funds came in lower amounts. Thomas pointed out Barack Obama had accumulated even more money than the Randolph campaign. John just shook his head in amazement. William gave a report on the status of the congressional term-limit effort in the states. William said twenty percent of the states had formally introduced legislation in their respective state houses. This legislation would require the state legislatures to send representatives to a special constitutional convention for the explicit purpose of voting for congressional term limits. Votes were scheduled in those states within the next two months. There was still a lot of work to be done in the other states, particularly the traditional blue states. John wanted to know if the campaign needed to hire someone to lead this effort. Hank stated current campaign rules prevented the Randolph campaign from hiring someone to work on this project. John asked William to find someone to lead the effort and let him know how much it would cost. He was willing to put up his own money to fund the congressional term-limit initiative. William said he would discuss this with him in a couple of days. Finally, Debbie spoke of the schedule for the next week, for the next four weeks, and for the next thirteen weeks. Hank called the period from October to December in the year before a presidential election "the quiet period." William said the Randolph campaign would continue to push forward. Debbie said the campaign would leave on Monday, October 3rd for Nevada. As they were finishing the conference call, John asked William to pick up the receiver and asked if he was free for golf the next day at Ford's Colony. William agreed.

Randolph One touched down at the Newport News airport at 5:30 p.m. on Saturday afternoon. Jenny met John at the airport, and they went to dinner at the Raleigh Tavern restaurant just off Duke of Gloucester Street. When they finished dinner and got back to The Willows, it was after 10:00 p.m. They talked for a while in the study and went to bed around midnight. Monday would start "the quiet period"—October to December—but the campaign was determined it would continue making noise.

Chapter 23

During the quiet period of October 1st through December 31st, the Randolph campaign was anything *but* quiet. It visited twenty-four states, not including Virginia. Of the early caucus/primary states, the Tier 1 states, John visited each of them once. Of the Super-Tuesday states, the Tier 2 states, the campaign visited 57 percent of them, which consisted of Alabama, Arkansas, Connecticut, Delaware, Illinois, Oklahoma, Tennessee, and Utah. Of the remaining "big" states or Tier 3 states, the campaign visited four of the five—Michigan, Ohio, Texas, and Pennsylvania. Finally, of the remaining states, the campaign visited Louisiana, Mississippi, Indiana, West Virginia, Nebraska, Kentucky, and South Dakota. By the end of December 2011, it had visited thirty-two of the fifty states at least one time and had visited Iowa, South Carolina, and Florida on seven different occasions each. John had grown accustomed to waking up in a different hotel in a different city.

During the quiet period, Debbie and Jen Harrison, Director of Scheduling and Advance, had put John in unusual situations. John had been on "The Late Show" with David Letterman and "The Tonight Show" with Jay Leno. He had been put on the "Regis and Kelly" show. He had been put on a live show with Paula Dean on the Food Network. John enjoyed this show as Paula Dean was one of his favorite cooks on the network. He was even on "The View." On this program which is known for its far-left extremist views spewed by Whoopi Goldberg and Joy Behar, John and the Progressive ladies got into a discussion on taxation. Goldberg said she did not mind paying more taxes as she could afford it. John stated taxes should not be considered like a charity—if one can afford a little more, one should give more to charities. John asked Ms. Goldberg if she thought the federal government did a good job of spending money. She did not answer the question. Ms. Goldberg kept saying she was agreeable with paying a little more, one of the tag lines of Barack Obama. Finally, John said if she wanted to pay more, as president he would make sure the IRS came and visited her to take some additional money. The crowd laughed, and Ms. Goldberg even smiled.

As for the "real" activities of the campaign, John stayed focus on the economy, the excessive government spending, the massive federal debt, and his plan for balancing the budget. John kept distancing himself from normal politicians and promoted himself as the "fix-it" guy. Even during the quiet period, the crowds were rather large. At one event in Miami, Florida, George estimated the crowd was over two thousand people. John lost count of how many people he had met on these trips. He liked talking to individual people and listening to the good things and the dreadful things going on in their lives. John also liked talking to teenagers. He liked to hear their perspectives. John knew teenagers' political points of view were often shaped by their parents whether for the good or the bad.

As for congressional term limits, there was a great deal of positive activity during the quarter. First, William recommended a woman named Nancy Cartwright to lead the effort. Nancy was a career-conservative political operative who agreed wholeheartedly with congressional term limits. She took over as National Director of "We Need Congressional Term Limits," a non-profit organization. The following shows the status of the initiative as of December 2011:

	Estimated Month To Get Bill Ready	Bill Proposed in Legislature	Bill Voted Upon	Bill Approved	Bill Rejected
Alabama		Sep-11	Nov-11	Nov-11	
Alaska		Sep-11			
Arizona		Sep-11	Nov-11	Nov-11	
Arkansas		Sep-11	Nov-11	Nov-11	
California					
Colorado		Nov-11			
Connecticut	Jan-12				
Delaware	Feb-12				
District of Columbia					
Florida		Nov-11			
Georgia		Sep-11	Dec-11	Dec-11	
Hawaii					
Idaho		Dec-11			
Illinois	Feb-12				
Indiana		Nov-11			
Iowa		Sep-11	Oct-11	Oct-11	
Kansas		Nov-11			
Kentucky		Nov-11			
Louisiana		Sep-11	Nov-11	Nov-11	
Maine					
Maryland					
Massachusetts					
Michigan					
Minnesota	Feb-12				
Mississippi		Sep-11	Nov-11	Nov-11	
Missouri		Nov-11			
Montana		Nov-11			
Nebraska		Dec-11			
Nevada	Feb-12				
New Hampshire	Feb-12				
New Jersey					
New Mexico		Dec-11			
New York					
North Carolina		Sep-11	Nov-11	Nov-11	
North Dakota		Nov-11			
Ohio	Mar-12				
Oklahoma		Dec-11			
Oregon	Mar-12				
Pennsylvania					
Rhode Island	Feb-12				
South Carolina		Sep-11	Nov-11	Nov-11	
South Dakota		Dec-11			
Tennessee		Sep-11	Dec-11	Dec-11	
Texas		Dec-11			
Utah		Dec-11			
Vermont	Jan-12				
Virginia		Sep-11	Dec-11	Dec-11	
Washington	Mar-12				
West Virginia		Sep-11	Nov-11	Nov-11	
Wisconsin	Feb-12				
Wyoming		Nov-11			
	23.5%	49.0%	17.6%	17.6%	0.0%
		72.5%			

In effect, 72.9 percent of state legislatures had either proposed or were close to proposing legislation that would require them to appoint people to serve as

236

representatives at a special constitutional convention for the purposes of proposing an amendment to the Constitution for congressional term limits. Of this number, 17.8 percent of the state legislatures had already approved the legislation. The goal was 100 percent, but the minimum needed was 66.7 percent. There was a long way to go in the next ten months. John had personally contributed $10 million to support this initiative and would contribute more if needed.

The polls had also been extremely favorable to the Randolph campaign during the quiet period. The following shows the polls' evolution during the three-month period:

Poll Date	Fox News 12/30/2011	Rasmussen 12/23/2011	Rasmussen 11/24/2011	Rasmussen 10/25/2011	Fox News 9/30/2011
Romney	11%	12%	12%	13%	14%
Cain	5%	5%	5%	6%	6%
Perry	5%	5%	5%	6%	6%
Randolph	58%	58%	57%	56%	50%

The Randolph campaign had continued to perform remarkably well against the other Republican candidates. With the exception of Romney, no other candidate was above 10 percent. John's polling numbers had increased by 8 percent during the three-month period. The "big mo" was obviously in the Randolph campaign. There continued talk that a couple of campaigns were very close to either suspending or ending their presidential aspirations. Hank had stated two of them were in serious debt, and they were "hanging on" in hopes of picking up additional contributions.

While the national polls are tremendously valuable, the key to the Republican nomination is winning the delegates allocated from the caucuses and primaries. John's numbers in Iowa, South Carolina, Nevada, and Florida were exceptionally good and showed him in first place. With the exception of New Hampshire, Randolph was leading in each state by a considerable margin. In New Hampshire, John was neck and neck with Romney but had continued to maintain a single-digit lead. Romney was the former governor of Massachusetts and owned a vacation house in New Hampshire. The Romney campaign was working very hard to win the New Hampshire primary.

Finally, contributions continued to be exceedingly strong. The following highlights the activity:

(000s)	Total Contributions	Total Loans from JR	Total Expenditures	Cash On Hand
5/31/2011	9,500.0	2,000.0	(2,300.0)	9,200.0
6/15/2011	4,125.0	-	(1,250.0)	12,075.0
6/30/2011	10,256.0		(2,250.0)	20,081.0
7/15/2011	18,566.0		(4,575.0)	34,072.0
7/31/2011	14,250.0		(6,875.0)	41,447.0
8/15/2011	23,758.0		(8,985.0)	56,220.0
8/31/2011	25,985.0		(10,215.0)	71,990.0
9/15/2011	32,855.0		(12,515.0)	92,330.0
9/30/2011	29,855.0		(11,985.0)	110,200.0
10/15/2011	27,558.0		(11,525.0)	126,233.0
10/31/2011	25,446.0		(11,385.0)	140,294.0
11/15/2011	26,778.0		(11,625.0)	155,447.0
11/30/2011	27,445.0		(11,725.0)	171,167.0
12/15/2011	21,554.0		(12,125.0)	180,596.0
12/31/2011	20,541.0		(12,200.0)	188,937.0
Total	318,472.0	2,000.0	(131,535.0)	188,937.0

During the three-month period, the campaign had brought in $149 million which easily outpaced all of the other Republican candidates. This was even slightly higher than the $142 million Barack Obama had brought in. At the end of December 2011, the Campaign had cash on hand of $188 million. It was still shocking to John the amount of cash being raised by his campaign, and William kept telling him that over $1 billion would be raised by the end of the campaign.

Therefore, the quiet period was not quiet at all for the Randolph campaign. The polling numbers were up, contributions continued to be extremely healthy, a great deal of progress had been made on the congressional–term-limits initiative, and the upcoming caucuses and primaries looked highly promising. William and Hank had already started working on the strategy for defeating Obama. The next ten months were going to be anything but boring.

Chapter 24

On Monday, January 2, 2012, John woke up at 5:30 a.m. He worked out, had breakfast, showered, and got ready for the day. In thirty-six days, the real start to the Republican presidential nomination process would begin. On February 6, 2012, Iowa would hold the first presidential caucus. Over the next six-week period, four states would have their say as to who the Republican candidate would be. Besides the Iowa caucus, New Hampshire would hold the nation's first primary on February 14, 2012. On February 16, 2012, Nevada and South Carolina would hold their primaries. While the Randolph campaign was leading strongly in three of the four elections (John was neck and neck with Romney in New Hampshire), one never knew until all of the votes had been cast and counted. Over the next six weeks, John and the team would literally reside on Randolph One, the campaign's leased Boeing 737. The current schedule had John campaigning five separate times in Iowa over the next six weeks, five times in New Hampshire, two times in Nevada, and three times in South Carolina. It was going to be extremely hectic over the next six weeks.

Promptly at 7:30 a.m., Charles knocked on the front door of The Willows. John met him at the door with his suitcase in hand. They loaded into a waiting SUV with one of the bodyguards at the wheel and drove to the Newport News airport. They arrived at the base of Randolph One and walked onboard. The airplane was airborne shortly thereafter. The first stop was Des Moines, Iowa. Randolph One landed at 8:30 a.m. local time, and one of the campaign buses met them. The bus was on its way by 9:00 a.m.

Caucuses are hugely different from primaries. In Iowa, there are 1,784 precincts in which residents go, listen to representatives from each campaign, and vote. At each of these precincts, they elect delegates to corresponding county conventions. There are ninety-nine counties in Iowa; therefore, there are ninety-nine county conventions. The county conventions select delegates for Iowa's congressional district convention and the state convention, which eventually chooses the delegates for the presidential nominating conventions. While only about 1 percent of the nation's delegates are chosen by Iowans, the people of Iowa take this first election of a presidential nominee very seriously.

The Randolph campaign spent Monday and Tuesday in Iowa circling the southeastern part of the state and visiting the cities of Des Moines, Iowa City, Cedar Rapids, Clinton, Davenport, and Ottumwa. In trips to Iowa over the next four weeks, the other parts of the state would be visited. The key to each of these trips was to meet as many people as possible and to talk about the economy and the nation's debt. The people in Iowa have traditionally been conservative in their political beliefs, and the messages that John had been preaching for six months were resonating remarkably well. John was whisked from one event to another, talking directly with the people of Iowa. On Tuesday night around 9:00 p.m., the bus pulled into the Des Moines airport. Randolph One was airborne shortly thereafter, on its way to New Hampshire for "Week One, Stage Two."

Randolph One touched down at midnight. The second campaign bus met the group and took them to a hotel in the Manchester area to rest. At 7:00 a.m. Wednesday, the Randolph team loaded into the bus and drove to the eastern part of the state. The campaign spent time in the cities of Rochester, Dover, Portsmouth, Derry, and Nashua on this trip, holding rallies and meeting as many people as possible. The next week, the campaign would focus on the western part of the state, including the cities of Manchester, Concord, Keene, and Laconia.

New Hampshire has historically been the first primary in the quadrennial American presidential election cycle. As a matter of fact, state law requires that the New Hampshire secretary of state schedule this election at least one week before any "similar event." A primary uses the same procedures as the general election—the winner of the popular vote takes the state. Interestingly, a state law also allows towns with fewer than one hundred residents to open their polls at midnight and close as soon as all the registered voters have voted. Historically, Dixville Notch and Hart's Location have been two of the first towns to tally their votes.

The Randolph team campaigned both Wednesday and Thursday in New Hampshire. On Thursday night, Randolph One departed for South Carolina. The bus that was in Iowa was driven to South Carolina and met the airplane at the Greenville-Spartanburg airport. The goal for this trip was to cover the upstate of South Carolina. This included visits to the cities of Greenville, Spartanburg, Anderson, and Rock Hill. On subsequent trips, the campaign would focus on the Piedmont Region of South Carolina and visit cities like Columbia, Aiken, and Florence. Finally, on other trips the campaign would focus on the coastal region and visit cities like Myrtle Beach, Georgetown, Charleston, Summerville, and Hilton Head. During the stay in South Carolina, John had the opportunity to meet with Senator Jim DeMint, one of the most revered leaders of the Tea Party movement and a staunch conservative. Senator DeMint and John agreed on fiscal matters with the exception of the implementation of the VAT tax. The gentlemen shared a cold beverage on Friday evening and discussed this subject. Of course, neither man budged on their respective positions. On Saturday, the campaign held a rally at the BMW Manufacturing Company in Spartanburg. Afterwards, the Randolph team visited the Beacon Drive-In, a famous, greasy hamburger joint, where John was greeted by over two hundred excited supporters. Finally, Randolph One was on its way to Virginia at 3:15 p.m. The flight landed at the Newport News airport at around 5:30 p.m. John spent the rest of the weekend with Jenny and the family.

Over the next three weeks (January 9th, January 16th and January 23rd), the schedule was similar to the first week of January. In each of the three weeks, the campaign was in Iowa and New Hampshire. In addition, for the week of January 9th, the campaign was in South Carolina, again, and in Georgia. For the week of January 16th, the campaign was also in Nevada and Utah. For the week of January 23rd, the campaign returned to South Carolina and visited Florida. The strategy was remarkably straightforward—Visit the early primary and caucus states so often the candidate was almost considered a resident of each of the states. While John never drove in any of these states, he felt he could maneuver around in each of them without a GPS or a map. The stump speech in each of the states was based on the economy and the massive debt. On the week of January 16th, the Randolph campaign stayed at the same hotel as the Romney campaign while in Nevada. The candidates even rode down the elevator together one morning for breakfast. By Saturday, January 28th, John was extremely tired from all of the travel. As Randolph One landed at the Newport News airport, John felt some relief. Next week, January 30th, would include only one state visit as Iowa would have a debate on Thursday night followed by the caucus the next Tuesday. As soon as the debate was over, the campaign would spend several days in Iowa visiting as many cities as time allowed.

On Sunday afternoon, John went to campaign headquarters and met with William, Hank, and Debbie. Debbie went over the schedule for the next couple of weeks in detail. William presented the latest polling numbers:

Poll	Fox News	Rasmussen	PPP (D)	NBC/WSJ	Fox News
Date	1/31/2012	1/25/2012	1/16/2012	1/12/2012	12/30/2011
Romney	11%	11%	12%	11%	11%
Cain	4%	5%	5%	5%	5%
Perry	4%	5%	5%	5%	5%
Randolph	59%	58%	58%	58%	58%

William stated the numbers were starting to be fixed as there had been little movement over the four-week period. He mentioned that the Fox News poll would be out on Tuesday. Hank presented the finance report for the first fifteen days of January:

(000s)	Total Contributions	Total Loans from JR	Total Expenditures	Cash On Hand
12/15/2011	21,554.0		(12,125.0)	180,596.0
12/31/2011	20,541.0		(12,200.0)	188,937.0
1/15/2012	35,446.0		(15,445.0)	208,938.0
Total	353,918.0	2,000.0	(146,980.0)	208,938.0

Hank stated the contributions and expenditures were both up and would continue to rise. Hank also mentioned the Randolph campaign's contributions were starting to match those brought in by Obama and the Democrats. In other words, the money trail was beginning to show there was a two-man race for president. John left the office around 4:00 p.m. and spent the rest of the day with Jenny. On Monday, John did a couple of television interviews from The Willows for the first time. John did not think Jenny appreciated all of the people in the house, but she did not complain. John and Jenny went to bed early that night.

The next morning, they were ready by 6:00 a.m., and Charles was there, as usual, very promptly. Randolph One took off at 6:30 a.m., and the campaign was in Iowa by 7:30 a.m. local time. The debate would be held at the Des Moines convention center on Thursday, February 2nd. The campaign spent the rest of Tuesday and Wednesday on debate preparations.

The debate included John, Mitt Romney, Herman Cain, and Rick Perry. It started at 8:00 p.m. CST and went exceptionally well for the Randolph campaign. John had hit his stride in debating, and afterwards all the commentators said John had won again. As usual, Jenny walked onstage after the event and waved with John. As they were leaving the stage, John shook the hands of Romney, Cain, and Perry. He wished them luck in the caucus which would be held on Tuesday, February 7th. According to the latest polls, John would win Iowa in a landslide. Hank even told John that Romney had left the state right after the debate to head to New Hampshire.

The campaign bus crisscrossed the state over the next several days, stopping in each town along the way. John shook hands until he felt his was going to fall off. He continued to meet and greet, engaging people along the way. Big Fred and the bodyguards continued to prevent people from getting too close, even though John "pushed" the bodyguards in every possible situation. As the day closed on Sunday, John and the team, including many local Randolph supporters and volunteers, were back in Des Moines at the hotel having dinner. The campaign had reserved the entire restaurant for the evening. John told the team how well everyone had done to get the campaign known in Iowa. He thanked each one of them for their hard work and many hours working for the campaign and told them that no matter how the caucus results worked out, he was immensely proud of them.

On Tuesday, February 7th, the Iowa caucus began and went throughout the day and into the night. By 8:00 p.m. CST, all of the news outlets had pronounced John as the runaway winner in the Iowa caucus. The results were even more pronounced than expected.

Results of Iowa Caucus	
Randolph	70%
Romney	10%
Perry	6%
Cain	3%
Other	11%

John gave an acceptance speech at around 8:30 p.m. CST. He received congratulatory telephone calls from each of the remaining Republican candidates. John thought that was classy. William corrected him and said they were positioning themselves for vice-presidential consideration. At 9:00 p.m., the campaign drove to the airport to travel to

New Hampshire. The New Hampshire debate was scheduled for Thursday, February 9th. The wheels of Randolph One were up by 9:30 p.m.

Chapter 25

On the way to the New Hampshire debate, Hank received a telephone call. He excused himself from the back office of the airplane. William and John continued their conversation on the strategy for the upcoming week. Hank burst back into the office and said he could not believe the call he had just received. He had just gotten off a telephone call with a representative of WMUR TV (WMUR and ABC were the co-sponsors of the New Hampshire debate). The other candidates had dropped out of the debate earlier that evening. Since John would be the only remaining participant, the debate was cancelled. Everyone in the back cabin looked at each other, utterly stunned. No one knew what to say next.

William was the first person to speak. He was most surprised Romney had backed out at the last minute. According to the latest polls, John had a five-point lead over Romney in New Hampshire, which was hardly a landslide. It was actually too close to call. As they continued to talk, Hank said not having the debate would actually be a negative for the campaign. John and William looked at him in astonishment. Hank explained that every chance John had to get his message out to the American people would help in the general election. By not having the debate which was, in effect, free media, John was missing out on letting people hear his ideas. William agreed with Hank. How could they still get the free media without having the debate? John suggested the campaign discuss the possibility of having a town-hall meeting. This would give the people of New Hampshire another opportunity to hear the Randolph campaign's Nine-Point Plan for Fixing America. William did not like the idea, because it would be another opportunity for the press and the progressives to try to stump him and make John look foolish. After discussing it further, they collectively agreed it was the proper course of action. Hank called back his contact at WMUR. At first, the television-station representative did not like the idea. Hank continued stressing the positives of such an event. Finally, WMUR said they would let him know in the morning.

Randolph One touched down around 12:30 a.m. EST on Tuesday in Manchester, New Hampshire. The team went to their regular hotel and got some sleep. The next morning, the group got together in the conference room that had already been reserved. Hank still had not heard back from WMUR, and he was worried the answer would be no. He felt as if they could see through the campaign's strategy of getting free airtime. William finally said they needed to get started, and they assumed the one-man town hall would happen on Wednesday, February 8th. John got onstage, sat on a stool, and William started firing questions at him. John answered the questions consistently using the responses he had given at previous debates. During one of the breaks, around 10:30 a.m., Hank's cell phone rang, and he walked out in the hall as everyone watched. A few minutes later, he came back in the room with a smile on his face. He had fantastic news—

both KMUR and ABC had agreed to a one-man town hall to be televised on Wednesday, February 8th. The campaign continued working throughout the rest of the day. John would have a target on his back at the town hall with ABC, one of the most liberal news organizations in America, throwing the arrows. He would have to be ready for a fight against a foe that had the questions beforehand.

On Wednesday morning, John continued prepping with William and Hank, but it was not the regular grueling session. At noon, John retired to his room and spent the afternoon talking with Jenny and reading a book. At 5:30 p.m., they had a private dinner in the hotel suite. Both ordered a fresh salad and grilled fish. At 7:30 p.m., Charles knocked on the door and corralled both John and Jenny for the ride to the convention center in Manchester, the location of the one-man town hall. They arrived at the convention center at around 8:15 p.m. John walked in and introduced himself to the interview panel. ABC had decided to bring in national figures for this event. George Stephanopoulos and Robin Roberts would ask questions to John. Some people may consider this a compliment. William and Hank felt it was a trap to catch John. ABC had made the change at the last minute. What measures the Progressives/far-left extremists would sink to in order to ensure that Barack Obama won re-election. As they walked in, Jenny and the rest of the senior campaign staff were led to their seats. William walked with John to the holding room off stage and told John to relax. This formal inquiry would dictate the rest of the campaign. Since John was the last Republican standing, this scenario would repeat itself until the national conventions. John was instructed to not lose his composure—simply answer the question. Whenever an unwanted question was asked, fall back to one of the elements of the Nine-Point Plan. When the panel tried to stump him with a question, simply get the discussion back on track. In the absolute worst case, take the discussion to what career politicians have done to this country. John asked William whether he was worried. William said if it were anybody else, he would be petrified. With John on the stage, he was totally at ease. Of course, William lied. As they shook hands, William told John to go get them.

At 8:30 p.m., John was introduced and walked onstage. In a nontraditional move, he walked up to the interview panel and shook each of their hands. As he walked back to the podium in the middle of the stage, he waved to the crowd. The audience, which was estimated to be over three thousand people, was enthusiastically in John's court. John looked at George and Robin, and saw they both were aware of the crowd's affinity for him. Shortly afterward, George welcomed the audience and those joining in via television. John did not know it at the time, but all of the news outlets had pre-empted their regular schedules for this one-man interview. CNN, MSNBC, and Fox were all carrying the interview. It was probably a good thing he did not know.

George asked the first question. *"There are a lot of people in America that are concerned you are not experienced when it comes to foreign matters. The US military is involved in Iraq, Afghanistan, and Libya. What experience do you have to handle the rigors of president in foreign matters?"*

John answered the question as follows:

Thank you, George, for the question. I wonder if Barack Obama was asked the same question when he was a relatively unknown junior senator from Illinois in 2008. This is the same person that spent his entire senatorial career either voting "present" or simply not showing up to vote. Merely visiting a foreign country does not make someone an expert on foreign affairs. I am not a politician. That is one of the truest statements any person can say about me. Does being a politician qualify you to be a good leader in military matters? Let's look back at what Barack Obama, the candidate, promised in 2007–2008. He promised all military personnel would be out of Iraq by the end of 2009. He also put forth a general exit plan for Afghanistan. Did either of these happen? Barack Obama took the combat forces out of Iraq, but left many military personnel. He also added 40,000 troops in Afghanistan. Was this consistent with what he promised as a candidate? Finally, can someone please tell me how America's vital interests are being compromised by the events in Libya? In two of these situations, I have shown Barack Obama lied to the American people and has potentially broken the laws of the land in the third. I do not have a military background. What I bring to the table is leadership skills. Does Barack Obama have these skills? Did he provide leadership in Libya? No. He allowed the US military to be directed by the Germans and the French. Both of these countries have significant financial investments in Libya. Barack Obama was bullied into providing support in a conflict where the US had no political, financial, or military interests. I have led a leading investment banking firm. I led that firm through the best of times and the absolute worst of times. I left the company in much better shape than when I took it over. It comes down to a very simple and direct choice for America. Do you want to double down on a president that was more interested in passing an immensely unpopular piece of legislation, ObamaCare; a president that cares more about passing legislation that appeases the union bosses, environmental groups, and other far-left extremist groups that call themselves Progressives? I promise the people of America I will rely on the military leadership on matters of national security, but I will not blindly follow. I will require a very clear engagement plan and, more importantly, a very clear exit strategy. If the benefits and costs do not measure up, I will not allow any military involvement.

The crowd in attendance roared in approval at the response.

George motioned for the crowd to quiet down. He asked them to hold their applause until the end of the town hall.

254

John had effectively used William's tactic of not answering the question directly. John's lack of experience in foreign policy was a weakness. Instead, John turned the question into a referendum on Barack Obama's foreign policy choices.

Robin Roberts asked the next question. *"The economy of America is still in very bad shape. Unemployment is still over 8.5 percent. How do you plan to put Americans back to work?"*

John stated:

Thank you, Robin. The biggest fallacy in America today is that the government creates jobs and enhances the economy. Barack Obama was not the first president to spew this nonsense, and I suspect he will not be the last. The federal government is a hindrance to the growth of the economy. For every dollar the federal government takes out of the economy, its performance diminishes. We need to continually explain the basic and non-complex truths that socialism does not work—European socialism is the plan of the Obama Progressives for this country. If you do not believe me, let's look at the facts. Barack Obama told the country if Congress passed the $862 billion stimulus bill, the country's unemployment rate would never exceed 8 percent. Three years later, it is 8.5 percent, and it has been as high as almost 10 percent. Why didn't that work? Barack Obama used the bank bailouts to fund one of his pet projects; he essentially gave both GM and Chrysler to *the unions. The debt holders and stockholders were bullied into accepting massive losses. It is astounding the banks have returned all the monies they borrowed with interest, and the only non-payers are AIG, GM, and Chrysler—all companies that Obama gave money to. Why haven't you, in the press, been more diligent going after the Obama administration about the losses created by these bailouts? Instead, the press has been focused on Wall Street, which paid back its loans with interest. The bank bailouts, including the theft of two car companies, were wrong in theory and in execution.*

In terms of lowering unemployment, the first step is to lower corporate tax rates. Currently, the corporate federal tax rate is 35 percent. This is the highest of the G-20 nations. If we lower the corporate tax rate to 20 percent, it will reduce tax collections by $95 billion. The CBO has shown that lowering the corporate tax rate will increase tax revenues by over $150 billion. A net $55 billion for lowering the tax rate would be the result. Why hasn't the rate been lowered is the question that you need to ask Barack Obama.

The crowd erupted again. Instead of quieting them, George asked the following question: *"Some have claimed while you led Goldman Smith, you allowed the company to invest heavily in mortgage-backed securities. You were part of the Wall Street group that just about brought down the home-mortgage market in America. How do you respond to these statements?"*

John replied:

*George, I would love to know who the "some" are in your question. I have made it abundantly clear the firm I worked for never allowed our capitalization ratios to exceed 16 percent. While this figure is higher than the 10 percent traditional commercial banks could have, we always had sufficient cash reserves to offset our debts. That is why, when I was CEO, we lagged behind the profits made by other investment banking firms such as Bear Sterns and Lehman whose capitalization reached over 40 percent. By the summer of 2006, my firm's capitalization ratios were less than 7 percent, which was lower than most of the large commercial banks. As the financial markets failed, including the home-mortgage market, the firm that I led was **forced** to take funds from the government which was led by Hank Paulson, Ben Bernanke, and Tim Geithner, who worked at the New York Federal Reserve. My firm was the second firm to return the money from TARP including interest. We did not **want** the bailout money, nor did we **need** it.*

Now for the claim you brought up that Wall Street brought down the home-mortgage market in America. What brought down the American mortgage market were Bill Clinton and the Progressives in Congress. The two events that occurred were the signing of the Community Reinvestment Act and the signing of the repeal of the Glass-Steagall Act. Bill Clinton signed the Community Reinvestment Act which required banks to lend to people who clearly could not afford a house. However, the houses could be flipped for a profit; thus the impact of foreclosures was minimized. If you compare the foreclosure rates before Clinton signed the Community Reinvestment Act and after, you will see a massive increase. The system worked as long as home prices continued to increase. When the opposite happened and home prices fell, home owners became upside down on their mortgages. This caused banks to foreclose on homes, but the banks had to take the losses now.

When Bill Clinton repealed the Glass-Steagall Act, investment banks were able to enter the home-mortgage market. The Glass-Steagall Act was put in place to make a distinction between commercial banks and investment banks. Investment banks, however, are not required to maintain certain liquidity ratios. As home mortgages started to fail, there simply was not enough capitalization to offset the losses. Both Fannie Mae and Freddie Mac provided a conduit for the investment banks to bundle mortgages together and pull more cash into the system.

It is as simple as that. Any other explanation is not truthful as to what actually happened. I am not here to preach to Americans. I am here to tell the truth. If we truly look at our souls and our own experiences, we know what happened. We extended our debt portfolios too much. I am not only talking middle-class Americans. I am talking to Americans who purchased second and third homes with little or no money down. All of these factors killed the home-mortgage market. I will point out, this is not my opinion, these are the facts, and they are irrefutable. Barack Obama and his Progressive buddies want to blame this group or that group. If we truly want to be honest with ourselves, all of us had a hand in the home-mortgage market collapse. Now we need to fix the problem and make sure that it does not happen again.

The crowd erupted again. George was waving furiously at them to quiet down, but they were not listening. The next question related to entitlement programs. Robin Roberts stated:

"Senator Harry Reid has made the claim that Social Security is secure for the next twenty years. Why would the Randolph plan include reductions in Social Security benefit payments?"

Thank you, Robin for the question. John was looking directly at Robin when he made this statement.

I will tell you any politician that does not factor entitlement-program reform in their solutions to fix America's massive fiscal problems is lying to the American people. Let me rephrase this again in order to prevent any misquotes of what I am saying. Any plan to balance our federal budget, any proposal that does not address the anticipated growth of entitlement programs in the next ten years, and any idea that does not make the hard choice to deal with entitlement programs is simply a means to ensure those promoting them keep their jobs, as opposed

259

to fixing the problems facing America. Any person who has a plan to fix America's fiscal problems without substantially changing our current entitlement programs is lying to you. I am telling you as directly as I can—Harry Reid lied to America when he said the Social Security program is secure. It is the same lie that nearly every politician has spewed for the last twenty-five years. When Barack Obama said our problems are revenue based and not spending based, he lied to you. We spend too much money, and there is no way for the current system to work in the future. The Progressives have continued the lie when they say anyone talking about reforming entitlement programs wants to take money out of the hands of recipients. Either they lied or did not bother to understand my plan. My plan is very simple. Are you listening? Can you hear me? If you are receiving Social Security payments today, you will see no changes. Let me say it again—you will see no changes. If you are sixty or older and have not retired yet, there will be no changes. These two statements are my promise to you, and I will never go against these promises. Now let's talk about what I am proposing. If you are between the ages of fifty and sixty, there will be a reduced benefit-payment. We will allow you to save for your retirement at levels higher than today through 401(k) or other deferred tax programs. If you are between forty and fifty, your payout will be lower than the group between ages fifty and sixty. We need to eliminate Social Security except for people who absolutely need it. We will *call it something else. We need to eliminate Social Security, but it will take over a generation to do so.*

Why does Barack Obama lie about my proposal? He does not have a solution of his own. It goes back to his lack of competent leadership. If you do not have a plan to fix a problem, you either blame someone else or criticize someone else's plan. We need a president who leads America, as opposed to our current president whose only way of dealing with problems is blaming others. Show us your plan for balancing the budget, Mr. President, or simply go back to Illinois and retire from public office. Mr. President, your Social Security payment under my plan would decrease, and I would eliminate your federal pension too.

The crowd went bananas again. John even smiled as the crowd started a "Randolph!" chant.

The rest of the discussion was more scripted. The questions were expected, and John answered them according to his previous stump speeches. At times, he was worried about missing traps in the questions being asked. He kept answering questions and waiting for the zinger. It never came. At the end of the one-and-one-half-hour town hall, John gave his closing statement, and thanked the panel and the audience for coming to listen to his plans for fixing America. Jenny walked onstage and waved to the crowd. The crowd erupted in a "Randolph!" chant. John walked over and shook the hands of George and Robin, the commentators. George whispered in his ear he was almost sure he would win in November. John pulled back and looked directly at him. John knew George had been instrumental in getting Bill Clinton elected in 1992. He smiled, leaned closer to George, and said:

George, thank you for the vote of confidence. I am still not sure. I am not a politician, so I am inexperienced at all of this, but my ultimate goal is to secure a much better future for America. Barack Obama does not have a plan, and his actions are killing the future of America. I am here to fix this. I will tell you right now I do not have all the answers, but I have a starting point. My twin brother, a liberal, is my chief of staff. If you want to give up your big money as a correspondent of ABC and work for little to nothing, I am offering you a job right now. Come work for my campaign and help us fix America.

John pulled back after this statement and looked George directly in the eye. George's face was completely white, and his expression was as though John had spat in his face. John pulled closer to his ear and said:

I am not kidding. I believe your first instinct is for the betterment of America and not the Progressive Movement in the country. I hope you will seriously consider my offer. I do not care that you are a Democrat. There are a lot of Republicans that do not like me either. I don't care. I want to fix America, and I need you to help out. I look forward to your affirmative phone call.

John pulled back again, looked directly into George's eyes, mouthed "I need you to help us fix America," and left the stage. John knew he had taken a whopping chance in that exchange. He had not talked this over with William or Hank, but John felt like he had "read" George very well. When he got to the back of the debate hall, he mentioned to Hank that George Stephanopoulos might be calling him. Hank immediately asked why. John just kept walking. They arrived at the SUVs and left for the airport. Everyone on the campaign staff felt extremely good about New Hampshire and was anxious to get to Nevada. William wanted a clean sweep in the early elections, and it was looking more and more probable.

They arrived at the Manchester airport and boarded Randolph One. They were on their way to Nevada by 10:00 p.m. on Thursday. Hank asked John again about the comment he had made about George Stephanopoulos, but John brushed him off. John knew he would have a lot to explain if George called. He fell asleep on the flight to Nevada. The town hall had gone better than anyone had anticipated. John had not only distanced himself from regular politicians, but he had also shown key differences between himself and Barack Obama. He had also used some forceful words in his answers. William and Hank discussed the town hall in private on the airplane. William was shocked at how the town hall had gone and was concerned the Randolph campaign might peak too soon. Hank told William of John's cryptic message about George Stephanopoulos on their way out of the convention center. He did not have the answers to William's many questions. William told Hank that he would find out what it meant. Both looked a little worried about the situation but were extremely pleased about the evening.

Chapter 26

Randolph One landed in Las Vegas at 2:00 a.m. on Friday. When they taxied to the private hangar, there were two Ford Expeditions waiting for them. John, Charles, George, and the bodyguards got in the first car, and the press pool got in the second car. William, Hank, Debbie, and Jenny stayed on the airplane and flew back to Virginia. The team arrived at the hotel at 2:30 a.m., and they all retired to their rooms to sleep. It was going to be a very short night.

John woke up at 6:00 a.m. PST and immediately called Jenny. No one answered. John determined she was still en route to The Willows. He went downstairs and worked out. Big Fred was with him because he did not want to argue with William about it. Neither of them worked up a serious sweat, because they were exhausted from the short night of rest. When John got back to the room, Jenny called and said she was at The Willows. She also said she was seriously regretting agreeing to this. John knew Jenny's way—when she became tired, she became difficult. John knew she did not mean it. John ordered room service, ate his breakfast of cereal and fruit, took a shower, and got dressed for the day. By the time Charles knocked on the door, John was ready.

John spent the next several days in Las Vegas giving speeches and meeting people. Nevada is a highly unusual state. There are two large cities in Nevada—Las Vegas and

Reno. The rest of the state is sparsely populated. The campaign spent Friday and Saturday in Las Vegas and Sunday and Monday in Reno. It was firing on all cylinders, and the crowds at each of the many events were getting larger and larger. On Monday night, Randolph One was en route to South Carolina. They would not get to South Carolina until very early on Tuesday morning. Tuesday, February 14th was not only Valentine's Day, but it was also the date of the New Hampshire primary. During the flight to South Carolina, John telephoned William and admitted he had asked George Stephanopoulos to join the campaign. William was clearly bothered by John's hiring decision. He was worried George would turn him down and tell everyone John had asked him to join the campaign. John told William that George was a smart guy, and he thought he could bring additional "new blood" to the campaign. William said he would let him know when George called and told him not to repeat this move again. Of course, he knew this would fall on deaf ears.

Randolph One touched down in Greenville, South Carolina at 4:00 a.m. They checked in at the Embassy Suites. Everyone got a few hours of sleep, but they were ready for a rally in downtown Greenville at 10:00 a.m. John did not think the day would ever end. By 8:30 p.m., the campaign was back in John's hotel suite watching Fox News' coverage of the New Hampshire primary. At 8:00 p.m. as the final polls were closing, Fox News was calling the primary for the Randolph campaign. The final results, which were published later that night, were:

Results of
New Hampshire Primary

Randolph	49%
Romney	32%
Perry	8%
Cain	4%
Other	7%

The Randolph campaign had managed to capture the first two Republican presidential contests. For the first time, a Republican candidate had won both the Iowa caucus and the New Hampshire primary!

On Wednesday, the campaign travelled by bus to Columbia where it continued to hold rallies and meet as many people as possible. The bus took the team to Charleston on Thursday, February 16th, which happened to be the voting day for the South Carolina primary. Polls opened in South Carolina at 6:30 a.m. The campaign bus went by two places where people were waiting to vote, and several people waved as they were standing in line. The campaign had scheduled a couple of rallies in Old Charleston and a rally near Patriots' Point, which is across the river from the historic district. John always liked visiting the old part of Charleston, in particular, the market area. John and Jenny had gone to Charleston on an anniversary getaway many years ago. They had stayed at the Church Street Inn which was right beside the market. At 7:00 p.m., the campaign went to the Charleston airport. Randolph One had flown over earlier that day from Greenville. The campaign loaded onto the airplane and took off for Newport News. On the trip back, which was about one and one-half hours, John was on speakerphone with William, Hank, and Debbie at campaign headquarters. Fox News had already projected the Randolph campaign would win both the Nevada and South Carolina primaries by wide margins. The final results, which were reported later that evening, showed runaway victories in both states:

Results of Nevada Primary		Results of South Carolina Primary	
Randolph	59%	Randolph	66%
Romney	19%	Romney	12%
Perry	7%	Perry	8%
Cain	5%	Cain	7%
Other	10%	Other	7%

John arrived at The Willows at around 9:15 p.m. Jenny, the children, and the grandchildren had decorated the house with "Congratulations" banners. William, Hank, Debbie, and the rest of the senior staff were there. Everyone was happy and enjoyed celebrating the momentous victories. The party did not break up until after midnight. John hit the bed hard and fell right to sleep. He was exhausted.

John did not wake up until after 7:00 a.m. the next morning. He worked out, ate breakfast, showered, and got ready for the day. He left The Willows around 9:30 a.m. and drove to campaign headquarters. When he walked into the office, the campaign staff looked up and started applauding. John smiled sheepishly, thanked them, and walked into the large conference room. William and Hank were sitting and working on something. John walked in and sat down at the table. Hank said he had heard back from George Stephanopoulos, and he had some questions. He wanted to know what his exact duties would be. Hank really did not know what John was thinking about in terms of his duties. John explained George would be an advisor. He would help with the messages of the week and keep the campaign from falling into traps. Since the focus of the campaign would soon change, the team needed another person to help defeat Obama. Hank and William started to throw out ideas around what George would do specifically. As they were talking, John walked out of the conference room and saw Thomas Philpot, the campaign Finance Manager, in one of the offices. John walked over to the door and knocked. Thomas jumped up and threw his hand out to shake John's hand. John asked Thomas about the February mid-month report which he showed him:

(000s)	Total Contributions	Total Loans from JR	Total Expenditures	Cash On Hand
12/31/2011	20,541.0		(12,200.0)	188,937.0
1/15/2012	35,446.0		(15,445.0)	208,938.0
1/31/2012	38,445.0		(21,554.0)	225,829.0
2/15/2012	40,542.0		(21,900.0)	244,471.0
Total	432,905.0	2,000.0	(190,434.0)	244,471.0

They discussed the tremendous jump in expenditures. Thomas told John that expenditures would continue to increase, and he was estimating that within the next sixty days they would be over $30 million every two weeks. John just shook his head. It was obvious he was an amateur when it came to campaign finances. John thanked Thomas for the report and said to continue the outstanding work. As he walked out of the office, he saw William at the conference-room door. William was motioning for John to return to the conference room.

John walked over, and William and Hank discussed what George's duties would be. He would be in charge of all media matters, assuming he agreed to come onboard. John said that was good. Again, William requested John leave the hiring to the senior staff. John laughed and agreed.

Debbie walked in and showed the team the latest polling data:

Poll	PPP (D)	NBC/WSJ	Fox News	Rasmussen
Date	2/16/2012	2/12/2012	1/31/2012	1/25/2012
Romney	10%	10%	11%	11%
Cain	5%	5%	4%	5%
Perry	5%	5%	4%	5%
Randolph	60%	60%	59%	58%

Debbie stated the campaign had finally broken 60 percent! She also said the media sources had started polling on a head-to-head with Randolph vs. Obama. The results were:

Poll	Date	Obama	Randolph	Undecided
PPP (D)	2/16/2012	45%	47%	8%
NBC/WSJ	2/12/2012	44%	48%	8%

She said both of the polls were within the margin of error. If the campaign continued to do well, William said the other Republican candidates would suspend their campaigns. After Super Tuesday, he expected most of them to end their campaigns.

Finally, Debbie went over the schedule for the next week. The campaign would obviously spend the entire week in Florida as the Florida primary was rapidly approaching. Randolph One would leave for Florida on Monday afternoon and the campaign would be there for the next seven days including the weekend. It would travel in one of the campaign buses all over the state, starting in Orlando, followed by Tampa/St. Petersburg, Sarasota, Cape Coral, Naples, Miami, Fort Lauderdale, West Palm Beach, Port St. Lucie, Melbourne, Daytona Beach, Gainesville, Jacksonville, Tallahassee, and finally Panama City. There would be rallies, luncheons, and meetings with potential donors. The message of the week would focus on the economy. Debbie went through all of the events. George was there and was taking notes, as was Charles. After they had finished, John asked to speak to William alone.

John and William started talking about what would happen after Super Tuesday. William shared with John a very sketchy view of the plan William and Hank had been working on for a couple of weeks. They would have it finalized in a week or so. William said the campaign would be very fortunate to lock up the Republican nomination so quickly. It would give them more time to focus on defeating Obama in the fall. William told John to focus on the next two weeks and get this part of the process behind them. John nodded. It was early Friday afternoon when John finished with all of his campaign meetings. John told everyone to have a pleasant weekend and walked out of the office.

He walked down the hallway to another office. This was the headquarters of "We Need Congressional Term Limits." John walked in and introduced himself to the receptionist. He asked to speak to Nancy Cartwright. A moment later, Nancy walked into the reception area and shook John's hand. She motioned for him to follow her. John walked into a large area with a lot of desks and a lot of people at those desks, on the telephone and computers. Nancy led John into a conference room and asked if he needed something to drink. He declined. She sat down and started to explain how the effort was going. She said February had been an exciting month for the cause. She stated as of today, 47 percent of the state legislatures had approved the measure requiring them to appoint representatives to a special constitutional convention. She expected by the end of April, there would be either approved or open legislation in 84 percent of the state houses. The biggest problems were California, New York, and New Jersey. There was not much traction yet in any of those states. The following was a breakdown by state of the current status:

	Estimated Month To Get Bill Ready	Bill Proposed in Legislature	Bill Voted Upon	Bill Approved	Bill Rejected
Alabama		Sep-11	Nov-11	Nov-11	
Alaska		Sep-11	Feb-12	Feb-12	
Arizona		Sep-11	Nov-11	Nov-11	
Arkansas		Sep-11	Nov-11	Nov-11	
California					
Colorado		Nov-11	Jan-12	Jan-12	
Connecticut		Jan-12			
Delaware		Feb-12			
District of Columbia					
Florida		Nov-11	Feb-12	Feb-12	
Georgia		Sep-11	Dec-11	Dec-11	
Hawaii	Apr-12				
Idaho		Dec-11	Jan-12	Jan-12	
Illinois		Feb-12			
Indiana		Nov-11	Feb-12	Feb-12	
Iowa		Sep-11	Oct-11	Oct-11	
Kansas		Nov-11	Jan-12	Jan-12	
Kentucky		Nov-11	Jan-12	Jan-12	
Louisiana		Sep-11	Nov-11	Nov-11	
Maine	Mar-12				
Maryland	Mar-12				
Massachusetts	Apr-12				
Michigan	Apr-12				
Minnesota		Feb-12			
Mississippi		Sep-11	Nov-11	Nov-11	
Missouri		Nov-11	Jan-12	Jan-12	
Montana		Nov-11	Feb-12	Feb-12	
Nebraska		Dec-11	Feb-12	Feb-12	
Nevada		Feb-12			
New Hampshire		Feb-12			
New Jersey					
New Mexico		Dec-11	Feb-12	Feb-12	
New York					
North Carolina		Sep-11	Nov-11	Nov-11	
North Dakota		Nov-11	Feb-12	Feb-12	
Ohio	Mar-12				
Oklahoma		Dec-11	Feb-12	Feb-12	
Oregon	Mar-12				
Pennsylvania	Apr-12				
Rhode Island		Feb-12			
South Carolina		Sep-11	Nov-11	Nov-11	
South Dakota		Dec-11			
Tennessee		Sep-11	Dec-11	Dec-11	
Texas		Dec-11	Feb-12	Feb-12	
Utah		Dec-11	Feb-12	Feb-12	
Vermont		Feb-12			
Virginia		Sep-11	Dec-11	Dec-11	
Washington	Mar-12				
West Virginia		Sep-11	Nov-11	Nov-11	
Wisconsin		Feb-12			
Wyoming		Nov-11	Jan-12	Jan-12	
	17.6%	66.7%	47.1%	47.1%	0.0%
		84.3%			

After discussing this in more detail, John thanked Nancy for all of her hard work and asked her to continue the fight. He also said he would continue to talk about the issue every week on the campaign trail. John left the office very pleased with the progress made.

He drove home to The Willows and shared all of this information with Jenny. John was looking forward to the weekend. The children and grandchildren were coming to dinner on Saturday. John was going to smoke baby back ribs. He was sure the grandchildren would stay over Saturday night. He was going to play golf with his son on Sunday after church. On Monday, John and Jenny would travel to Florida and campaign for the next seven days. The weekend went as expected. John liked spending time with the family, and he enjoyed cooking dinner—in particular anything smoked. After two weeks on the road eating restaurant food, John appreciated home cooking even more. After church, John lost to his son in golf, as usual, but still enjoyed the round. On Sunday night, John and Jenny packed so they would not feel rushed the next day.

On Monday around 3:00 p.m., Charles was at The Willows to collect John and Jenny. They drove to the Newport News airport. Randolph One was in the air by 3:30 p.m. on its way to Orlando, Florida. When they arrived at the airport, one of the campaign buses was there to take the group to a hotel. The week in Florida had begun.

The week progressed just as Debbie had described. John and Jenny did not know where they were at any given time. More than half of their waking hours were spent on the bus, and since they were in the back, they could not see which city they were pulling into. Over the weekend, they were in Daytona Beach. A rally was held on the beach. Other than being terribly windy, it was a marvelous event. The trip around Florida ended as expected in Panama City on Monday, February 27th. The next day, Floridians would vote in their GOP primary. The polls showed the Randolph campaign was vastly ahead of the other candidates. The bus arrived in Tallahassee, the location of the nearest airport. Randolph One had flown over from Orlando that morning. John, Jenny, George, Charles, and the bodyguards including Big Fred got on the airplane and took off for Newport News at 6:00 p.m., arriving a little after 8:00 p.m. Charles took John and Jenny to The Willows. John and Jenny went to bed before 10:00 p.m. as they were both exhausted from the trip around Florida.

The next morning, John drove to campaign headquarters. He met with William, Hank, and Debbie who said that starting on Wednesday, February 29th, the campaign would visit thirteen states over the next nine days. They would visit, in order: Tennessee, Georgia, Alabama, Arkansas, Missouri, Illinois, Oklahoma, California, Texas, Michigan, Ohio, New York, and finally New Jersey. The message for the nine-day period would be the economy and the amount of debt the country had accumulated on Obama's watch.

That evening, while John was packing for the long trip, he watched the Florida primary results. By 8:00 p.m., Fox News projected John Randolph the winner of the primary by a very wide margin. The next morning, the final results were reported:

Results of Florida Primary

Randolph	70%
Romney	12%
Perry	4%
Cain	3%
Other	11%

John received congratulatory telephone calls from William, Hank, and Debbie. John went to bed very early to be ready for the next nine days.

Chapter 27

John woke up at 4:30 a.m. on Wednesday, February 29th. He ate breakfast, showered, and got dressed. Charles was at the front door at 5:30 a.m. They drove quietly to the Newport News airport and parked at the private airplane hangar. Randolph One was there, and they boarded the airplane. Hank, who was going in the place of George, was already onboard. The airplane took off at 6:00 a.m. and would log a lot of air miles over the next nine days.

On the first leg of the trip, the Randolph campaign flew to Nashville, Tennessee and held several rallies around the city. Less than eight hours later, Randolph One was back in the air to its next destination. John wondered what real benefit could come out of such quick visits to these states. William had told him that local news outlets, both television and newspapers, would cover the appearances, and it would be reported on that day. It showed the campaign had an interest in that state. John was not sure, but he trusted the experts.

Over the next eight days, the campaign visited Georgia, Alabama, Arkansas, Missouri, Illinois, Oklahoma, California, Texas, Michigan, Ohio, New York, and New Jersey. John woke up in a new state every day. On Friday, the campaign visited three states in one day. It was quite a tiresome adventure. During the first part of the trip, Hank told John that George Stephanopoulos had agreed to come to work for the campaign. The press release announcing the addition would be delivered after Super Tuesday (Tuesday, March 6th) so as to not take away from the news cycle.

Most political commentators had already predicted all of the Super Tuesday states would be big wins for the Randolph campaign. They were surprised it was visiting each of the states. During the trip, John had a senior-staff meeting while they were in the clouds above Nevada. The newest polls were out:

Poll	Date	Obama	Randolph	Undecided
Fox News	2/29/2012	44%	48%	8%
Rasmussen	2/24/2012	44%	49%	7%
PPP (D)	2/16/2012	45%	47%	8%
NBC/WSJ	2/12/2012	44%	48%	8%

The campaign was holding its ground, and the polling numbers were strong. They all wondered what the numbers would be once the only focal point was defeating Barack Obama. They also wondered what would happen when Obama and his hit squad fired all of their weapons at the Randolph campaign.

Thomas Philpot gave the February 2012 finance report:

(000s)	Total Contributions	Total Loans from JR	Total Expenditures	Cash On Hand
12/31/2011	20,541.0		(12,200.0)	188,937.0
1/15/2012	35,446.0		(15,445.0)	208,938.0
1/31/2012	38,445.0		(21,554.0)	225,829.0
2/15/2012	40,542.0		(21,900.0)	244,471.0
2/28/2012	42,445.0		(25,886.0)	261,030.0
Total	475,350.0	2,000.0	(216,320.0)	261,030.0

John could not believe the campaign had already received contributions of almost one-half a billion dollars and had spent over $200 million. It was mindboggling even for an experienced finance guy.

Finally as the nine-day trip ended, Randolph One was on its way back to the Newport News airport. John was utterly exhausted as was the entire travel team. They arrived at midnight on Tuesday, March 6th. Charles, along with Fred, took John back to The Willows. John walked in very quietly, got ready for bed, and passed out in the bed beside Jenny who was already asleep.

John woke up at 6:00 a.m. the next morning. Today was Super Tuesday, the day in which fourteen states held their primaries. California and New York would be among the states voting today, and these states carried a lot of delegates. John went downstairs, worked out, had breakfast, and took a shower. Afterwards, he got dressed and drove to campaign headquarters. Hank was already there. John wondered how everyone else on the campaign staff had so much more energy than he did. He walked in and said hello to a couple of the campaign workers. He went back to the conference room where William and

Hank were sitting. Across from them at the table was George Stephanopoulos. John walked over and shook his hand and welcomed him to the team. He sat down at the conference room table and listened to the discussion about the strategy after Super Tuesday. They had made a change. Originally, the campaign was to focus its attention on Barack Obama starting April 1st. They had decided they were going to move the date up. Starting the week of March 12th, the Randolph campaign would focus its entire attention on putting Barack Obama on the unemployment line.

William told John that the campaign would spend its time focused on all the interviews it could over the next two weeks. The only travel would be to New York or Washington. This would give the campaign time to put a new schedule in place for the next five months until the Republican national convention, which was the week of August 27th. William went ahead and warned John that the travel schedule would be heavy throughout the summer months. He also wanted John to talk to Jenny about traveling and campaigning separately from John. John knew Jenny was not going to like that. John asked the "brain trust" to make sure congressional term limits stayed at the forefront, because this was extremely important to him.

George said John would be negatively vetted by the Democratic Party as soon as the votes were counted on Super Tuesday. There would be things brought up that he would have probably forgotten. The campaign needed a quick-hitting response team in place. George said he wanted to vet John first to get in front of any negative attacks. John said there was nothing in his past that would be negative, other than what had already been exposed. George said there would be things. George told John that the Democrats would have a very well-funded research machine looking into every time he had paid a bill late, any person he had ever offended, and every transaction he had ever done. This would be the most comprehensive colonoscopy he had ever had. John thanked him for the vivid verbal image and agreed to be vetted by the Randolph team.

William said the final touches to the plan would be finished next week, and they would discuss it then. John said goodbye to everyone and went to back to The Willows. He told Jenny everything that had been said. Jenny did not like the idea of campaigning separately, and she certainly did not want to give speeches. John tried to reassure her, but he could tell she was anxious about it. John said they would know more next week, but he knew Jenny was going to be asked to do it.

John and Jenny, along with the bodyguards, went out on a boat ride late in the afternoon. Until the Super Tuesday results were in, John would not believe he had won all of those states. For dinner, John made almond chicken and baked potatoes. They talked until around 7:00

p.m. then went into the parlor to watch the results. They turned the television to Fox News, as usual.

As soon as the polls were closed at 7:00 p.m. EST, Fox News declared the Randolph campaign the winner in Connecticut, Delaware, Georgia, New Jersey, and New York. At the 8:00 p.m. EST hour as the polls were closing in the central-standard time zone, Fox News declared John the winner in Alabama, Arkansas, Illinois, Missouri, Tennessee, and Oklahoma. The rest of the night kept repeating itself. By 11:00 p.m. EST, John was the projected winner in all fourteen Super-Tuesday states. John received congratulatory phone calls throughout the evening from members of the campaign staff as well as friends and family members. John and Jenny were in bed by 11:30 p.m.

By the next morning, the final results were in, and the Randolph campaign had won by whopping margins in each state:

	Randolph	Romney	Cain	Perry	Other
Alabama	61%	11%	3%	5%	20%
Arkansas	63%	12%	3%	4%	18%
California	52%	14%	6%	9%	19%
Connecticut	55%	21%	3%	4%	17%
Delaware	49%	16%	3%	9%	23%
Georgia	62%	9%	2%	5%	22%
Illinois	53%	14%	2%	9%	22%
Missouri	64%	12%	3%	5%	16%
Montana	65%	10%	3%	4%	18%
New Jersey	57%	15%	4%	5%	19%
New York	50%	20%	7%	4%	19%
Oklahoma	62%	13%	3%	4%	18%
Tennessee	65%	12%	4%	3%	16%
Utah	68%	20%	4%	3%	5%

It was a massacre. Hank called John in the morning and told him that Romney had already announced he was going to suspend his campaign. Hank expected Cain and Perry would do so by the end of the week. This was a massive boost to the Randolph campaign. Hank did not know when a candidate had ever had the nomination wrapped up this early in the process.

On Thursday, March 8th, Michigan, Ohio, and Texas held their primary elections. As it had Tuesday night, Fox News projected John the winner as soon as the polls were closed. What was significant about this night was John formally had enough delegates to be the presumptive Republican nominee for president. The next morning, the final results were reported:

	Randolph	Romney	Cain	Perry	Other
Michigan	65%	16%	4%	5%	10%
Ohio	63%	11%	5%	4%	17%
Texas	65%	8%	6%	18%	3%

On Friday, March 9th, Herman Cain and Rick Perry formally ended their campaigns. The Republican Party had only one candidate, and it was John Robert Randolph. Now it was time to take on the most formidable political machine ever created—the "Obama for Re-Election Express."

John wondered what the next eight months were going to be like. He had been campaigning now for almost one year. He had started out as a complete nobody in the political system and had won the Republican nomination in a decisive manner. John worried that the climate was getting ready to change drastically. Up to now, the Republican candidates were fighting to find favor with people who generally thought the same way they did. Most Republicans/conservatives believe in smaller government; most believe in opportunities versus entitlements; most believe in the exact meaning of the Constitution as opposed to ever-changing meanings; and most believe in individual rights versus rights based on current whims and polling data. Now, the Randolph campaign had to appeal to Independent voters, who could be very fickle in their selections but were absolutely necessary for a Randolph victory.

In the battle for the Republican nomination, the Randolph campaign had focused on the Nine-Point Plan for Fixing America. This agenda was very well received by conservative voters. How would it be perceived by Independent voters? Would they like some parts and truly despise others? Would their hatred over entitlement reform throw the election to the Obama administration? John worked himself into a frenzy by considering all of the possibilities.

He was also worried about the Democratic establishment, precisely the Progressive Movement. He knew they would bend the truth, try to divide, and do whatever was necessary to win a second term for the most progressive candidate since Lyndon Johnson, and maybe Franklin Roosevelt. John expected the onslaught to start very soon, and he foresaw the Randolph campaign wasting time and money refuting untruths and mischaracterizations. In an environment in which the incumbent's record was so inept, tricks, schemes, lies, and unjustified outrage were the only tools left at their disposal.

At the same time, John thought about what the voters had just decisively communicated to the electorate. The Republican voters had just overwhelming decided they wanted an outsider, a former businessman to be their nominee for president. They had made it abundantly clear that they were tired of the ways of the past, of continual gridlock, runaway spending, massive deficits, and unthinkable debt levels, of a poorly functioning economy, and a Progressive agenda that did not speak for the majority of Americans. They believed the Nine-Point Plan could fix the problems facing America. They wanted John to represent them and to ensure and to protect the future of America. John was truly honored and humbled by the confidence the Republican voters had placed in him.

As John walked downstairs to the kitchen, he saw Jenny sitting in the parlor. They smiled and greeted each other. John sat down beside her and said the easy part was over. Jenny's mouth fell open. The last twelve months had been very tough on the family, and John's retirement had been anything but. He told her that he could not win this election without her. He told her that a lot of people were putting their trust and faith in him, and the task seemed overwhelming. John and Jenny prayed for strength, conviction, and wisdom for the next eight months, but they did not pray for a victory. That was ultimately in God's hands through the voters.

John drove to campaign headquarters on Friday afternoon. He asked if William could assemble the team in the main office area. About fifty people walked over and faced John. He cleared his throat and said:

As most of you already know, we have secured the necessary votes to be named the presumptive Republican nominee for president of the United States. First and foremost—thank you! We would not be here today without your hard work. But I must point out, the hard work does not end today—it is just beginning. And I suspect it will be harder over the next eight months. Some of you in this room were here twelve months ago as we started this roller-coaster ride. It was a little scary back then as we went to Iowa, then to New Hampshire, and then South Carolina to introduce our campaign to people who had never heard of us. No one knew how it would end. As we started to gain some traction, others of you came onboard to help us. You brought new ideas and methods for us to get the message out. As we started to collect massive contributions and started winning caucuses and primaries, the number of people in this room exploded. I am here to say again, Thank You, Job Well Done!

This campaign has never been about me—it has been about fixing America. Our Nine-Point Plan has been chosen by the Republican voters as the way to fix America. We need to stay the course, because I believe all of America will embrace our plan once they learn more about it. The plan may have been hatched by a few, but hopefully it will be embraced by all.

Starting today, we begin the fight against Barack Obama, a sitting president. Barack Obama is an eloquent speaker; he is an effective campaigner. He has massive amounts of money supporting him; he has most of the news organizations squarely behind him; and he has the Progressive Movement behind him, willing to do or say anything to get their agenda passed. What he does not have is a plan to fix America. We have that. And finally, he does not have you, this team, supporting him either.

I will make a promise to you today and I ask you to make a commitment to me. My promise is I am going to continue to work as hard as possible to become president of the United States and to fix America for us, our children, and our grandchildren. That is my promise to you today. I ask you to continue working as hard has you possibly can. I know the hours will be long, and the work will be exhausting. If we both keep our promises, we will win this election, and together we will fix America.

Thank you again for all that you have done and all that you will do. Let's make Barack Obama a one-term president and put America's future first. God bless each of you and your families. Tomorrow starts our next chapter in fixing America. Let's go and win this for America!